DATE DUE

MY 29 '97			
8/8/97			

DEMCO 38-296

ABOUT SCHMIDT

About Schmidt

LOUIS BEGLEY

ALFRED A. KNOPF   NEW YORK

1997

THIS IS A BORZOI BOOK
PUBLISHED BY ALFRED A. KNOPF, INC.

Copyright © 1996 Louis Begley
All rights reserved under International and Pan-
American Copyright Conventions. Published in the
United States by Alfred A. Knopf, Inc., New York,
and simultaneously in Canada by Random House of
Canada Limited, Toronto. Distributed by Random
House, Inc., New York.

Library of Congress Cataloging-in-Publication Data

Begley, Louis.
    About Schmidt : a novel / by Louis Begley.—1st
ed.
        p.   cm.
    ISBN 0-679-45033-5
    1. Fathers and daughters—New York (State)—
New York—Fiction. 2. Middle-aged men—New
York (State)—New York—Fiction. 3. Retirees—
New York (State)—New York—Fiction. 4. Law-
yers—New York (State)—New York—Fiction. I.
Title.
PS3552.E373A64 1996
813'.54—dc20   96-8244
                                              CIP

Manufactured in the United States of America
Published September 1, 1996
Reprinted Twice
Fourth Printing, February 1997

For P., A., *and* A.

Già che spendo i miei danari,
Io mi voglio divertir.

—DON GIOVANNI

ABOUT SCHMIDT

I

SCHMIDT'S WIFE had not been dead more than six months when his only child, Charlotte, told him she had decided to get married. He was finishing breakfast at the kitchen table. The "Metropolitan" section of the *Times* was in his left hand; as on every Saturday, he had been poring over the mutual fund quotation table to check the prices of two investments, one in small capitalization companies and the other in international equities, both of which he had bought on his own initiative, out of conviction, and had come to regard, irrationally, because the rest of his money was managed with reasonable success by a professional whom he left quite alone, also out of conviction, as the weather vane of his financial standing. The small capitalization fund was down, by ten cents. He thought that made it a loss of about fifty cents for the week. The international stocks were down too. He put aside the paper, looked at his daughter, so tall and, it seemed to him, painfully desirable in her sweat-soaked running clothes, said I am very happy for you, when will it be? and began to cry. He had not cried since the afternoon when the specialist confirmed the advice he had previously given to him

over the telephone: Don't think of an operation, why muti-
late Mary, it won't give her even one good year, we'll keep her
as comfortable as possible. Meanwhile, you two try to have a
good time. He held Mary's hand until they were out in the
street.

The morning sunlight was blinding. He put Mary into a
taxi—ordinarily, she would have walked home, but he saw
that she was shaken, almost disoriented—caught one himself, proceeded to the office, told his secretary he didn't want
to be disturbed, shut the door, called David Kendall, the family doctor who was also their friend, heard that he and the
specialist had discussed the advice before it was given, and,
lying facedown on the couch, wept like a boy, the parade of
his life with Mary passing on the screen of his burning eye-
lids like some refurbished newsreel. That day he had been
mourning the end of his happiness. But today it was the im-
minent collapse of a bearable existence he had thought he
might be able to sustain. He didn't need to ask Charlotte who
the man was: Jon Riker had been around for a long time before Mary began to die. That very minute he was probably
shaving, in Charlotte's bathroom.

In June, Dad. We want to talk to you about picking the day.
Why are you crying like this?

She sat down and stroked his hand.

From happiness. Or because you are so grown-up. I'll stop
now. Promise.

He blew his nose elaborately, using a piece of paper towel
he tore off the roll on the upright holder next to the sink. Of
late, he was finding himself reluctant to use the handkerchief
he always carried in the pocket of his trousers, saving it for

some unspecified emergency when having a clean handkerchief would save him from embarrassment. Then he kissed
Charlotte and went into the garden.

Jim Bogard, the new gardener he had hired at the beginning of the season, and his crew had been at work all week.
He noted once more with satisfaction that dead leaves and
broken branches had been raked, even from the mulched
flower beds around the house and the more inaccessible
spaces beneath the azalea and rhododendron bushes. The
wilted yellow tops of Mary's lilies had been cut so close to the
ground that one could not suspect the presence of the bulbs
underneath; the Montauk daisies looked like topiary porcu-
pines; the hedges of honeysuckle that enclosed the property
on three sides, leaving it open only to the saltwater pond that
lay beyond a stretch of fields beginning to turn light green
with winter rye in this mild weather, had a prim and angular
look. If his neighbor Foster decided to subdivide, or a devel-
oper finally got to him, it would not be difficult to plant out
whatever monstrosities they might build: at worst, they
could put up two or three houses. Of course, the feeling of
open space and the view would be lost. This was a subject of
worry for him each year, when the potatoes had been taken in
and farmers had time to turn their minds to money and taxes.
He had been thinking of it during his last visit to the tree
nursery, and noted the great number of mature bushes for
sale and their prices, which weren't so high as he had expected. Should he take the initiative and talk to Foster about
his plans? Mary had never wanted to tie up such a large part
of her own money in the Bridgehampton property, and she
didn't want him to use his money, but Charlotte, really Char-

lotte and Jon—he would have to accustom himself to that formulation—might see the problem differently. One never regretted a purchase of land made to protect one's property.

He walked around the house and the garage, examining them closely. Here and there, Bogard's chattering Ecuadoreans had missed an apple. He picked up as many as he saw, threw them on the compost heap, and inspected, one by one, the garage, the pool, which was under a new cover he didn't like, and the pool house—really a strangely minuscule barn—they had been able to convert into a cottage and finish just before the thunderbolt of Mary's illness struck. It had been her project: Schmidt preferred to have Charlotte and her guests in the house, under the same roof as he—which wasn't awkward since Mary required these young men to use the bedroom and bathroom with the shower stall off the kitchen—so that to see Charlotte at breakfast required no prearrangement. He could linger quite naturally with his newspaper at the kitchen table or in the wicker rocking chair and listen while she talked on the telephone or with the visiting friend, absorbing the texture of the day she planned.

Once the upstairs bedrooms in the pool house, with their *Town & Country* bathrooms, and the red-tiled kitchen next to the changing rooms had been completed, the mornings became awkward for Schmidt. In theory, Jon Riker still occupied these new quarters alone, or with guests he and Charlotte had invited, but Charlotte would make breakfast there, and something inside Schmidt recoiled from the idea of simply walking in and sitting down with them. Mary had done it quite naturally and laughed at his formality. But he detested surprising others as much as being surprised himself. In his opinion, the whole point of giving the young people a separate house was to ensure their privacy. He was not to go there unless he had been invited; but since it was very rare that an invitation issued, he would try to get around his own polite rules by telephoning to ask whether they would like him to bring the paper. Sometimes he got the paper early, before there was any sign of activity in the downstairs of the pool house. Jon was asleep, and, one could suppose, Charlotte as well—in Jon's bed. Then that pretext was unavailable, and he would watch miserably as Charlotte took the copy of the *Times* he had bought for them from the kitchen table, carried it across the lawn, and disappeared behind the forbidding door of the other house.

Schmidt couldn't deny that the pool house turned out to be a blessing during Mary's illness. It had let Charlotte and Jon continue a relatively carefree sort of life alongside theirs, without calling attention to the disparity, and without unduly tiring Mary or forcing Jon to come face-to-face with the indignities, at first small, and then so shattering, of Mary's struggle. By then Charlotte had told them she was moving from her studio on West 10th Street into Riker's Lincoln Center apartment, and the fiction that she slept in her room in the big house while he spent the night in a lonely bed, perhaps working on documents he had brought from the office, had to be abandoned. There was nothing to be done: to suggest that she no longer bring him to the country would have been a useless provocation, one that would have surely made her decide to stay in the city. As soon as Mary died, though— in fact, the evening of the day they all came down from the city for the funeral—Charlotte moved Jon to the main house, into her sunny room with its bow windows and the blue Chinese rug Schmidt had bought for her at an estate auction in Amagansett, a room so particularly comfortable because it was in the more solid part of the house that had been added at the turn of the century. And that's how they had continued to live: his daughter and her lover separated from him by the stair landing and the upstairs hall between their room and the one where he slept, which he had shared with Mary. Schmidt did not protest; so far as he was concerned, the house was now much more his daughter's than his. Charlotte's plan, she had told him, was to continue to use the pool house for younger guests—her and Jon's friends—so that Schmidt's light sleep would not be disturbed by the pulse of alternative rock or the thud of bedroom or bathroom doors being shut without the care he had instilled in his wife and daughter. That was considerate, and Schmidt welcomed the restoration to the weekends of the morning ritual he liked. How was he to avoid, though, the sense that in these arrangements he was the *tiers incommode*?

Altogether, the house looked good. Mary and he moved to the country soon after he had negotiated an early retirement. Schmidt had found it indecent, yes more indecent than unbearable, to go to the office day in and day out, ostensibly affable from habit and collected the moment he set foot in that place, as though all were not in ruins, actually attend to work, and at times allow himself to become so caught up in a client's problem that he forgot Mary and, in any case, for long hours did not think about her, while she, virtually alone, was stretched on the rack. He put the Fifth Avenue apartment on the market. That it was much too large for them had become evident once they stopped entertaining; the wind that blew from Central Park down the side street was so strong that already in the winter of Mary's first operation the doorman needed to put his arm around her to keep her from being blown over while she took the few steps to a taxi; besides, with the abrupt diminution of the income Schmidt received from the firm, the expense of keeping and running that large place had become uncomfortably noticeable.

It was understood that the house near the beach was the place they both liked, in all seasons and every kind of weather. When Mary worried that he would feel trapped in Bridge-hampton, and disoriented without his long-established week-day habits, he reassured her: he had spent more than enough years behind a desk, and they weren't really giving up New York. The two-hour bus ride to the city was itself a habit as comforting as any other; in time, they might look for a pied-à-terre, perhaps in one of the new condominium buildings people claimed weren't all that shoddy, and become the own-ers of a dashing pad on a high floor, surrounded by the sky and humming with central air-conditioning and kitchen and laundry machines no one had ever used before. Of course, they both knew there wouldn't be time for that. Mary's strength had lasted, miraculously, until the essential furni-ture and objects had been transported to the country and ac-commodated in the house. Afterward, waiting for the end was enough to keep them busy.

Decidedly, there was nothing wrong with Jon Riker. Schmidt had invited him to dinner one night—along with a group of other associates and two investment officers of a Hartford insurance company they all serviced—without in the least imagining that Charlotte would find him remarkably attractive. In fact he was surprised at her turning up, after Mary had warned her that the party would be business entertainment, one of those rank-has-its-obligations affairs older partners have to suffer through once in a while to make the hardworking young fry feel appreciated. But the next morning Charlotte said she was glad she had come. She thought Jon looked like Sam Waterston; that was her pronouncement, enough for Schmidt to get the picture. She had graduated from Harvard the previous year and was still living at home. The time to say what he really thought about Jon as his daughter's prospective beau was then, or over the course of the next few weeks. But he never told them—either Charlotte or Mary. He gave them only his office point of view: an excellent young lawyer, almost certain to become a partner, except that he works much too hard. How will he find time to take Charlotte to the movies, never mind movies and dinner! Schmidt had behaved with decent consistency, of which he was rather proud, just as he would later, when he became Riker's principal, probably indispensable, supporter for partnership. Luckily for Riker, that process took place, and was concluded favorably for him, before he began sleeping with Charlotte; anyway before the word had gotten around or Mary had opened Schmidt's eyes, so that the firm did not need to face the dreaded question of whether the rule against nepotism was about to be breached.

But even if Charlotte had not just informed him that she and Jon had made their decision—now that he thought of it, couldn't Riker have gone to the trouble of coming to Charlotte's father to ask for her hand?—and it weren't too ridiculously late to speak to Charlotte with the utmost candor, there was still nothing he could say against Riker, or, more precisely, against the marriage, that wouldn't seem to her, and perhaps even to him, once the words were out of his mouth, quirky, possessive, smacking of jealousy or envy. What could he say beyond admitting that, outside the office, he didn't care all that much for the qualities that in time would make Riker such a useful, reliable partner in that beloved firm—which Schmidt was coming to realize he missed principally as a source of income and a porous barrier against self-doubt—and that they surely weren't the qualities he had hoped to find in a son-in-law? According to an Arab proverb that one of his partners with oil-rich Middle Eastern clients had assured him was genuine, a son-in-law is like a pebble, only worse, because you can't shake him out of your shoe. Schmidt knew that the Romans, on the contrary, had prized these intruders. If one really loved a woman, one loved her the way a man loved his sons and his sons-in-law. Since he regretted not having sons—at work, he had had a tendency to develop a strong affection for the best of the young men who worked with him, a feeling that was generally reciprocated until the associate he had singled out as his right hand and object of loyalty became a partner and no longer needed a father figure in the firm—he had hoped to have Roman feelings for the man who married Charlotte. But how was he to bestow them on Jon Riker?

The stuff he had written about Riker, with considerable eloquence, in the critiques that, according to office procedures, followed the completion of each important assignment, was true enough: with variations appropriate to the occasion, it was like what he had told Charlotte and Mary and what became, in due course, the necessary mantra of slogans he repeated wearily at firm meetings when Jon came up for partnership. These slogans were not contradicted by Riker's other attributes, which Schmidt liked less but hadn't felt compelled to mention because they had little to do with the criteria according to which his partners judged candidates. For instance, the narrowness of that strong intelligence: What did his future son-in-law think about, apart from client matters and deadlines and the ebb and tide of bankruptcy litigation (Jon's annoying specialty, the domain of loudmouth, overweight, and overdressed lawyers, thank God Jon didn't look or sound like them), spectator sports, and the financial aspects of existence?

Jon's talk about finances was sort of a mantra too, one that Jon repeated and Schmidt despised. After his clerkship, should Jon have taken a job with a firm that paid associates more than Wood & King did? How should he evaluate the loss of income resulting from his choice, if there had been one, against the possibly lower probability of partnership at some other more lucrative place—but had he "made partner" there, what a bonanza! Now that he was a Wood & King partner, was his generation's share of income sufficient (here the pocket calculator might come out of the neatly organized attaché case, Charlotte's lavish offering), or was too much going to older types (like Schmidt, but that was left unsaid), who had not had the decency to get out when their productivity declined? Should he buy an apartment or continue to rent, was it to be a condo or a co-op, how much would it cost him to be married if Charlotte stopped working, what price tag to put on each child? The evidence of Jon's having read a book since the first volume of Kissinger's memoirs, Mary's Christmas present, was lacking. On long airplane trips, of which Jon took many, Schmidt had noticed that Jon did his "homework"—an honorable enough occupation—caught up on advance sheets, read news magazines, or stared into the middle distance. There was no pocket book tucked into Jon's litigation bag or in the pocket of his belted raincoat that looked like a Burberry. Such had been Schmidt's personal observations during the early years of their working together, when they often sat side by side in the plane, Schmidt struggling, once his own "homework" was done, to stay awake over some contraband belles lettres. Discreet interrogation of Jon had revealed only one subsequent change in his traveling habits: as the proud owner of a laptop computer, he could also use the time to write memos to files and work on his checkbook. What was this young man if not a nerd, or in the slang of Schmidt's own generation, apparently coming back into use, a wonk, a wonk with pectorals? His Charlotte, his brave, wondrous Charlotte, intended to forsake all others and cleave to a wonk, a turkey, a Jew!

Schmidt kicked the last of the stray apples. His anger was like a bad taste in the mouth.

That final indignity was unmentionable. He could not have spoken of it to Mary: a word against the Jews, and she brought all the sins of Hitler on your head, but this marriage was not a matter of civil rights or equal opportunity or, God help him, the gas ovens. To the best of his recollection, no matter how deeply or how far back he looked, Schmidt was sure he had not once in his life stood in the way of any Jew.

But now he was discovering that what didn't count at W & K (which had certainly filled up with Jews since the day he had himself gone to work there) and what could even furnish him at times some eyebrow-raising sort of amusement, as it had when Jews, beginning in the seventies, had begun to move into his Fifth Avenue apartment building, or joined one of his clubs, did count heavily when it came to his family, or what was left of it! This marriage would turn Charlotte, his one remaining link with life, into a link with a world that wasn't his—the psychiatrist parents he had so far escaped meeting, grandparents on the mother's side whom Jon occasionally mentioned, possibly uncles, aunts, and cousins he hadn't yet heard about. What might they be like? That contact with them would be unpleasant, that it would put a strain on his quiet good manners and composure, he was quite sure. Before long, they would cover Charlotte like ooze from the sea; they would absorb her and leave him out; never again would he be alone with her on his own ground; the pool-house kitchen and its hostile threshold were the microcosm of his future.

He tried the cellar door cover. It opened, which meant that he had forgotten to check it after Bogard and his men had finished raking. Perhaps now that Bogard had proved himself he should be allowed to lock the cellar from the inside and then leave through the house. Might as well give him the keys too; Schmidt couldn't be sure of always being there to open the door. When he entered the cellar, his mood lightened. The place was impeccable; the effort he had put into arranging it had not been wasted. The dehumidifier humming beside the shelves on which he stored the reserve of cleaning supplies and canned goods did such a good job, drawing the moisture even from the crawl space, that as an experiment he had moved the paperbacks from Fifth Avenue to a new set of shelves he had the handyman build on the opposite wall. Their pages hadn't curled, which was more than could be said for the books and magazines in the house; perhaps he could put in the cellar as well the art books and those of Mary's accumulated hardcover volumes he didn't need to have at hand. The temperature was about as low as it would get, and that was good news for the wine, also moved from the city, where he had been forced to keep it in a warehouse because the basement in the Fifth Avenue building was so stiflingly hot, to the cellar's windowless continuation under the new part of the house. In the summer the coolness of that space was delicious, reminding him of the way movie theaters had felt during New York summers before window air conditioners had become customary in apartments. He sat down in the rocking chair near the workbench and shifted his weight. Not a squeak; it was a solid piece—his father's, as was the oval woven-ribbon rug that the old man had had in his bathroom. The tools were in near-perfect order; the seniors among them, hammers, pliers that might have belonged to an old-time dentist, and little saws, also came from his father's house on Grove Street. What a contrast between the cellar of that artisan's federal Greenwich Village house and this! There had been no way to keep the damp out of it, or, for that matter, visiting rats, although Pasha the cat had worked hard.

He found the box of small cigars on the workbench, lit one, and threw the match into the wastebasket, a habit of which Mary had been unable to break him. Next time he came down, he would bring an ashtray, by way of remembrance and apology. And then the thought he had not allowed to form while he was touring the garden was complete, impossible to set aside for some later hour when he would have a drink in his hand and music in which he could lose himself on the turntable. Clearly, he would have to leave this house: the only trick was how to do it without Charlotte's knowing it was because of Jon, or, if that realization could not be avoided, to do it in such a manner that she would take it as a good development for her father, a sign of returning optimism, something on the order of her own decision to found the next generation of the family, with him now willing to stand on his own feet in a new life. A preposterous idea, but it would not be the first time he had successfully put on an act for the benefit of his wife and daughter.

The problem of the house was not new. Schmidt had perceived its unpleasant outline during the first meeting with Dick Murphy, the trusts and estates lawyer at Wood & King who had drafted Mary's and his wills when they decided they ought to sign such instruments, amidst the requisite jokes about whether they were of sound and disposing minds. He had stared at it during each subsequent discussion of revisions and codicils occasioned by the rising tide of their fortunes, and changes in the tax law, and when he arranged for them to see Murphy before Mary's exploratory operation, at a time when the doctors were still hopeful. It came to this: the house wasn't his and it was too valuable by far. It had belonged to Mary's maiden aunt Martha, her father's sister, who had brought up Mary after her mother died of pneumonia in 1947.

Mary had just turned ten. Martha was the only relative,

apart from some elderly distant cousins in Arizona, Mary's father having been killed in knee-high water off Omaha Beach, in the first attempt to land. From the time Schmidt and Mary were married, they had spent their summer vacations with Martha; in due course, Martha became Charlotte's god-mother; it had taken all the powers of persuasion of Martha's lawyer to keep her from leaving the house to a four-year-old Charlotte. In the event, the house and everything else Martha had went outright to Mary. Everything else consisted of a sum that was small even in 1969 dollars. Martha had been used to living very comfortably, spending her capital; the trust from which she also received income terminated on her death and was distributed to those distant cousins. But by the beginning of the seventies, Schmidt was earning enough to pay for the upkeep of the house. Thus Mary's cash inheritance grew, and she had been able to put aside a good part of what she earned as an editor distinguished for her sure literary taste in an otherwise brutally commercial publishing house. The convention between her and Schmidt was that she paid for her own clothes and hairdresser, the few lunches or taxis for which she was not reimbursed, gifts (which were sometimes startlingly extravagant), and charities Schmidt didn't want to support. He took care of the rest. Still, as Murphy said, she had only a little over a million dollars. Martha had brought her up to be old-fashioned about money, which to her meant investing in treasuries and only the highest-rated municipal bonds. On the other hand, given its location, the house was probably worth two million; if she was to leave it and the money to Charlotte, as she intended, the tax would be more than a million, and how was Charlotte to pay it unless she sold the house, which was the opposite of what Mary wanted? The only sensible plan, Murphy pointed out, was to leave the money to Charlotte and the house to Schmidt. In that case, he explained, there would be no tax on the house, as a bequest to a spouse. Later, there would presumably be enough in Schmidt's estate, when he died and she inherited, to pay the tax. She would be coming into some leftover money as well, enough for the upkeep on a big house. Then Murphy—Schmidt could have strangled that Irish oaf—put to Mary the question he had already raised with Schmidt privately and Schmidt had asked him to stay clear of: Tax planning aside, why shouldn't her husband own the house he had lived in each summer and on most weekends for more than a quarter of a century and in which he had invested a great deal of his own money? He recited the modern heating system and insulation, the endless roof repairs, and, most recently, the new larger pool and pool house. Couldn't Charlotte and, in time, her husband and children, use the house the way she and Schmidt had used it while her aunt Martha was alive, and inherit only on Schmidt's death?

There were at least three reasons why Schmidt hadn't wanted Mary to be backed into that corner. She wasn't well, the question was so obvious there was no need to ask it, and he was sure he knew the unpleasant answer. She had never told it to him, and it wasn't for Murphy's ears, but he knew that before she died, she intended to settle an old score. As for the taxes, they didn't worry her. She could have no doubt that Schmidt would pay them himself before he saw Charlotte sell the house. Therefore, it made him squirm, first to hear Mary carry on about the solemn promise she had made to Martha, and how Charlotte could get a mortgage to pay the taxes, and then Murphy's solution, never mentioned to Schmidt previously, and inspired, it seemed to him, by the two vodka martinis Murphy had drunk over lunch at the Racquet Club. How neat! Mary would leave Schmidt a life estate in the house! That did it! The word given to the aunt wouldn't be broken, since, as a matter of law, Charlotte was the heir. Because Schmidt had the house for life, it would escape taxation when Mary died, and, when Schmidt died, the tax would fall on his estate.

Except that I don't fancy playing the dowager on my daughter's property, and he wouldn't have minded pointing out to Murphy that if he had kept his mouth shut, Mary might have left the house to her husband after all, was the rejoinder Schmidt would have liked to make, but what was the use? Apparently, he was to continue to be a slave to a house that would never be his own.

Thus, when Mary turned her eyes on him—there were tears in their corners, and he couldn't help thinking of her contact lenses and how lucky it was that she still cared about her looks—and smiled, saying, Mr. Murphy is right, don't you think so? he smiled back and said, Yes, that's just fine.

That was that, but he saw the way to undo it. For Charlotte's wedding present, he would surrender his life estate and pay the gift tax on the entire value of the house. He was sure that was how the tax law still worked. The market was down, but not for properties of this quality. It would have to be a big payment. He would call Murphy and go over the figures, but, whatever they were, his heart told him he could and would do it. There was another aspect of the situation to be considered. If he moved fast enough, and bought another place for himself, there was tax he could save some money on, the tax on the gain on the sale of the Fifth Avenue apartment. He had bought it the year of his and Mary's marriage, with the money he had inherited from his mother. It was large and elegant, so that, even after he became a partner, there was no need for them to move. But the price that had made him gasp at the time turned out, in hindsight, to have been nothing at all, less than one-fiftieth of the sum for which he had been able to sell the place. He had literally rubbed his hands together with glee watching the value of that place go up, realizing that it was his real nest egg. Yes, in terms of what his investment adviser liked to call preserving family wealth, the result wouldn't be all that bad—he would use up the gift tax exclusion and pay about seven hundred thousand in gift tax, save some of the million dollars in tax on the gain on the apartment, and hand the property over to Charlotte at a time when gift and estate taxes were high but not so high as one might fear they would become in the future.

Where the proposed transaction departed from a pleasant capitalistic model was in its effect on his income: he had planned to pay the gains tax and add what was left from the sale of the apartment to his capital. And he hadn't intended to buy for himself a house that cost as much as the astonishing price the apartment had commanded, which was what he would have to do if all of the capital gains tax was to be saved. In fact, he had had no thought of buying any house; his plan, to the extent such a thing existed, had been to live right where he was, in a place he had become used to thinking of as his home, to which he was attached, and which also happened to offer him, not to put too fine a point on it, the birth-right—or is it the dream?—of every American retiree: a house that's all paid for. He went back to his calculations. In order to carry out his new plan in full, he would have to take almost three million dollars of his cash and invest it in Charlotte's taxes and the purchase of a new house he didn't want and, in theory, didn't need. That money, placed in municipal bonds, could be expected to produce an income of one hundred fifty thousand per year, tax free. Now it would no longer be forthcoming. He would still have the payments from his firm—one hundred eighty thousand dollars per year—and the income from the balance of his savings, perhaps another one hundred fifty thousand tax free if he invested that money in municipals as well. It occurred to Schmidt that, to the average American, this would seem a pretty good deal for a single sixty-year-old codger with no dependents, but was the average American accustomed to living as Schmidt lived? Had he worked as hard?

Moreover, his unsympathetic fellow citizen might not know that Wood & King had so organized its affairs that payments to retired partners stopped when they reached the age of seventy. That was five years after the normal retirement age. Therefore, the deal Schmidt had negotiated was generous in its own way. The pension was reduced, because he was leaving the firm early, but it was to continue until the same magic age. The reason for the generosity was no secret: it was to compensate him for gracefully leaving when he might have remained for another five years, like his contemporaries drawing a top share of the firm's income. They didn't mention that consideration in their talk, neither Jack DeForrest, the presiding partner, nor he, but he imagined that Jack had already been spoken to by many young partners—Jon Riker probably leading the charge!—anxious to warn DeForrest that if he stayed during those final years, Schmidt would be coasting. They wouldn't have suggested he was a shirker; to allude to the effect on him of Mary's illness and the declining role in the generation of revenues for the firm of the sort of financial work he handled would have been more than enough. Well, Schmidt had wanted to put down the burdens of his profession. It wouldn't be necessary to push him out the door; that was one less worry for Jack.

Schmidt recalled that when, as a very young partner, he had voted in favor of the W & K retirement plan, this quaint—so he thought—notion of stopping pension payments after five years had made him laugh. Jack DeForrest, his law school classmate and then his closest friend, was sitting next to him at firm lunch. He had whispered to Jack, This is neat! The vestry of St. James really believes that a man's life is three score and ten! It so happened that Messrs. Wood and King, both present at the table, and both past the canonical age, were members of that august New York institution. Because they were the founding partners, the retirement plan treated them differently from everybody else—with exquisite courtesy that Schmidt, ever filial, had applauded. As for himself, how was he, then in his thirty-sixth year, to imagine that one day the fabulous frontier of his seventieth birthday would not seem distant at all, and he would be obliged to contemplate the financial disadvantages of living on beyond it? All he knew then was that he had, so far, managed everything very well; there was no reason why he wouldn't continue to be both lucky and happy.

As he rocked on in his chair the course he must follow seemed both clear and inevitable. Damn the taxes and the loss of income. He would give the house to Charlotte and move out. Living under the same roof with Jon Riker married to Charlotte during vacations, all summer weekends, and however many other weekends in the year they would want to use it might have been contemplated if it were on his own terrain, in a house that was really his, where he made the rules. But never in a fake commune, where he felt the obligation to consult those two about calling the plumber, repainting the house blue, or ripping out a hedge! He wasn't going to try to save the capital gains tax on the apartment. Instead of sinking two million dollars into a house like Martha's, he would buy a shack in Sag Harbor, among Mary's former publishing colleagues, give up shaving and visits to the barber, putter around in L. L. Bean togs, and get his summer meals at book party buffets if the invitations to them didn't dry up! Then if Riker someday decided he could at last afford to procreate, he, Schmidt, would still be able to offer his grandchildren an occasional treat. The great adventure of trying to live out his sunset years was yawning before him.

He went up the cellar steps and entered the kitchen. Now Riker was at the table, a plate of unfinished poached eggs before him. Steel-rimmed, slightly tinted glasses on his nose, attaché case at his feet, he stopped correcting a thick draft.

Charlotte's in the shower. Has she told you? She thought I should speak to you first, but I knew you would want it to be her. I hope you approve my making her an honest woman!

He stood up and held out his hand, which Schmidt shook. The long fingers that explored Charlotte were hairy between the first and second joints. Where does the ring go, on the right or left hand? No doubt, Jon would wear a ring. It occurred to him, not for the first time, that this large, very handsome young man's hairline wasn't what it used to be. Probably he worried about it; a small pocket mirror might be lurking in one of the pockets of that attaché case.

Nicely put! Thanks for the old-fashioned sentiment. Congratulations!

You are the first to know, Al. I haven't even told my parents.

Schmidt disliked being called Al, slightly preferring Albert, which was his given name and, therefore, couldn't be helped. He wondered why Riker wasn't handling him better. A tiff with Charlotte over breakfast, while the paternal heart was breaking in the cellar? Getting even, because of the bizarre flashback to the days when, as a young associate, he had been afraid of Schmidt? Second thoughts?

Then pick up the telephone. It's past ten. And don't use your credit card.

Thanks, Al. I'll do it from the room. That way I'll catch Charlotte before she comes downstairs and will get her to speak to them too.

Do that. Since when do you call me Al?

Just testing. I want to see how much a son-in-law can get away with. Don't be such a sourpuss!

Schmidt took the breakfast dishes off the table, scraped the egg yolk from Riker's plate, and rinsed them. He genuinely liked cleaning up after meals. From the start, in the early division of chores between him and Mary—it was important to her that Schmidt share equally in the housework and looking after Charlotte—he had asked that doing dishes be included in his assignment. The activity soothed him, as did washing off the kitchen floor and counters and sweeping anyplace at all. They were simple, uncontroversial tasks, in which it was possible, provided there was enough time, to achieve, when one stood back squinting at the clean surfaces, a feeling of perfection, an illusion that order had been reestablished. He referred to them as his occupational therapy.

Of course, during the week there had never been much housework or looking after young Charlotte of the sort that weighed down many of their friends. They had had a cleaning woman from the time they got married, every weekday, since Mary was working at her first junior editorial job and brought manuscripts home, and he kept the usual New York lawyer's late office hours. When Charlotte arrived so did a nurse, a grim but very gentle fat Texan lady once married to an air force warrant officer, who stayed with them until Charlotte went into the second grade at Brearley—the only southern nanny known to Schmidt who was certifiably white—and a succession of housekeepers, periodically up-graded to keep up with Schmidt's income. Neither the housekeepers nor the nurse worked on weekends, and the housekeepers prepared dinner but didn't serve it, Mary and Schmidt ate so late. The result was that Schmidt's dishwash-ing was the principal domestic task performed during the week, Mary being in charge of putting away leftovers, mus-tard, and chutney when they ate curry. She did that well; Schmidt had always been a dismal failure at filing, and orga-nizing little dishes covered with aluminum foil reminded him of that. Weekends were more complex. They went to the country unless there was a party or a concert they really couldn't miss. If Schmidt had to work in the office on Saturday or Sunday, which happened dismayingly often until he no longer felt he was a young partner and began to have papers brought out to him by messenger, Mary would take Charlotte alone, with the baby-sitter. There was a succession of those, as well: Hunter College students working for lodging and pocket money and later, when they decided Charlotte should learn French, au pairs. Corinne had been one of them.

If he was stuck working on a Saturday morning, he would try to catch an afternoon train and join them, and, when it was too late for that, he would go out sometimes early on Sunday to get in a set of tennis or a long walk on the beach, and help Mary with the drive to the city. While Martha was alive, work-sharing rules did not apply in her house. She thought Charlotte should be in women's hands—her own, Mary's, and the baby-sitter's—unless the child was going to the beach or to her pony lesson, or to the afternoon movie show in East Hampton, each of which was a proper occasion for a father to appear. And there wasn't any question of sticking one's nose into the kitchen and doing the work of Martha's cook and the cook's assistant, each as adamantly Irish as their cigarette-smoking, hard-drinking employer.

Mary and Schmidt kept the cook until her retirement; it was unthinkable that she be let go. Would she return from Florida to look after Schmidt, now that he had been put out to pasture? The question had teased him. Afterward, they kept the house going as best they could, with the help of a squadron of Polish women who arrived once a week in battered Chevys, Diet Cokes in hand, hair in curlers, their outsize rear ends and bosoms restrained by resort wear in which lime, shocking pink, and orange predominated—women who whizzed through the place and departed three hours later planting moist kisses on Mary, Charlotte, and even Schmidt.

It astonished him, how he had come to believe in the absolute necessity of Charlotte's being taken to the country each weekend, and to feel uneasy himself, at loose ends, uncomfortable with city smells and the Sunday look of streets, if he happened not to go away. And yet, this was a habit acquired only upon marriage. Schmidt's parents had not owned a place in the country. Unless one counted attendance at law school reunions and out-of-town Bar Association meetings as vacations, his parents took none. They didn't agree with Schmidt's father, and his mother didn't like the expense. Saturdays and Sundays were spent in the city; Schmidt learned about grass and trees in Central Park and about swimming in a large reedy pond to which an establishment upstate called Camp Round Lake had a right-of-way. He had been a camper there from the age of eight, and later, until his second year at Harvard College, a counselor.

The champagne flute snapped in his fingers as he was rubbing it under hot water to get Charlotte's lipstick off. He scooped the broken glass from the drain with a paper towel and saw that it was rapidly turning dark red. The cut in the palm was clean but deep, apparently not the sort that could be taken care of by pressing a wad of paper toweling against it. He looked for the Band-Aids he thought he had last seen on the shelf above the sink. They weren't there. Meanwhile, unmanageable fat blood drops kept reappearing on the floor, on the counter, and on the open cabinet door, faster than he could wipe them with the sponge he held in his good hand. It was a ridiculous situation, fit for a sorcerer's apprentice. He was beginning to feel shaky.

Dad, what have you done to yourself? Sit down right away, make a fist, and hold it up high. I'll bandage the cut.

Just a broken Pottery Barn champagne glass. Four dollars and seventy-five cents. Don't they crush glasses at Jewish weddings for good luck? I guess I'm getting in practice.

He looked at Jon.

You've got a long way to go, Al! It's the groom who crushes the glass with his foot, not the disappointed father with his hand, and the bride and the groom first drink wine out of it. Remember, wine not blood. Jews aren't big on drinking human blood, but they're very big on guilt. So they drink the wine to show that they are about to experience the greatest possible joy, and right away the man has to break the glass, as a reminder of the destruction of the temple. That makes them guilty about being happy and brings them back to reality.

Charlotte had finished wrapping his hand with gauze and adhesive tape. She kissed him on the top of the head, which was a caress that always made him melt.

Let me finish the dishes, she said, and please keep that hand out of the water until the cut closes. You should probably take it to a doctor and have it stitched.

Never! Can't break my lifetime record of no cutting and sewing my skin for such a trifle. Thank you, sweetie, for being so good to the old grouch. And thank you, Jon, for setting me straight. By the way, how do your parents feel about your marrying a shiksa? Have you spoken to them? Will they allow it?

Not as broken up as you about her marrying me! Albert, will you come off it? Charlotte and I have been together for almost four years. We love each other. We live in the same apartment! And you've known me for ten years!

Yes, of course, Jon. I am very glad. I just need time to get used to the concept.

Dad, Jon's parents would like you and us to have Thanksgiving with them.

This was a development Schmidt recognized immediately as natural, but he hadn't foreseen it. Mary had reigned over Thanksgiving, Christmas, and Easter. Of course, they had spent those holidays with Martha, while she was alive, and they continued spending them in her house afterward, except for one Thanksgiving when Charlotte had the chicken pox. During their good years, they usually had invited young people from Schmidt's office. There never had been any question of Charlotte's being elsewhere; therefore, if Riker was right about the length of his tenure, he must have had each of those holidays with them at least four times.

That's very kind. I don't blame the Doctors Riker for wanting Jon for once to spend a holiday with them, but it may be a bit soon for me to go visiting over Thanksgiving. That doesn't affect you, sweetie; of course, you and Jon must be together.

And then he added, because the thought had suddenly occurred to him, Unless you want to invite the Rikers here, Charlotte. Between the two of us, I bet we can roast a turkey.

You'll hurt their feelings. They said my grandparents are even coming to New York instead of the usual family gathering in Washington. My brother will be there too.

Schmidt had forgotten to put the brother in the family album. This would be the boy who jumped ship from Wharton and was working for a trade association—also in Washington. Was he married? Might he be gay; was that what Mary had told him?

Let's not decide today. This is only the third week of October. We have lots of time before us.

That's all right, but please, Albert, please don't spoil this for us, and for yourself too.

II

THE FOLLOWING TUESDAY, Schmidt received a telephone call from Jon Riker's secretary. Jon had asked her to give Mr. Schmidt a message: Neither he nor Charlotte would be coming out for the weekend, they were staying in town, and Jon wondered whether his parents should expect Mr. Schmidt for the Thanksgiving meal, lunch being at two-thirty.

I've got the message, Schmidt told her, making his voice sound light and cheerful—almost elated, as if the best thing in the world had just happened to him. It was a tone he thought he had perfected in the fallow period of his practice and used to thank potential clients when they called to say that Schmidt's presentation had been excellent, really most impressive, but other counsel had been chosen for the project Schmidt had hoped to get for Wood & King.

And do tell me, does Jon now get you to make all his personal calls? he continued, but no sooner had he spoken these words than he was ashamed, because Riker's secretary was a nice woman, who was already working at W & K when Riker got there and understood the insult as well as Schmidt himself. Of course, she couldn't know—so he hoped—that a warning shot had just been fired across his bow. Therefore he added, It's perfectly all right. I was trying to tease you. We sunset people will do anything to keep amused!

Oh, Mr. Schmidt, you really must forgive us! You know how Jon is. He came in this morning very early and left typed instructions for the whole day, and ever since he has been in a meeting with clients that will run late. It's been like that since last week! That's why I thought it was better to call you myself, instead of reminding him to do it. He will be very sorry when he learns that you were annoyed.

That's what he mustn't learn. Remember, we are covered by secretary–former partner privilege! Your lips are sealed. Now could you switch me to Mr. DeForrest?

It had occurred to Schmidt that, since W & K was probably paying for this call—he was willing to make a small bet that Riker had instructed his secretary to charge to the firm as a business expense telephone calls and faxes to this retired partner, even though he was his father-in-law-to-be—he might as well make it a long one. The profitability of the firm was no longer his problem.

Dealing with Mr. DeForrest was a pleasure, if the purpose wasn't to defend one's usefulness to W & K, which that potentate measured in terms of hours billed to clients, or to negotiate the terms on which, having understood that the defense had failed, one would be prepared to leave the firm. For one thing, he still adhered, as had Mr. Wood and Mr. King, to the custom of answering the telephone himself, unless there was someone in his office, or he was working on a problem so complex that he could brook no interruptions.

The great mind must have been momentarily in repose, for the first ring had not run its course before the receiver emitted a familiar, preventively jovial roar, followed by: Schmidtie, you rascal, don't keep me in suspense one second longer. Tell me right now that you're coming to us for Thanksgiving. Dorothy will be so pleased! We could never get you to join forces with us before!

I was calling to say that the prospects aren't good. Jon Riker has invited me to his parents', and I am not sure I am up to that. If I were to go to your party instead he'd be really put out.

Aha, Jon has finally popped the question!

Something like it, but please don't put it in the office bulletin!

That's for him to do. Can't Dorothy and I pull rank? Perhaps we could ask him and Charlotte too, since it's a special occasion. You know, I've been trying to limit these gatherings to the management group and some of the seniors. I'll want to think about that one, perhaps talk it over with Harry.

Don't. I am sure Jon would be flattered, but this is not the right time. Why don't you and Dorothy give me a rain check?

Schmidtie, you don't need one. Just pack your toothbrush and pajamas and come for a sleepover anytime you like. Have you got a minute?

Without waiting for an answer, the voice continued, increasingly friendly. I suppose Jon has told you that the management has been looking at the firm retirement plan? There is a strong feeling here, and not just among the younger partners, that we should make sure the burden falls fairly. We have a committee studying the problem, and they've got a consultant to do some actuarial studies and advise us on what the peer firms are doing. You understand this is a continuing process, and we haven't made any decisions on what we will be recommending to the firm, but as a first step we would like each retired partner to get on board.

Get on board what?

The process, and the underlying principle—that there is no objection to changes we may want to make to achieve greater fairness.

I think you had better write to me, Jack. I don't think I can discuss changes before I know what they are. Anyway, I don't see what this has to do with me. My arrangement with the firm is a contract, one that I negotiated with you.

It still comes under the retirement plan, Schmidtie. You know that. There are mechanisms in the plan to permit the firm to make changes at its discretion, but we don't want the process to be divisive. That's why we are asking you fellows to sign on. I've got to say I am a little surprised that you of all people are getting excited. You've been able to salt away quite a bundle, and really you have no expenses or capital needs!

I haven't gotten excited yet, and maybe I won't, after I see what you propose. As I said, I don't understand how it can or should apply to me.

All right. I just hope you won't screw it up with the firm, Schmidtie. You've had a good cruise here, and people like you. Don't spoil it! Do you want to be switched to anybody else? The invitation to Thanksgiving still stands; do you want to reconsider?

No to both questions, but thanks again for the invitation!

The universality of the advice to watch his step was impressive. Schmidt went into the kitchen and poured himself a large drink of bourbon and sat down with it at the kitchen table. The rain, which had begun as a lackadaisical drizzle in the morning, had turned into a torrent. It pounded on the windowpanes. Schmidt didn't own a cat or a dog; no need to worry about a pet being outside in foul weather. The roof on the main house had been redone again at the end of the summer. The technologically advanced pool-house roof was still under guaranty. There were no known leaks anywhere, certainly not in the cellar, not in the garage, where the Toyota Schmidt had given to Mary and the VW Golf he had given to Charlotte slumbered alongside his own Saab. No, there was decidedly nothing to worry about. In fact, this savage rain was a fine thing, giving the trees, the bushes, and the more serious perennials one more chance to drink up before the ground froze. Yet everything was badly wrong.

Schmidt knew that lurid confrontations, browbeating of adversaries followed by buttering them up, ambushes miraculously avoided, dramas played out in conference rooms against a backdrop of piles of unfinished sandwiches, during tête-à-tête chats among principals that one lawyer only has been invited to join, games dangerous like a hand grenade from which the pin has been pulled or, on the contrary, banal and tepid, because their issue has been determined in advance, held no starring role for him. They had all been scripted with Jack DeForrest in mind or, even more likely, the ubiquitous Lew Brenner, W & K's own Jewish Al Pacino, stiletto or charm ready for whomever it might concern, and other imperturbably self-assured and yet esurient men just like them, partners in a posse of firms, each of which claimed primacy in the profession, the right to be the first to go through every door. Schmidt too had been at the top of the profession, but the peak he had scaled—representing two of the largest American insurance companies in their most complex private loans—had been eroded over the course of twenty years until it took on the gentle look of an ancient hillock comfortably lost in a verdant landscape. To retain his standing as an alpinist, Schmidt would have needed to find another range and an ascent of such difficulty that there was no room left for another climber. It was no one's fault. The same change in capital markets and the practice of law was humbling other grand New York lawyers: insurance company money was a river that had abandoned its old bed and was flowing away from the transactions in which Schmidt had excelled. Many lesser lawyers, in New York and other cities, some of them cities where these insurance companies had their head offices, were pleading to do on the cheap those deals that remained to be done. Schmidt's clients were loyal and grateful, but they had been sending him less and less work and, red-faced, sometimes had bargained over fees. No one denied that his work was faultless, but, except in the most unusual and progressively rarer cases, were the higher quality, and the margin of added safety it brought, worth the price? Schmidt's watchful partners were taking note. He was a proud man. If certain dealings with Jack DeForrest had not miscarried, if it hadn't been for Mary, if shoring up his position at Wood & King had seemed a matter of life or death—it couldn't have, given what Schmidt was learning about dying—he might have had another go at the Himalayas. But he also knew that the qualities that had made clients seek him out were going out of style, just like the transactions on which he had honed them: legal and textual analysis rigorously applied to each sentence another lawyer had written until all mistakes and ambiguities had been caught and corrected, eerie precision of draftsmanship capable of shrinking arcane provisions to one-third of what they would be in anyone else's document and making them inescapably comprehensible, and total fidelity to the fuddy-duddy institutions he served. Schmidt had not had to cajole or threaten to win in negotiations: it had sufficed that he was always demonstrably and impeccably right. Thus, he had been moved, beyond anything he had ever experienced in his career, when, at a dinner at the "21" Club celebrating the completion of one of his transactions, the legal department of the insurance company that was his client presented him with a plaque showing a knight-at-arms, with his name at the top and underneath it the words "Dieu et mon droit." A tribute, the general counsel explained, to the power of Schmidtie's right reason and, he added laughing, his crushing rectitude.

No, he must not quarrel with Riker. His deepest need was to be at peace with his daughter, to maintain a state of wordless complicity with her, like those rare moments of surrender when the surf that rakes the Atlantic beach is transformed into tiny, glittering ripples, and one can float on one's back, eyes open to the late-September sky. Instead he had been churlish with the boy, Charlotte surely thought he had, and on the day she had told him they would be married! It didn't matter that the vulgar boy had provoked him. Coming from himself, ill temper was unforgettable, if not unforgivable. If he didn't manage, for reasons that couldn't be stated without aggravating the case, to return to treating Riker as he used to in the office, indeed at the breakfast and dinner table under his own roof during all those years when, after all, he was sleeping with Charlotte, if he behaved as though Mary and he hadn't imagined and accepted the conventionally desirable result, he would force her to take Riker's side against him, to behave, quite properly, as though the insult had been directed at her. This was the kind of misery that Mary could have cured, even as she could unravel desperately tangled kite strings and make things all right between him and Charlotte, now talking to one and now to the other, keeping their confidences, until at last, hours or many days later, one of them was coaxed into saying the obvious, necessary words that meant nothing but brought them back into sunlight.

And a quarrel with DeForrest and the management committee over the pension plan? He could imagine how Riker might explain the two sides of the argument to Charlotte. Charlotte didn't doubt that he had more than enough money. How could it be otherwise? Money had not been a subject Mary and he discussed in Charlotte's presence—they hardly ever talked about it even when they were alone. His mother's squalid nagging about money had been the constant background noise while he lived with his parents; he didn't want to be reminded of it in the life he had made for himself. To be sure, he had occasionally informed Charlotte that he wasn't rich, in a tone, he realized, about as convincing as that of his ritual injunctions not to speed on the eastern end of the Long Island Expressway because she was bound to be caught, but considering how Mary and he had lived, in such material ease and without going into how that ease was financed, as though bills didn't exist, could she have resisted the conclusion that in fact he was rich, and his disclaimers of wealth or anything like it only a part of his perpetual scoffing and self-deprecation? What would she think of her father when she heard he was digging in his heels to resist—uselessly, in all likelihood—prudent measures the partnership wanted, ones that had been designed, with expert help, to make sure that retirees weren't a millstone tied to the young partners' collective neck?

He looked at the kitchen clock. Charlotte would have left her office, and probably gone to her dance class, would now be at home waiting for the hardworking Riker's late meeting to end, microwave oven at the ready. What did they put in it? Surely not little steaks; it would have to be grilled tuna—of course, cooked sushi! Instant tortellini! A lot of good it had done, poor Mary's ban on TV dinners, frozen veal parmigiana with potato croquettes, takeout or delivered pizzas, and those little carton rhomboids of chicken with water chestnuts from the Chinaman on Third Avenue. Linen napkins, the table set as if for a picky grown-up, even if Charlotte was having her dinner alone, as she often did because he, Schmidt, had worked late for many years and Mary had book parties she had to attend—all that effort rewarded by her blooming into an iron-pumping yuppie! Their daughter in Lycra leotards, waiting for her bankruptcy maven to come home! And he—probably accustomed to eating in his shirtsleeves, ballpoint pens and pencils sticking out of his pocket, unbathed and unshaved!

Quiet, Schmidtie. That's not the way to domestic tranquillity.

Almost surely he could catch her at Jon Riker's apartment, before he came home; perhaps it was better than talking to her at the office. There, she might put him on hold and attend to more pressing business! On the other hand, he was coming to realize that what he had to say, that he would be delighted to accept the senior Rikers' invitation to eat their turkey—subtext, meet them and their relatives—could be said anytime, the sooner the better, and quite usefully in fact when Riker was at home, provided he could resist adding a crack or two to the acceptance. Yes, even if he was speaking to Charlotte when she was alone, he'd have to be careful to hold the irony. Then the evident, symmetrical solution presented itself: He could leave the message with Jon's secretary without speaking to either of them!

He dialed the secretary's number, got instead her voice mail, and, overcoming an urge to giggle, said, Please tell Mr. Riker that Mr. Schmidt accepts with pleasure the invitation to Thanksgiving lunch so kindly extended by Mr. Riker's parents.

Now that was done; he could see there was no other way out of the Thanksgiving mess, short of a well-staged last-minute sore throat or bronchitis. A lugubrious solution, but one that needn't be rejected out of hand. In the meantime, he would call Charlotte at the office and invite her to lunch the first day she was free. It was impossible to face Jon Riker, the Riker parents, and the Riker relatives and friends before he had talked to her. About what? There was time to figure that out, and why not have lunch with his daughter, even if he had nothing new or urgent to say? He might let her talk about her life; she ought to have a great deal to tell him. It seemed to Schmidt that he was behaving intelligently, as though he had sought Mary's advice and followed it.

Schmidt detested leftovers and cluttered refrigerators. He shopped separately for each meal and bought staples every two weeks at the grocers' cooperative in the village. Held back by the weather and the weight of his sadness, he hadn't left the house all day. The only place where he might still get food was the delicatessen with a misleading Russian name that sold cold cuts and shamelessly marked-up groceries. Cold cuts didn't tempt him. He could dine on the sardines, hard-boiled eggs, and bread he already owned and had paid for, and wash them down with bourbon or the Côtes du Rhône he hadn't finished the night before, when he had cooked hamburgers. Schmidt's feelings about leftovers didn't extend to unfinished bottles of wine, provided the wine hadn't waited more than two days and, during warm weather, was kept in the refrigerator. He had eaten sardines, hard-boiled eggs, and bread for lunch, but lack of variety was no objection; after all, he ate the same thing for breakfast every day, and sardines and eggs were food he liked. The alternative was to go out to dinner, not to a friend's house, since no friend had suggested it, but to a restaurant. He got the ice, the bottle of whiskey, and a glass, and carried them to the living room. The fire was laid. He had done that after clearing the breakfast dishes and making his bed in the morning. It took with the first match. He poured a drink and sat down on the sofa that faced the fireplace.

To go out, actually to speak to someone, even if it was only the waitress, to hear the sound of his own words, struck him as desirable. It might make him sleep better. It wasn't a question of having a hot meal; he could take care of that by making scrambled eggs, instead of having them hard-boiled. The cost of the meal shouldn't deter him, although the local restaurant prices were absurdly high in relation to the quality of the food and the service. He had done more arithmetic since the meditation in the cellar: he wouldn't need to apply for food stamps or live like a hermit, provided he bought an inexpensive, simple house. The yearly saving on upkeep alone would pay for many outings. But if he were to have dinner at O'Henry's, which was surely where he would go since he liked his conversations with Carrie, the waitress whose name he had recently learned, chances were strong he would, on the way to his table, be inspected by the Weird Sisters. These were the three writers' widows who lunched and dined there most days—every day, he was willing to bet, unless one of them or one of the larger circle of similarly situated hags was entertaining at home. He knew them, had known them for years, and had always greeted them with a smile and a wave of the hand and passed on. Mary occasionally paused for a few words—they were of her world—while he waited at a respectful distance. He had understood that he was in fact invisible to them, as a lawyer, a married man, and the husband of an editor who had not had the honor of publishing the works of their husbands. His new person seemed to be acquiring an alarming opacity; after a few more smiles, a hoarse summons to join them might issue. Could he refuse without giving offense? He might get away with it the first time, but politeness would require that he ask to join them himself the next time he arrived, if it wasn't obvious that they were at the point of finishing their meal. Unless his having been a lawyer was a fatal social bar, his presence would not be without precedent. At lunch, there were occasionally men at their table. Two of them were also known to Schmidt. They were both local writers, gaunt, tall, and trembly, of whom one must believe that their work was done in the early morning or late at night, before the prandial intake of martinis or long after it had been slept off.

Schmidt wasn't sure he would thrive in this particular seraglio. He feared that, except when free legal advice was needed—how to recover the deposit on the tour of Sri Lanka, booked just as the Tamils had gone on their most recent rampage and canceled only two days before flight time, or in which court a libel action might be started to restrain the publication in Ukraine of a biography of the late husband that alluded to his taste for little boys—the treatment reserved for him by those hags, and even more so by their men friends, would be patronizing, of a sort to make him regret his presumed wealth, flat stomach, and as yet unredeemed failure to tend the thankless Muse. There were other disadvantages. For instance, did he want the overly familiar owner who seated guests when he wasn't too busy downing a shot at the bar or watching a momentous pass on the television screen to direct him automatically to the widows' table? Was he ready to do the arithmetic when the time came to split the check and measly tip among the revelers, to keep track of who had drunk how much of what? It was a case that called for the application of Groucho Marx's rule: If that club would have him as a member, he didn't want to join. "People" might think he had become a hopeless case, ready for AA and the social worker. But were there people likely to turn up at O'Henry's—other than Carrie, the waitress, and Mr. Whittemore, at whose store across the street he bought liquor in transactions marked by mutual respect—about whose opinion he gave a hoot?

He couldn't think of anyone. Martha's friends, who had taken up Mary and him with old-lady graciousness, were dead or resided in nursing homes or distant retirement communities. It was true that, in principle, anyone with a house nearby, or even a chance visitor capable of identifying the Weird Sisters and their entourage, might go to O'Henry's, for hamburgers with chili, which were good, or, in the case of resident squares and summer people, for the regular sightings of local litterateurs. But Schmidt no longer had contacts with squares of his own class who owned property nearby. They had ceased when the tennis club refused to admit as a member the Jewish laryngologist who had bought, overpaying considerably, a large house across the street from the club entrance, especially in order to be near the courts on which he had hoped to play. Mary was on the admissions committee and, upon the fatal blackballs being cast, resigned in the name of the whole family. Schmidt hadn't complained—not even about not having been consulted. Later tennis stopped being an issue because Mary had to give it up, they had thought only temporarily, after the false alarm of her angina that was exacerbated by the anguish over her family history of heart disease. Schmidt hadn't wanted to play, if it meant leaving her alone; she loved the game with such a passion. In the meantime, Schmidt and Mary's social life continued among Mary's friends: other editors, writers of all stripes, and literary agents, and their hangers-on, so many of whom lived nearby. They were by and large more interesting than the squares, and often played good tennis. Some were rich as well as glamorous and could organize games on their own courts. Frankly speaking, Schmidt was not displeased when the subject came up, because a gossip column had mentioned some lunch on a terrace overlooking the beach, to note that his partners envied his fancy connections. Obedient to unwritten rules that govern such matters, none of them dwelled in the surrounding woodland, their habitat being nearer the city, chiefly in Westhampton. It had occurred to Schmidt recently that his social situation had changed: he might rejoin the tennis club. But Charlotte's marriage plans were going to throw a monkey wrench into that project; he had no intention of becoming Riker's Trojan horse.

It was Schmidt's belief that he had no friends of his own in the agreeable circle that had been his and Mary's. He had entertained most of Mary's pals and colleagues as her husband, and it was in that capacity that he had been entertained by them. They had been popular hosts: the fact that their parties were held at an old house of considerable distinction, and the food and drink they served were more than a cut above usual book party fare, didn't hurt. But he realized that their guests came, and invited them back, because of Mary: she was a powerful editor and she was genuinely liked. Her own authors, of course, were assiduous; so were many others who aspired to be published by her. The invitations to large parties continued during the summer that followed Mary's death. Mostly Schmidt declined or, having accepted, at the last minute decided to remain at home. He didn't like to find himself standing on those broad lawns or under well-pruned trees, glass in hand, on the edge of the crowd as though its roar were a centrifugal force that had expelled him, too sad or too timid to push his way to the hostess or to break into conversations—groups didn't open to include Schmidt; journalists didn't race to greet him—that had no relation to his grief. Besides, he was certain that any effort he made would leave him fearing he did not have sufficient respect for Mary. He might have wanted to go to some of the small weekday or Sunday-night dinners Mary and he used to attend; but, with a few exceptions, which he was able to relate afterward to the presence at table of an unaccompanied female houseguest, his telephone didn't ring. He wasn't invited. Possibly it was because he hadn't been seen at the larger gatherings; people could well think he had decided to travel. The continuing flow of invitations to such events didn't contradict his theory. He was simply on the list for the Xs' or the Ys' standard summer parties, invitations to which were typically addressed and mailed by the secretary of one of the members of the household. There was no more to it than that. At one of the book parties he did attend, the hostess, a literary agent who represented several of Mary's authors, directly after offering Schmidt condolences and the usual odious apology for not having expressed them in writing, made a remark that offended him, and stuck in his mind.

You must be the hottest property around! An eligible new widower living in his own house in the Hamptons! Only one child, and fully grown! The females must be camping in your driveway!

I am too old, he had replied, whereupon his hostess said

that was nonsense, offering him the example of Ed Tiger and Jack Bernstein, both of whom were older than Schmidt and had just procreated. If you fall in love with a younger woman, anything can happen!

Perhaps, but Schmidt wasn't ready, certainly not for a member of the younger generation with her own children to raise or, worse yet, an urge to beat the chronological clock. That was, he believed, the way one put it. And it seemed to him that he was unlikely ever to be tempted, either by the houseguests to whom he owed his presence at those dinners, or by this cheerful literary person or the other women of his acquaintance, assuming that, even if married, or *en ménage*, they were all indeed candidates for his bed, and perhaps his hand, simply because he was in theory available and not yet on welfare. Time had not singled out these women particularly for harsh treatment. Rather, it seemed to Schmidt that loss of the ability to attract was an affliction as generalized among his female coevals as thinness of hair, the sclera and teeth turned yellow, sour breath, flaccidity or gigantism of breasts, midriffs gone soft and distended by wind, brown splotches and deltas of minute angry veins around the knee and on the calf, disastrous, swollen toes verging on deformity displayed in sandals or throbbing in the prison of black pumps. To tease Mary, he used to tell her what, in fact, he thought was the truth: that his own loss of libido, from the effects of which she was exempt (and this was so until the time, almost at the end, when pity for her body overwhelmed both desire and habit) had less to do with his own aging than with the aging of the women around him.

How could one, he would ask, referring to one or another of their friends, how could one want to have sex with her, es-

pecially for the first time? Can you imagine the terror of finding out what's under her clothes as one fumbles with hooks
and buttons, the terror of what one's fingers will touch once
the crotch has been reached?

Schmidt was the first to agree that there wasn't much to
recommend in his own face, mouth, torso, or extremities. As
a younger man he used to preen in every mirror; that was one
bad habit he had finally broken. The consequence appeared
to be that often, at the end of the day, he did not remember
whether he had shaved and would have to raise his hand to his
cheek to feel the stubble. He thought that if he were a woman
he would not want to find a body like his in bed. If that
wasn't the inevitable reaction of all women, nature had somehow steeled them against ugliness—a blessing as great as the
ability to make complaisance pass for desire. Why had nature
not made life as easy for men?

Cheered by these thoughts, Schmidt brushed his teeth,
put money and a credit card in the pocket of his trousers, and
set out for O'Henry's. At times like this, he knew he moved
like a puma. He removed his dripping oilskin at the door, held
it aloft in his right hand, concealing his face as he passed the
restaurant bar. Then, at once, he began a smooth, unbearably
long reach for the coat rack, making it last until he had
crossed the stage, away from danger, to the far end of the
room. There Carrie, rising on her toes, relieved him of his
burden. Schmidt wished it were a heavy Venetian cloak, reek-
ing of wet wool, the corner of which he could lift until there
was only a slit left, through which his eyes could fix and hold
hers. She led him to a table. The view of the Weird Sisters
and of the small cloud of smoke that hovered above them was

unobstructed. But the continuing serenity of their repast reassured Schmidt: they hadn't penetrated his camouflage.

By the time she had served him the chopped steak, which was his main course, the crowd at the bar was thicker and very noisy, but a sleepy, negligent, late-evening calm had possessed the dining area. The two Oriental busboys were setting up with paper tablecloths and paper napkins for the next day's lunch. Carrie lingered at Schmidt's table, her hand on the back of the empty chair. He observed her attentively, as had become his custom each time she served him: skin almost green in that light, black hair with tiny curls that she wore in a long, tight pigtail, large dark eyes, under them circles that deepened with fatigue, and someday, if her features retained their absolute purity, would perfect her resemblance to Picasso's *Woman Ironing*. She is younger than Charlotte, he thought, not more than twenty, and yet so very tired. She was some sort of Hispanic. Or it could be Negro blood. Her voice told Schmidt nothing of her origin: raucous as though she had worn it out wailing, it was also completely flat, neither educated nor vulgar. Waitresses at O'Henry's wore black pants under their long, white aprons. He wondered about her legs.

You've had a long day, he told her.

Yeah. She tossed her head as though to rouse herself from sleep. Big crowd at lunch for such a lousy day, and a big crowd at dinner.

Her neck also was admirable, like the neck of a tired swan.

Is there someplace you can rest between the two meals?

He imagined her asleep in the seat of her car, that long neck thrown back, mouth open, droplets of sweat on her upper lip.

If I don't have to shop, sometimes I go home. I live in Sag Harbor.

There were houses in Sag Harbor with peeling motorboats on trailers parked to the side, where electrified Santa Clauses went up early and kept on blinking until the spring. He supposed one could rent a room in some of them. But perhaps she was someone's daughter, or lived in such a house with a peanut-butter-skinned husband who delivered bottled gas? Or did he work with his hands and service garden irrigation systems? No, in that case she would live in Hampton Bays. That was a place he passed on the highway, where he imagined blue-collar locals necessarily had their dwellings. He never had stopped there.

That's very convenient—and pretty!

I like it. My girlfriend helped me find an apartment.

So she was single and did not live with her parents. Would Charlotte have said, My girlfriend? Possibly; come to think of it, he had heard young women lawyers in his office say about their vacation, I am going to walk in Bhutan with my girlfriend. So the usage had to be widespread.

Well, I used to live in New York. Now I live here.

I know that. She laughed. You are popular in Bridgehampton. I guess everybody knows about you.

I see.

That was, indeed, how he had always imagined it: the synod of local thieves gloating about how much money they made off him! Merely paying bills on time wouldn't buy good service in Bridgehampton, certainly not popularity. Schmidt, the winner of the respectable summer crowd's spending contest! He was tempted to suggest she tell the boys that the party was now over; it had been nice while it lasted, and he was glad they had enjoyed it.

What's the matter? Have I said something wrong?

A large man stopped waving his credit card in the air. Instead, he snapped his fingers. She began to make a face and then immediately smiled, only the curve of that truly admirable neck—she had inclined her head slightly to the side—giving a hint of her discouragement. As she left Schmidt's table, she let her hand brush his shoulder and whispered, I'll be back!

During slow moments, which grew longer as he finished his meal, and then smoked and drank many cups of espresso, she came back to stand beside the empty chair at Schmidt's table and talk about herself as if it were the most natural thing in the world. He learned that Carrie was short for Caridad, that her mother was Puerto Rican but her father wasn't, that the father's name—she giggled before she pronounced it—was Gorchuk (Schmidt concluded he couldn't be colored, more probably some sort of Russian, which conclusion led him to wonder whether he was a Jew) and that he had worked for the school system in Brooklyn, that her mother always spoke to her in Spanish. Also, that after one year at Brooklyn College she had stopped—temporarily—taking her present job to earn some money, as her parents couldn't give her any. Later, she would study to become a social worker, and get a job with the city, but she really wanted to be an actress.

A banal story, thought Schmidt, but better that than discovering she was the dropout daughter of a Mexican investment banker! Probably half the kids in his old firm's mailroom had a story just like that, but her job, on her feet ten hours each day, six days a week, that was quite different from goofing off at Wood & King. It seemed to him that she had a lovely way of not being downtrodden. Quite the contrary, there was a sort of personal elegance, something spunky, almost proud, about her that he had noticed right away, the first time he saw her taking orders and rushing about with plates spilling over with French fries.

She began to yawn each time she stopped at the table. The party was over, but not quite yet: Schmidt left a large tip, shamelessly larger than usual. What was he to do? She was working for tips, wasn't she? Some puma! He allowed himself to speed home on the wet back road.

III

No, there wasn't a single day before Thanksgiving she could have lunch with him. Her team was working on the tobacco campaign, night and day.

Then I'll see you and Jon on the weekend, Schmidt volunteered. He will probably have work from the office as usual, and, while he slaves away, you and I can go for a walk on the beach. It's been a long time since you and I have had a talk. I've missed that.

Dad, have you given up reading the *Times*? Everybody's joined the crusade against smoking. We are working to stop them before they cart you off to a concentration camp for reeducation.

Schmidt made a point of laughing.

Seriously, you've got a personal interest in what I'm doing! Dad, I'm almost sure I'll be in the office both weekends. Jon will probably have to be at the office too—unless he's down in Texas. If I don't have to go in, I think I'll just crash.

Then you should really find time to see me in the city. It doesn't have to be lunch. I said lunch because I wanted to take you out for sushi, but if you've given up raw fish it can be anything else you like. Charlotte, I need to talk to you. The meal doesn't matter.

It won't work, Dad. I've no time to relax or think about anything except tobacco right now. What's the use of talking when I'm like that? If you want to discuss Jon and me, it would be better to wait until you've been to the Rikers' home. By the way, has Jon's secretary told you how thrilled they are that you're coming to Thanksgiving?

That made him mad.

Yes, I got that message as well. Don't you think it might have been nice—I don't want to say polite—for you or Jon to tell me?

Dad, I would like a small present, how about ten dollars, for each time your Mrs. Cooney called me with messages from you or Mom! But mostly from my loving father! It was like a joke at college! These pieces of paper from my roommates or at the *Crimson:* Miss Schmidt, your father's office has called again to inform you that the car will meet you at Islip, Mr. Schmidt's secretary hopes Miss Schmidt will be pleased to learn she has two tickets for the Grateful Dead, Mrs. Cooney has Miss Schmidt's blood test results if Miss Schmidt would like to call! The best was the one about how Mrs. Cooney wishes Miss Schmidt to know that Mr. Schmidt will be available this afternoon after four to talk to her about her mother. That was right after we had the first scare! Give Jon a break!

I was and I am your loving father, and I was doing my best. It wasn't easy just then, between my work and Mary, and trying to make sure you and I stayed in touch, and running this house and the apartment.

Well, I am your loving daughter and I am very busy, and

Jon is going to be your son-in-law, and he is busier than you ever were!

Has Jon told you so?

He doesn't need to. I live with him, remember?

This conversation makes me wonder whether there is any point in asking to see you or going to visit those Riker parents who are so thrilled at the prospect of my visit!

Dad, we can see each other and talk, if you feel like talking, after Thanksgiving when I have time. I'm not sure though that there is any point unless you make Jon and me feel you are happy about our marriage and want us to be happy together. It isn't just the way you were last Sunday. You've been carrying on like this since the day of Mom's funeral. You never speak to Jon except to say something nasty, and the rest of the time you put on your looking-right-through-him act.

My goodness! I hadn't suspected you had so many grievances—old and new! We had better hang up now, while we're still on speaking terms.

The storm had blown out to sea at last, and the kitchen was yellow with sunlight. Schmidt found it hurt his eyes. He sat down in his chair at the table, turned his back to the window, and lit a cigar. He had a deal with a discounter who mailed cigars to him in a private-brand box. The advertising hinted they were in fact Cuban. It didn't make much difference; for the price, the taste wasn't half bad. Tobacco campaign indeed! Didn't she remember he never touched the garbage her client sold? Who would have thought a summa in comparative literature, faultless French, summer internships Mary found for her with those famous small newspapers—all that enthusiasm, all those gifts—would lead straight to the sewer. Sure, Wood & King defended asbestos cases! There was no need to remind him; he had never been proud of it. They also tried to get serial murderers off death row—pro bono! But they didn't try to sell the public on the idea that asbestos was a great product. Besides, what did his work, or his firm's need to cover the overhead, have to do with how she had decided to live? Nobody had tried to open the doors to a better or wider world for Schmidt—certainly not his old man!

He felt tired, hardly able to move; his bones ached. How many more years of this? He was sixty and in good health: Ten? Fifteen? Twenty-three, like his father? Each day like this or worse, probably much worse? Old heartaches, stale disappointments, arguments lost long ago—why did they come back to stick their tongues out at him over and over? A career in public relations! His daughter choosing an occupation both mercenary and parasitic. Necessarily, it had hardened her, given her a tolerance for vulgarity and meanness. The marriage to Riker would finish the job. This piece of blackmail was conclusive proof. Riker, not Charlotte, had invented it. Had he brought the parents into it, consulted them? He must have told her it was time to break her father. Tell the old boy he has to toe the line or he won't see you! These were steely negotiating skills, the killer instincts he had himself babbled about at firm meetings when that circumcised prick was up for partnership.

He heard car doors slam. Wednesday—it must be the Polish cleaning brigade. He was too nervous to shave, too nervous to remain in the house with them. The forward observers, Mrs. Zielnik and Mrs. Nowak, poured into the kitchen and caught him by the arms. Kissed, he fled upstairs, wiping his cheeks on his sleeve. The bed in Charlotte's room was unmade. That was good; they would know it was time to change the nuptial sheets. In the corner, he saw Riker's running shoes, on top of them thick socks—unwashed, he supposed. At arm's length, holding them with the tips of his fingers, he carried these articles to the bathroom, dropped them on the floor, lowered the toilet seat and cover, and without looking, flushed, just in case. A contraption for cleaning gums, familiar to Schmidt from drugstore window displays, but new in this place, stood on the shelf. Fearful of electrical fires, he unplugged it. Beside it, in a glass, two plastic attachments for use in the mouth, one with a blue and the other with a pink base. Conjugal hygiene! No doubt one sat straining on the crapper while the other performed advanced oral ablutions. Back in the bedroom, he stripped the blankets and threw them on the floor. There they were, the weekend stains—like a kid's wet dreams in camp.

By the time he had put on his heavy sweater and descended the front stairs, the vacuum cleaners were in action. Waving with one hand, pointing to his ears with the other, to make sure they understood there was too much noise for conversation, he passed through the front hall. He had avoided the weekly update on Mrs. Zielnik's eczema and the pesky bladder of Mrs. Nowak's husband. That was something to be grateful for.

He heard the sea from the road, before he got to the residents' parking lot. Mauled to the bone by the storm, the beach had become a narrow, abrupt strip. Neat clumps of seaweed, like little brown nosegays laid out in parallel arches, marked the successive limits of the ocean's heaving advance. Schmidt left his loafers in the dune and walked east, along the edge of the surf, where the sand was hardest. There was no pause between the breakers, no rest from the sucking that followed every crash. He could not imagine making it through that water, heavy with sand, rushing in confused circles while it gathered its force for the next strike. Why hadn't he done it, right after Mary died, the way he had imagined it? The scene was out of the Woody Allen movie that looked like Bergman, only the figure on the screen would be he: A thin, fairly tall man, to judge by his posture no longer young, in cotton trousers and a large parka, stares from this beach at just such a sea, but the light is less strong. One senses that it's daybreak. He stands at the edge of the water. A disorderly wave far ahead of the others swamps his Top-Siders, wets him to the knees. The man doesn't retreat; with his sleeve, he wipes the mist of tears from his face. Then he does take a few steps back, looks to the left and to the right and at the sky, runs heavily, but that's the best he can do on the wet sand in shoes that are already like weights, and plunges into the surf. Even in these ridiculous clothes, one can tell he is an experienced swimmer. He makes it over the top of the first wave, and then the second, as though he were romping with grandchildren; the third is too high, so he dives through it, recovering in time to take on each newcomer until he is free, at last able to start swimming. He does an improbable sort of crawl, arms in those baggy sleeves lifting in a laborious wobble, the head bobbing up irregularly, quite out of control. At a certain point—the strangeness of the scene subverts the absent spectator's and perhaps the man's own sense of time—he seems to have had enough. He goes for the shore, and he is intelligent about it. On his back, keeping an eye on those breakers, he does a tired swimmer's float. A huge one comes. The man repeats his diving act until he catches a wave badly: a frantic arm is out of line. Still, he comes up, for a moment that's brief like a shriek, in great disarray, no longer swimming. Then there is absolutely nothing.

Why hadn't he?

Some seagulls flew overhead, in full cry. Such a very clear day! Already, he could see the house at the edge of Georgica. Too bad only he was taking advantage of the sunshine to walk on the beach, but what could one expect? The locals were busy unplugging toilets or filling oil tanks and sending bills for the same, writers were writing or getting a cup of coffee at the candy store, the Weird Sisters were on the telephone, retirees with apartments in New York or Paris were in those apartments getting dressed for lunch, and the other old farts had lost the ability to move or the habit. They might be playing canasta at the Seagull Motel! Mary had liked walking on this endless beach even more than he. A place of no abiding footprints: Why hadn't the ocean saved him from trudging here alone, his thoughts dispersed and black? Had he lost his nerve? That might be the truth, disguised as pity for his own body, still undamaged, still eager, like a dog that won't come to heel, eager to gallop about, a soggy tennis ball in his teeth, so unprepared for the rolling and scraping against the ocean floor, for the swelling and the evisceration. *Pace* Woody Allen, it was possible to be less brutal. There were pills: all those leftover pills in paper cups. It turned out that Mary didn't need everything the surgeon had provided. He had told himself he should bury her, that it was wrong—cruel, really—to leave it to Charlotte to clean up after both mother and father, to muck out their private, unspeakable debris. But it hadn't taken long before he recognized the true shape of his disgrace: curiosity, and longing for solitude, both obscene as an itch. For so many years, in effect, his entire adult life, he had lived at Mary's side. Could he not sail alone beyond the pillars of Hercules and taste the apples of the western garden before the waves closed over his head?

He had never promised Mary he would do it, although the temptation had been great. Solicitude—she was so tired— had held him back, and his own dislike of pathos. Such little courage as she still had shouldn't be used up in vacuous re- monstrances: No, you mustn't, you are still a young man, think of Charlotte! Yes, I must, I won't live without you! Yet, until the end, he had intended to do it, at the right time, without making it harder for her.

Hee! The ocean is still wet, the painkillers are nice and dry!

The Polacks would be at his house for one hour more. That was the message Schmidt read on the face of his watch. A meal in their presence was unthinkable. Comments on his nutrition. Or Mrs. Subicki, her rear end cascading off the seat of the kitchen chair drawn up companionably beside him, legs in elastic kneesocks stretched out, monstrous feet un- shod for comfort, would reach into the Gap shopping bag for a bologna and mayonnaise on white, already half consumed on the previous job, and finish it pensively. The hard-boiled eggs and sardines could wait—for his supper or the next day's lur .1.

It wasn't the Sisters who harpooned Schmidt. He hadn't even noticed whether they were at their usual place at O'Henry's. Sure of himself and nimble, Schmidt had evaded the owner's greeting and was moseying toward a table in the land of charity, near the one at which he had sat the previous evening—itself occupied by two males of the minor insurance agent genus—it being equally out of the question, Schmidt thought, to sit elsewhere, and let the sweet child fear she had been wrong to be so friendly with him or that she hadn't been friendly enough when she said thank you for that tip, and to say point-blank to the busybody owner that he wanted to be served by Carrie. Instead, he heard the familiar, droll voice of his college roommate. A pleasantly stocky man with a face like Michael Caine's and layers of beige cashmere on his body rose to embrace him. A lucky roll of dice in the housing office had joined them in their freshman year; untroubled affection kept them together until they graduated.

At last! My faith was about to be shaken! Half past two and no Schmidtie! Mrs. Cooney would not have allowed such a thing to happen.

You are right! I don't know what to say. I'll just say that I am terribly sorry.

Cooney II or *The Return of Cooney*! Which title do you like better? Can we install that saintly woman and her telephone in your pool house? I yearn for her calls: May we confirm lunch today at twelve-thirty? Or my favorite: We are on a conference call with a client. Will you forgive us if we are fifteen minutes late?

There was a bottle on the table Gil had been working on. Too bad about Carrie; how could Schmidt get Gil to move to another table when he had already ordered? Perhaps it was just as well. She would be watching from the door leading to the kitchen and perhaps she knew—if not, she would find out!—who Gil was. Schmidt's prestige was about to sky-rocket.

A drink of cheap red wine? All the decent bottles are out-rageously overpriced.

He poured Schmidt a glass.

Thanks, I have stopped drinking at lunch. No, I do want it. Gil, I am not just late. The truth is that I had forgotten we were having lunch. The only reason I'm here and haven't stood you up altogether is that I had to get out of my house. The Sikorski squadron is in it, moving the dirt from one place to another. I have so few appointments these days I don't bother to look at the calendar.

Yet another reason to make Cooney come back. If you have nothing to do, why haven't you called us? You know Elaine and I would love to have you come for a meal. We want you at every meal!

I don't know any such thing. You and Elaine are always working. I don't want to interfere with the birth of a new masterpiece.

We eat—just like everybody else!

This was disingenuous of Gil, but Schmidt had no desire to say so. In his opinion, the only reason it was possible to maintain that they were still intimate friends was that he had taught himself to observe certain conventions carefully. One of them, which under present conditions clearly needed up-dating, was to believe that deep down in her heart Elaine liked Mary and him more than the glamorous people, her real friends, she and Gil lived with day in and day out, and that she regretted—oh how bitterly!—the mysterious, irresistible forces that interfered, absolutely prevented, Gil and her from "playing" with the Schmidts. In her language that meant doing together the sort of things one might expect of couples bound by a special, secret predilection: casual dinners after an off-Broadway show, vacation trips to the Andes, and what have you, not merely seeing Schmidt and Mary at large gatherings—principally screenings of Gil's films and the receptions that followed. Another convention regulated Schmidt's lunches with Gil. Soon after Gil's *Rigoletto* had made it to Cannes and won, Schmidt sensed from remarks Gil let drop about certain friends that it was on the whole better not to call Gil first but to wait until the suggestion to have lunch came from him. And yet, experience with disturbingly long periods when Gil gave no sign of life whatsoever, even when there was no reason to think he had taken offense or was out on the Coast, suggested that if Schmidt wanted to avoid a de facto rupture he himself would have to make a move at some point. That this was the correct line of conduct Schmidt had no doubt: Mrs. Cooney, who understood a lot more than she let on, had tacitly validated it. She would mention casually, but probably in accordance with one of the schedules she kept in her desk drawer, that she had noticed several openings in Schmidt's calendar and ask whether he mightn't like her to call Mr. Blackman's assistant—since they hadn't heard from him recently—and set up the usual. That would be lunch at twelve-thirty, eaten, depending on whose turn it was to invite, at Schmidt's club or at a restaurant in the Seagram Building that was treated like a club by Gil and a number of other sleek men and women with idiosyncratic eating habits the headwaiter had memorized or entered in a computer.

Why Gil should consider Schmidt's calculated reserve natural in so old a friend, why he should go off the air abruptly and without any explanation, were questions to which Schmidt thought he had the answer, one that made him sad. It had to be the slow onset of a combination of absentmindedness and indifference so profound that, unless Gil's assistant told Gil, in accordance with her own schedule, that it was Schmidt time once again, or, increasingly rarely, Gil himself suddenly wanted to exchange a certain kind of gossip, the way Schmidt might feel a craving for knockwurst and potato salad, he wouldn't think of Schmidt at all. Schmidt supposed it was no different from the way he sometimes forgot to send his annual contribution to Harvard College, Planned Parenthood, the Armenian Jazz Festival, the Girl Scouts, etc., a failure that the Mrs. Cooneys who worked for those institutions were paid large salaries to prevent, even as they took care not to irritate him by overly frequent appeals. The value of his link to Gil was such that Schmidt accepted the humiliation like bad weather. It had not, for instance, prevented him, at a time when he was more ignorant about death, from being pleased to imagine that, when the time came, it was Gil whom Mary would unhesitatingly summon to his bedside. That nice prospect no longer mattered. If Charlotte and Jon did any summoning after packing him off to the hospital, it would be that clown Murphy or some other lawyer of his ilk.

Is there a new film in the works?

Yes and no. I have a proposal and a script I should take seriously, but there is something about it I dislike. Elaine has a proposal too—for a show she might organize at the Whitney. We are holed up here, fiddling around and drinking. I write things down and cross them out. What about you?

There is nothing left to fiddle with! I am discovering that it's difficult to wean myself away from being a lawyer. I wonder about clients, the firm, whether Mrs. Cooney likes living in Santa Fe, and on and on. I could take the jitney into town, go to firm lunch, and find out, but I hate going to the office and I hate calling up my former colleagues. It makes me feel like an unwanted ghost! I remember what my father used to say after he quit: everything keeps going around and around.

I told you to take a leave for as long as necessary to look after Mary, and not even think of retiring. There is a race of men—all federal and state and bank employees, and most dentists—who are born to retire. They aspire to retirement from the moment they are born. Youth, sex, work, are only the necessary intermediary states: the subject progresses from larva to pupa to nymph until, at last, the miracle of metamorphosis is complete and gives the world the retired butterfly. Golf clubs, funny shoes, and designer sunglasses for the dentist, campers and gas-fired barbecue sets for the employees at the low end of the pay scale! You and I belong to a grander race. We need to be kneaded by misfortune and modern medicine before we are ready. Praised be the Lord, I am happy to announce that you strike me as unripe for a living death. What you need is a job. I'm going to think one up for you.

Schmidt felt his heart pound. Gil was going to offer him

work: ask that he negotiate the financing for his production company's next movie deal. Or some sort of consultancy—if only it wasn't a purely legal job. Then he could take it without running afoul of the no-practice rules of the W & K retirement plan!

No dice. All Gil had to offer was advice to be endured patiently. Isn't that man DeForrest who runs Wood & King your friend? Can't you work something out with him? If they don't want to redistribute partnership percentages, why shouldn't you go back as a partner on salary? A sort of senior adviser?

Schmidt laughed.

It's too late for that. Too many irreversible steps have been taken. I have bargained for a pretty decent deal by W & K standards, I have no clients left—they too have been redistributed and seem quite happy. Where would I live in the city? Let's talk about something cheerful: like the Blackman children!

We'll do the children in due course. You have a problem. Quite seriously, Schmidtie, isn't there anything you want to do? How about a foundation? Even better, go on some boards. What's the name of that lawyer with bad skin who raised money for Reagan? That's what he has done.

You've put your finger on my problem! All I've done is work for W & K. I am a product nobody needs. That's why you can't get me back on the shelf. I have thought about foundations. And even if there were some harmless small outfit that would hire me, I am not sure I'd go for it! In the first place, there is the practical angle: it would cost me more to move back to the city and take such a job than it would pay. More important, I've always disliked charities and the sort of people who run them. It's my vision of hell. You raise money and set aside a fat slice for salaries and overhead. The next thing you know, you have to invent programs so that what's left can be spent on them. Then da capo! Jaw-breaking boredom!

Seeing Gil's blond face darken, Schmidt added with alacrity: I don't mean all not-for-profits, for instance not the home for actors with Alzheimer's you support, that's quite useful, and I don't dislike all foundation presidents, just most of them. The simple truth is just as I said—nobody wants me. Not my firm and neither foundations nor boards. I haven't had the right extracurricular activities, so I don't have the right profile!

Schmidtie, what you don't have is the right attitude!

Believe me. I am like some guy on a bus who got up to pee and comes back to find that his seat has been taken, along with every other one. What can he do? Get off? You know what that means in the case of the one and only bus ride. It's better to look stupid and hang on to a strap. What do I care if I look stupid!

You certainly shouldn't have gone to pee while your pal DeForrest was getting himself elected presiding partner of your firm. I've never understood it. You as much as told me the job could have been yours; all you had to do was to say you wanted it. Then you would be running the firm and asking your partners whether their clients or anybody else needs them!

Schmidt salted his French fries. He had been picking at them daintily, with his fingers, as though he really meant to leave them on his plate. They weren't bad. To hell with abstinence. He decided he would eat them, down to the last one. What would he get in return for denying himself a little fat? Sometimes Gil's memory was more irritating than charming. One could go for months without seeing him, and he would take the conversation up just where it had ended, remembering tidbits one wished had been forgotten or never mentioned.

That's precisely it. DeForrest wanted the job. He wanted it more than I. In fact, I'm not sure I had a reason for wanting it. I might have only wanted to be sure I could get it. That's not enough.

And DeForrest?

He had this ambition to be presiding partner for years; at times he seemed quite childish about it. Also, he had gotten rather tired of practicing law. It's something that happens to lots of lawyers, but it hadn't happened to me. So it was natural he should get the job. Besides, he had all sorts of ideas about what should be done—quite a manifesto. I had no program—I guess I would have just tried to keep things as they were.

What would have been wrong with that? You always liked that firm, and you seemed to make enough money. Do you wish now you had been less accommodating?

Not really. DeForrest might have put up a fight and won. That would have been very tough on me and bad for the firm. Anyway, I would have left just the same, at the same time, and I would be in the same spot now.

Schmidt was stuck with this answer. What was the use of admitting that he had stood aside because Jack DeForrest had told him over and over they would each have what they wanted most? Schmidtie, you want to shape the practice and

that's what you should do, leave the administrative headaches
to me, you don't like that stuff. An unofficial, happy duumvi-
rate. It hadn't worked out that way, though; there was no
sharing with Jack. Overnight he had been diminished, and it
escaped no one that something had gone wrong: Schmidt remained just as he had been, with his own clients and his own
shrinking practice—for the likes of Riker to carp at.

He smiled at Gil and helped himself to half of what remained in the bottle.

Let's sound that cheerful note. How are the sublime Blackman girls?

Still working hard at their dead-end magazine jobs. Refusing to be grown-ups. Lisa is without a boyfriend and becoming frantic about it. Nina has found a new one who doesn't
earn a living and never will. To be precise, he is having his
voice repositioned—from baritone to tenor, because he
thinks he looks more like a tenor. By an Albanian coach! And
his father is an Orthodox priest in Scranton! I wonder what
the paternal voice is like. Lisa and Nina haven't stopped playing with dolls. Perhaps they had too many dolls' tea sets.

And Elaine's kid?

Schmidt had forgotten her name, something that never
happened to Gil.

Lilly. Lovely Lilly. No change. She's a harmless, dull child.
I wish she spent more time with her father. It would make it
easier for Elaine and me to travel. His girlfriends are practically her age! I tell Elaine that's built-in company for Lilly
and should make it easier for him to take care of his daughter.
She doesn't see it that way. Why do you and I always carry on
about our children like a couple of barnyard hens?

Because we love them.

No, it's guilt. I have a reason—I abandoned mine and their mom and have lived with silly Lilly and her mom, so I can't grow up and act like the father of grown-up women. But you? You and poor Mary were always perfect, and at least there you have got what you deserved—the beautiful, intelligent, and completely successful Charlotte! Any news?

She told me last weekend that she is getting married. No surprise there: to Jon Riker.

Ah, Schmidtie, how right and how wonderful! Your family has been reconstituted! I shouldn't have had to drag this out of you.

I was going to tell you but we got bogged down in my sorrows.

What a relief! Both of them have real, grown-up jobs, and they are getting married instead of playing house! I was wrong—you don't need a job, you have one! You will be the indispensable baby-sitter! I assume that Mary knew. That must have made her very happy. Elaine will call you. She will be thrilled. And a little envious!

In fact, I don't know whether Mary knew. I rather think they made up their minds afterward. And the truth is that I haven't taken the news well. We've had a sort of quiet but deadly tiff, and I don't know how to end it.

Tell me about it—everything.

Pride and a shared preference for dryness in discourse: Schmidt could not have brought himself to tell Gil that what had happened to their friendship made him suffer, or that for a moment he had hoped to work for him somehow. Everything else was fair game; one accomplice confessing to the other. In consequence, they were often indiscreet. Thus

Schmidt had told Gil about Corinne. And Gil, newly famous and newly rich, had come to Schmidt, although Schmidt had been the best man at his wedding and it wasn't Schmidt's sort of work, to say, I deserve to be happy and instead I am wretched, I must divorce Ann, handle it for me. Schmidt negotiated the arrangements with more zeal than if his own money and rights to children had been on the line, obtaining a perfect success, and wasn't surprised that Ann never spoke to him or to Mary again.

He wanted to answer Gil, but only in part; he wasn't going to say that he didn't have enough money. Therefore, he told Gil about the house not being really his and how he couldn't live in it with Charlotte and Jon, once they were married, on those terms, that they were trying to extract from him a show of enthusiasm it wasn't in his power to give, and about the Thanksgiving lunch with the Riker parents, which had turned into a test by fire.

Have you told Charlotte that you will give her the house and move out?

No. I couldn't explain it very well on the telephone, and I was afraid if I didn't make myself quite clear she would feel it was some sort of abrupt, hostile action. She will need some money from me. I have to talk to her about that as well. I don't want her to refuse my money.

I think she will see your leaving the house, not wanting to try to share it with them, as hostile, however much you explain. Can't you let up and work out some rules for when they come? After all, it will only be some weekends, when the weather is good. I can't imagine they will be spending every weekend here, with you.

Mary and I spent every weekend in this place, even

when Martha was still alive, and our summer vacations as well.

That was you and Mary! You had Charlotte right away, and that was once upon a time, in the Hamptons of the sixties! What a lovely picture in Technicolor. Flaxen-haired children back from pony lessons or the beach, clean and dressed. In the club car, the paterfamilias asleep after the third gin and tonic, mouth open. Suntanned Mom, legs freshly shaved, at the station waiting in the Chevy with the top down—or did she take the Ford station wagon?—worried about the lasagna in the oven and whether it's that time of the month. The au pair has just enough time to get into the bathtub in the master bathroom and do her toenails. Where is my camera? I'm ready to film! This script will be different. I see Charlotte and Jon on the Colorado River or waist deep in powder snow at Alta—pleasures you and Mary have never known! Meanwhile you'll take care of the trees and the cracks in the swimming pool.

Very nice, Gil. Do make that film. The trouble is that it will be even more difficult to clear out of there later, after I have fixed the one or two things that are left to fix. Right now, this is still a summerhouse, even for me, and I have a little snap left in my garters. But that isn't really the nub. You know how I am: if a corner can be found, I'll back myself into it, even if no one is coming at me. I just don't seem to know how to change the way I feel.

But as yet you haven't said anything to Charlotte—or Jon. And you really don't know the parents?

Never seen them. We don't bother about the background of our young lawyers or partners either, and we certainly don't interview the parents to see whether we approve! I believe they're psychiatrists, both of them—of the analyst kind.

You approve of Jon. But haven't you been curious about the father and mother? This is the guy your daughter has been living with for some time!

Mary was beginning to be tired by the time they got really serious. As a matter of fact, though, I am not curious and I don't approve! I don't approve of Jon, and I don't approve of Charlotte. That's one more hurt.

How can you not approve of Charlotte? She is one hundred percent all right. She has always done what you and Mary wanted, and she has done it faultlessly. And that boy is your partner! A partner in the prestigious New York firm of Wood & King. Isn't that what the *Times* squib will say? I would think that was eminently respectable.

On the surface. I hadn't expected to see Charlotte turn into a smug, overworked yuppie. I'd rather she had a dead-end magazine job, if that was what she really enjoyed doing. A job like Mary's, like your girls'—perhaps that's why I envy you!

Schmidtie, you don't know what you are talking about. The jobs Lisa and Nina have are the only employment they could get. Sure, they like magazines and people who write for magazines. But they can't write, they can't edit, and they refuse to learn about production. They are tourists in the magazine landscape, like someone on a safari admiring elephants from a Land Rover; the basic difference is that they are doing their looking from the lowest rung of the research department. What they earn isn't enough to pay the rent—let alone for the whole-grain cereal for them or the smelly gravel they feed their Abyssinians! I support them and the Orthodox priest's son. The only alternative would be a rich boyfriend or husband. There is no such animal in sight.

You can afford it, and so could I, though less well. Never mind, this isn't some adaptation of an Ibsen play you are about to film. If you want to know about Jon, he is all right but not what I hoped for either—not for my son-in-law or the father of my grandchildren or the guy I want to live with in a house that's morally my daughter's.

Let's get some more coffee, said Gil. Maybe we could use a brandy. I'm not working this afternoon and this interview isn't nearly over. What's the matter with Jon? Isn't he exactly your kind, the sort of fellow you were at his age—a brilliant young lawyer on the way to fame and fortune?

I haven't found either. No, I wasn't like Jon. Not inside— you, of all people, shouldn't define me by my profession. I'll tell you a guilty secret: I was a romantic when I was in college; when we met, more of a romantic than you, and I've never stopped being one. Jon never began. It's a real difference. He has all he needs to be a W & K partner, but there are other things that W & K doesn't care about and I do. Such as the value to be accorded to material success. Maybe it's his background, the taboo subject in the office!

Background? He is the son of two doctors, and you don't even know them! I am beginning to think their Thanksgiving is something you should thank God for. Go to the lunch graciously, and try to behave yourself once you are there. The parents will fall for your faded charm. That and a home-cooked meal will get you out of your corner.

I sort of doubt it.

And then Schmidt no longer cared whether he broke one of Gil's and his rules.

Gil, he said, I am lonely and lost. Don't badger me. I feel like a big enough fool already. Mary wouldn't have let this happen. I make no sense without her.

I think we will have that brandy.

Gil drank his, ordered another one, and told Schmidt, You are right. You are lost—I mean in your feelings—without Mary. You are probably also right about that house. If you have a new place to live, one that you have put together yourself, you can make a less complicated new start. You can motor over to your baby-sitting job. But there is some stuff going on between you and Riker that's like a subplot I don't understand. What do you have against him? Am I hearing code words: Psychoanalyst parents? Background? Not romantic? Schmidtie, have you been hinting that the boy is a Jew?

He is.

And is that upsetting you, the last of the Grove Street Schmidts is marrying a Jew?

That's the least of it.

Gil finished the second brandy.

Schmidtie, you're keeping me in suspense. This is where you are supposed to remember suddenly that you are speaking to a Jew. You should turn red and say, Oops, I don't mean your kind, you are so different!

As a matter of fact, you are.

You mean famous, known to you for forty-three years, and, above all, a sort of artist!

Isn't that better?

Not really. In any case, I don't want you to be my father-in-law. Call me when you come back from Thanksgiving. If those Riker parents haven't got you on their couch I may try mine.

They were the last lunch guests still in the restaurant. Their waiter had disappeared. Gil paid at the bar, interrupting a low-voiced colloquy between the owner and a pensive fat woman in a jersey dress almost the same shade of green as her rubber shoes. Her hands were badly chapped. In one she held a watery whiskey and in the other a filter cigarette. The Black & White ashtray beside her was full of butts—hers by the look of the lipstick smudges. A few stools away, the video store man and a companion Schmidt feared might be a child pornographer were staring at their draft ales. No conversation there. It occurred to Schmidt that the woman might be the owner's sister, come to visit from Montauk where she managed a cabins-in-the-dunes sort of motel for low-ranking Mafia types, or his bookkeeper. The former hypothesis would account for their having the same pig-blue eyes with no lashes, the latter for the attention with which he had been listening.

The light outside was still very strong. Schmidt stooped more than usual, because Gil had draped his arm over his shoulder. This was a notable gesture of solidarity, not to be interfered with.

Hi, Mr. Schmidt.

This was Carrie, on the sidewalk, out of uniform, in black wool tights and a red ski parka. The legs were good: long neck and long thin legs. Thin but differentiated—harmonious calves, knees that didn't draw attention to themselves, and strong, bold thighs rising toward the zone of mystery under the aforesaid unseasonable garment. Surely, the poor child yearned for a warmer climate, but then, why not wear trousers? Don't look a gift horse in the mouth, Schmidt! Hasn't your wish been granted? At last, you've seen her legs.

She did not have the look of someone about to cross the street. Did that mean she was waiting for a ride?

I saw you were paying so I waited to say hi.

This is Gil Blackman, Carrie. Carrie kindly stops to chat with this old man as he eats his lonely hamburger and has one drink too many.

Just make sure you come back soon!

That hoarseness—then it wasn't just her evening voice. Schmidt wished she would say something more; any words would do. Late night, barroom scales. A muddy Honda Civic with a dented rear fender and a scratch along the door on the driver's side was parked at the curb. She unlocked it, eased herself into it with the grace of a swan on point, arms tremulously lifted in a gesture of farewell, and started the motor. The wheels turned. As the car was pulling away she lowered the window and called, Have a nice evening! For the second time in the space of five minutes, Schmidt had got his wish.

Not half bad!

A sweet child.

Arm in arm they reached the parking lot.

Well, here I am.

Here was a long Jaguar. Gil sighed, raised his eyebrows, and hugged Schmidt. Onset of atavistic sentimentality? Effect of Schmidt's impending admission to the tribe via Charlotte, though presumably only as a corresponding member? The priest of Midian was blessed with seven daughters. What became of him after the connection with Moses? Did his herds multiply? These were questions to be researched.

Be of good cheer, Schmidtie. Think grandchildren, ocean and pool, and baby-sitting. And that doesn't mean you should look right away for a second Corinne, you old goat!

Schmidt ambled over to his car, wishing Gil hadn't said that. The memory was distant; he thought it still had the power to move him because he had been so careful not to summon it too frequently, guarding it like a bottle of old brandy, not to be often uncorked. The summer in question had begun badly, with rainy weekends and mosquitoes. Far too early, a hurricane struck. They lost the landing on the pond that Foster had given Martha permission to build and maintain, the sailing dinghy, and a copper beech as old as the house itself. Falling, it blocked the garage, and if it hadn't been for Schmidt's car, which he left during the week at the station, they would have had to rent a car or make do with bicycles until Foster's handyman sawed the huge tree into a supply of logs that lasted two winters or more. It was the first time Mary had obtained the right to work at home during July and August, so they could dispense with day camp and give Charlotte a real season at the beach. But Mary had just settled down with Charlotte and the new au pair, Corinne (Schmidt's vacation was scheduled for August), when she began to suffer from migraines of a severity she had never experienced before, which left her staggering from nausea and fatigue. The first attack was enough to make her withdraw from the club tennis tournament and stay away from the beach. The glare, the beating of the waves, and the wind all seemed unbearable. The west porch was screened; that's where she tried to read manuscripts a few hours each day. When she met Schmidt at the station she asked him whether he thought she had a tumor. He was able to reach David Kendall in Westchester that very evening; Kendall in turn called the neurologist. Mrs. Durban, the cleaning lady, agreed to sleep in the house and keep an eye on Charlotte and Corinne, and on Sunday night Schmidt took Mary with him to the city for tests. They saw the neurologist together the following Wednesday. As he had expected, the results were negative. He thought the headaches were the by-product of a mild depression linked to or aggravated by office tensions at Wiggins, the publishing house where Mary worked. Evidently, the depression should be treated, beginning in the fall—when the psychiatric profession returned from Wellfleet. For the time being he would equip her with tranquilizers to take during the day and sleeping pills guaranteed to give her a sound night's sleep. He advised her to sleep as much as possible. That was a form of psychotherapy in itself, and not the worst one either.

Although Schmidt was working on a ship mortgage financing that had to be signed up before the end of the month with only a first-year associate—the firm was unusually busy and, with half the lawyers on vacation, understaffed—he took Mary back to the country that afternoon. There was no point in suggesting that she stay in the city until Friday. She had already told him about Charlotte's worried little voice on the telephone, the manuscript she had forgotten to put in her overnight bag and left on the hall table, and her suspicion that Mrs. Durban was raiding the liquor closet. And there was no possibility of her returning alone. He had seen the hurt look on her face when he ventured a question: Would she prefer to drive his car from the station, or have him order a taxi to meet her? He took it back at once. Of course, he would take the train with her to Bridgehampton and spend the night. He too wanted to see Charlotte. It was stupid not to have thought right away of the early train. He would catch it, and be in time for the meeting at the bank.

She thanked him and then added: Isn't this nice for you? You will be able to explain to all your partners and all your friends that you aren't just overworked. You also have a wife who is sick in the head. They will feel sorry for you.

That piece of nastiness surprised Schmidt. Nothing of the sort had been a part of their discourse; he didn't know how he had deserved it. Was she off her rocker more seriously than the neurologist had hinted? He decided it was like one of those moments when a searingly bitter bile comes up, unexpected, from one's stomach into one's mouth. Depression could mean loss of self-control. What else was there she was hiding?

As soon as it was time for Charlotte to say good night he got Mary to go upstairs as well and, while she was getting ready for bed, made her a cheese sandwich and a bowl of tomato soup. When she had finished, he gave her one of the new sedatives. The effect was almost immediate. Mary was lying on her back. Mouth open, she began to snore, as Schmidt's father used to do, whatever the position or circumstance in which he had happened to fall asleep, and, faithfully, every night while Schmidt had lived at home. Each creak in the floor, each clearing of the throat, could be heard throughout the Grove Street house. In his room, separated from his parents' by a narrow corridor with a red runner, Schmidt would listen and imagine his mother's resentful, forever obsequious figure cowering at the edge of the black bed. It was a noise Schmidt had studied. Negligible at first, and almost amusing, like the whirring of a hobbyist's model airplane or the buzz of a mad fly, one doesn't mind it because it will end very soon, as soon as the toy engine runs down. Instead, the noise gathers strength, turns fearsomely rowdy and urgent, vastly larger than the placid, self-satisfied body from which it issues, and only a stake driven through the sleeper's heart will make it stop.

And this was Mary, who forced herself to stay awake in trains and buses, maintaining that one mustn't sleep in public! He sat down on the bed. Knowing how embarrassed she would be to know she had snored, he pinched her arm and shook her, then tried turning her on her side. Nothing. A drunken and implacable satyr crouched inside her, playing the same scale over and over on a scandalous pipe.

He put his hand under the light summer blanket, found the hem of her nightgown, pulled it up, and stroked her thighs. When he tugged and pushed, they parted. She had been shaving them since she was a girl but of late used wax. Her headaches must have made her neglect that chore. The stubble was rough, reminding Schmidt of the first time she had allowed his hand under her skirt. His eyes on Mary's face, watching for a change of expression, he uncovered her legs. Like her buttocks, the thighs were heavy, as though formed for the saddle. Mary was ashamed of those thighs, but they and her rear were Schmidt's joy. Still careful not to awaken her, he lifted her knees until she was ready to be mounted, continued stroking the insides of her thighs, moving up gradually, and then opened the lips. She was dry. He licked the middle finger and began a circling motion. There was no quickening in the tempo of the snoring, in fact no change at all, but she began to wet abundantly, and he moved his finger, and later two, easily up and down between the lips and inside her, and then lower. Without warning, pleasure overcame him with such force that he didn't even have time to put his other hand inside his trousers. When the spasm was over, he placed one of her hands, which had remained crossed over her stomach, where his hand had been, drew the covers back across her body, and turned off the reading lamp. Although the blinds were lowered, the room remained light, the days were so long. Mary's face was completely still. He wondered whether snoring so loud and so long—he supposed that, like the old man, she would keep it up until the morning—ever damaged the vocal cords. But perhaps they weren't involved, and all that rasping and sawing took place somewhere behind the nose. He checked her hand. Its position hadn't changed, but the fingers had a comfortable, lively look about them. Mary claimed that she never touched herself. He wanted her to learn to masturbate, in the hope that it might unlock her, make it easier for her to come instead of being so generous and telling him not to worry, she had really liked it anyway.

He swam laps in the pool and changed. Then he went into the kitchen, feeling a great hunger. No one was there; presumably, Corinne was still putting Charlotte to bed or had gone straight to her room, which was at the other end of the pantry. The glass of bourbon he poured for himself warmed him. Standing at the stove, he ate the rest of Mary's soup and the cheese and was about to put the plates and the casserole in the dishwasher when she stopped him. Monsieur shouldn't wash dishes, she said to him, that's my work.

He looked at her with curiosity. The girl was barefoot. That's why he hadn't heard her come in; quite possibly these were the first words she had ever addressed to him directly. He had been getting home late since the beginning of June, when she arrived, and on weekends she had seemed more timid than her predecessors. In any case, she had hardly any accent in English, and, according to Mary, her French was very pure. Perhaps being half Indochinese accounted for her shyness. He couldn't remember what Mary had said about her father's having been an official in the French administration in one of those places of which he, Schmidt, was good and sick: Vietnam, Cambodia, or most probably Laos. Whichever it was, he had married a local woman of good family and brought her and the child back to France quite late, some years after Dien Bien Phu. Then he died.

I don't mind at all cleaning up after myself, he replied. In fact, I think one should.

Please. Monsieur should be in the salon.

He made himself another bourbon—on second thought, took the bottle and the ice bucket—and avoiding the living room, went into the library. It was his and Mary's favorite room, especially pleasant in the summer, when all the windows were open. Seeing that she had turned on the lamps, he decided Corinne was a pearl: apparently good with Charlotte, beautiful, silent, and thoughtful about the house. Installed on the sofa, he closed his eyes. Should he in fact sleep here? Or perhaps he could take the big guest room and tell Mary that he had gone there so as not to disturb her. Sleeping through her snoring was out of the question, and so, it seemed to him, was telling her that she snored if he wanted her to follow the neurologist's orders.

Excuse me, Monsieur.

She was there, with a small glass tray of egg canapés. He noted that she had changed: she was wearing sandals and a white cotton dress instead of blue jeans.

I thought perhaps Monsieur liked these. He hasn't had dinner.

I do. Thank you.

She put the tray before him, and spoke again. I wonder if Monsieur would allow me to sit with him.

Of course.

Do you mind if I put on some music? I like Mozart very much.

She pronounced the name without the *t*.

Please play whatever you like most.

She had evidently been listening to their stereo because she picked out the record without hesitation. It was the horn concerto. He told her he was fond of it as well.

Thank you.

She sat down on the sofa beside him. There was a strong smell of almonds. She saw him sniff and said it was her hand cream. Some people think that Asian skin has an unpleasant odor.

What a dreadful thing to say and what nonsense!

I have made you angry. But it's something we worry about.

I'm not angry at all. Anyway, it's very nice smelling cream.

She smiled at him and sniffed her own arm.

Was this girl a flirt? If she was, there would never be a

Schmidt laughed. It's a fine book to look at together. I am ashamed that I've never been to that place. Perhaps we should take Charlotte.

The book was very large. She opened it so that it lay across both her knees and his, and she began to turn pages. The dress was sleeveless. Schmidt took a gulp of the bourbon; he was beginning to be unable to think of anything except the warmth and almond fragrance of that arm. The photograph she was looking at was of the edge of the gorge. She pointed with her fingers at the tiny figures of tourists on mules, and asked, Would Monsieur allow me to come   ?

I would insist on it, Corinne. You sho   p saying to me, Would Monsieur this, a   Monsieur th   ase call me Schmidtie, just like everybo   oes.

I don't dare.

Don't worry about it. It's p   f being in Ame   ca.

He moved his arm so it was   ainst hers, skin to skin. She gave him a look, and he thought she might be blushing, but he couldn't be sure.

What was he doing? Was it possible that he was making a pass at the au pair and that the au pair would go along with it? Disaster was certain. It was like sleeping with your secretary, a brutish act first consummated in the office, on the floor if there is no couch, later God knows where. Her studio apartment in Jackson Heights. At night, you leave just before she does, and catch a cab a couple of blocks away from the office, so that other people who worked late and are waiting for cabs won't see you. That hideous story about Coulter's wife finding a used condom in the pocket of his pants when she was sending his suit to be cleaned: he was sinking to the level of Coulter.

better opportunity. He mustn't miss it. Then, wondering whether he should, he asked would she like some of his bourbon or wine. You can try what's in my glass, he told her. If it tastes good, I will get you a glass of your own.

She took a sip, said it was strong but she liked the sweet taste, brought a tumbler from the kitchen, and held it out to him to fill.

Now let's listen to the record, he told her.

She nodded, all at once looking worried.

It's all right. You haven't disturbed me. We can listen and also speak from time to time.

She gave him a grateful smile. He had guessed right. She was flirting with him. Reaching for a canapé, he moved slightly nearer to her.

Excellent! My favorite food to go with whiskey.

He put his hand, palm down, between them on the sofa. There were two canapés left on the tray. Why don't we finish them? he asked. His voice had acquired an unnatural timbre. Perhaps she wouldn't notice.

She nodded again.

He returned his hand to its place on the sofa. A moment later, when he glanced in its direction, he saw that hers was lying beside it, a tiny space away. What was the next step?

Would you like to look at a picture book while we listen to music? he asked her.

Oh yes. Which one?

You choose.

Here too she knew what she liked. She took from the shelf, without hesitation, an album of photographs of the Grand Canyon.

time on the question. It was the beginning of August. Mary told him he should take his vacation anyway and not change his plans in order to spend the holiday with her. The way it had worked out, she could leave without worrying whether Corinne and Charlotte, alone in Bridgehampton, would be able to cope.

Before Mary left for the Coast, he had continued to go up to bed with her, every evening, right after their early dinner. The effect of the pills remained quick, but Mary did not want to postpone taking the sedative until they made love. She was afraid of any pause between lying down and falling asleep.

Let's do it while I am dozing off, she told him, I like it that way, it's cozy. I think I sleep better. I don't mind if you read afterward. You can turn the light on or go downstairs.

Schmidt liked it too. He would turn her on her side, press against the cold bottom, find his way, and lose himself in pleasure. Was this not the true magic flute? Thrill bordering on pain, modulated, rising and falling, uninterrupted until the climax. Mercifully, the snoring had abated. He would wipe himself on the top sheet, to leave his mark for Mary, and, without washing, tiptoe down the stairs.

I go to my fairy temptress as I am, he would say to himself. Time has stopped.

That Charlotte would not hear him moving about, he was quite sure. The stair carpet was thick, and he was very careful. Terror lay in the thought that she might come to Corinne's room because a bad dream had awakened her.

Corinne told him not to worry. She always knocks. I will ask her to wait and take her upstairs. You must lie very still, under my spell.

May I speak to you from time to time? she asked. I feel so timid.

The girl was only teasing. He moved his arm away. Of course, he told her, always. Charlotte is crazy about you, and Mary and I are very happy that we found you. Or that you found us.

His voice had returned to normal. In a moment it would be possible to close that book, get up from the sofa, and go to bed in the guest room. Perhaps he would take another bourbon upstairs with him.

You were so kind   day. I watched you. You are kind to everybo   u are mad at me.

I'm not. How   ere to be mad about?

Because I   orried that Madame will find out. Bu   worry, you don't have to.

He thou   gh at her, but she raised her face to hi   clea   ing that instead he kissed her. At once,   nond ar s were around his neck. Somehow she had   .ered into his lap and glued her body to his. He realized t at she had taken over the kiss, pressing so hard that he thought all of her tongue was swallowed in his mouth. Some time passed, and, without speaking, for that kiss was not to be interrupted, she tugged at his wrist and led him to her room.

I am a fallen man, he whispered to her.

A couple of weeks later, Mary decided to accompany one of her authors on the West Coast leg of his publicity tour. His book was unexpectedly climbing to the top of the best-seller list. The migraines had stopped—excitement over a big commercial success, rest, the pills, or all three working in combination. Who was to say? They didn't spend much

VIII

TELEPHONE CONVERSATIONS the next day.
Although it's past ten, Schmidt is in bed, perhaps asleep, covers wound around him tightly, like a shroud, to keep the warmth in, to shut out the need to get on with the day. Summoned, he reaches for the receiver, the phone kept somewhere on the floor beside the bed: that is how Schmidt guards against knocking over the glass of water on his night table, spilling the contents on his book, losing his reading glasses, and making the battery pop out from his alarm clock, which it does at the slightest shock. It's Gil, not Charlotte.

You were great. There's no one else I can talk to about her.

Ah, the girl.

I don't think I got across how wonderful she is. I could be doing anything at all—shaving, crossing the street—and suddenly I think of her. It's as though I had a second heart. One for everything in my life that's known, that's as it should be, and one for her.

You did get it across. I understood that.

I have a letter from her—the first one! She timed it so I would get it this morning. There's no risk; she knows I al-

ways get the newspaper and the mail myself. It's terrific—
short and funny. I feel like jumping up and down. She wrote it
to make me feel good! Why shouldn't I let her?

No reason. I envy you. Just be careful about Elaine.

I am, even about how I use the telephone. She's out shopping, for party favors. What about the island?

I'll call you later.

And that man?

I'll call about that too.

Do. This afternoon. I told Elaine about him. She said I
should have brought you back home with me, and made you
sleep here.

Please thank her, she's a love. Of course, so is the girl!

Complacencies of a meaningless Sunday. Schmidt drives to
town. On the main street, in the sharp light, a dark crowd en-
ters the Catholic church. Their cars have filled the parking
spaces along the sidewalk, but there is room in the lot behind
the hardware store. The candy store owner saves *The New
York Times* for Schmidt. Although, contrary to his custom,
Schmidt is unwashed and unshaved, like the numerous Jewish
and somewhat less numerous Gentile males who also get their
paper and drink coffee at the counter of that establishment,
he decides to take breakfast in a booth. Pancakes, bacon, and
syrup, in place of the week-old English muffin waiting in his
fridge. At once, he feels he has eaten too much. Analysis of
the Willy Smith trial in the "Week in Review": Will the jury
acquit him? Gil probably knows the oaf; surely he knows the
senatorial uncle. Another aging satyr in search of young love.

After breakfast, Schmidt visits each of the town's three
parking lots, leans against the fender of a car that strikes his
fancy, and, thus exposed, waits.

Terror lay also in Corinne's becoming pregnant. She used no precautions and cried the one time he withdrew before the end. He supposed that ejaculating first in Mary reduced the risk for Corinne, but over twelve months—that's how long she was to stay with them—the odds had to be against them.

If that happens, I will go away, she told him. You will never hear from me again.

Toward the end of Mary's absence, they took Charlotte to Montauk, to eat lobsters in a restaurant on the pier. On the way home, she fell asleep in the car and then was too excited to go to sleep right away. There was a new moon. She asked if she could wish on shooting stars. The sky was crisscrossed by them. Schmidt felt tired from the drive; he had drunk most of the bottle of a German white wine. He shrugged his shoulders and said she and Corinne could do as they wished; he was going upstairs. That was an additional treat for Charlotte. The wind had died completely. Under the open windows, the girls were giggling. He listened for their whispers and, from across the pond, the thud of the surf. The screen door slammed. That would be Corinne, about to put the child to bed. She must have read to her. It had taken a long time. Finally, the bedroom door opened. He held out his arms for her and felt that she was already naked.

Wait, she whispered, I have to put a towel under me. And then, Right away, please, now!

We shouldn't, he whispered back, this will make a mess in the bed, but she put her hand on him, and he found he couldn't refuse.

It was the blood on the mattress cover, which Corinne thought she had scrubbed off, that Mrs. Durban found and brought to Mary's attention the morning after her return, while Schmidt was at the club, playing singles with the knee surgeon who had won the previous year's tournament.

Charlotte is in her room, having a tantrum, because I have just put Corinne and her suitcase on the train for New York, Mary told Schmidt when he came home. If you have to screw some bitch in my house, at least don't leave stains on my bed.

You are quite right, he replied, and went to the pool to swim.

Later in the day, Mary fired Mrs. Durban.

The woman is a drunk, she told Schmidt. It's practically Labor Day. I will make do with the Poles until I find someone with proper qualifications.

That evening, after he had given Charlotte dinner and gotten her to go to sleep—Mary had remained in the bedroom with the door closed—Schmidt went out on the back porch to smoke. Should he sleep in the guest room? What could he say to Mary? He wondered whether Corinne would leave a message at his office. It might be best if she didn't. In that case there would be no way he could find her.

He heard footsteps. It was Mary.

It's chilly out here, she told him. Don't you think you should come to bed?

IV

THE CLUB where Schmidt might ordinarily have whiled away the interval between his arrival in the city and lunch was closed, its members unlikely to eat the Thanksgiving meal away from their homes or homes of relatives or friends. Unless, of course, they had no family or company or friends. In that case, Schmidt imagined they preferred to bury the shameful secret and shun public places, emerging from their dwellings only at the hour when the lunch or dinner that their self-esteem told them they should have attended would normally be over, having taken care they were appropriately dressed for the occasion. And if they lived in a building where the doorman and elevator men noted each coming and going, and therefore would know, with derisive precision, that Mr. or Mrs. So-and-So was in town and in normal health, and yet had had no visitors and had not gone out to a party? Did those poor souls save their dignity by repairing to Chinese restaurants located somewhere in the boroughs, places where their presence, so puzzling to themselves, aroused neither curiosity nor pity in their boisterous fellow diners? Or was it easier in such a case to find an early show in a midtown Broadway movie theater, thereby adding to anonymity the protection of darkness? What would Schmidt have done, if he were still living in his apartment and had chosen not to go to the country, where on the whole it's easier to hide, and had not been the object of the solicitude of his daughter, of the parents of the man resolved to make an honest woman of her, and, by golly, even of his former presiding partner?

The problem's beautiful complexity procured for Schmidt a moment of elation and hastened his progress toward the Harvard Club, a temple of gregariousness located but a few blocks from where the bus had deposited him. Memories of bulletins received in the past, touting the holiday menu, made him confident it was open, the membership apparently exempt from the scourge of false pride. He was no longer a member there, hadn't been for years, but that was no reason why he shouldn't, for old times' sake, visit the men's room, and perhaps even enjoy a short snooze in the library. The hall porter was new to Schmidt or had undergone a face-lift. He shook the man's hand and walked on to the great hall. Where once the only sound had been that of dice rattled in leather cups or of a bell furiously summoning a waiter to bring another martini to a grim-faced player bent over the backgammon board, gamboling little girls in pastel tights and their doting relations were in full cry. Like a blind man without a cane, Schmidt made his way through the Howard Johnson merrymaking to the beery smell of the urinals, the soap, and the cheap black combs in jars of disinfectant, one of which he washed and dried and then passed through his hair. Ten thousand hungover men of Harvard had peered at themselves in this full-length mirror. It was not one that flattered: he looked worse than even the sour person wearing his own clothes he had glimpsed returning his own stare from a Fifth Avenue store window. The way his recent loss of weight had shrunk his cheeks, and the set of his lips, closed from habit over uneven, discolored, cigar smoker's teeth, and promising nothing, seemed especially regrettable. He practiced lifting their corners. The two-hour bus ride had introduced a disorder in his dress. He opened his belt, unbuttoned the fly, shook his trousers and smoothed his shirttails, rebuttoned and rebelted himself, and centered his necktie. The tweed suit had been his father's. It never wrinkled. His brogues gleamed.

There's enough fancy stuff on me to lodge and feed a homeless family for a month, thought Schmidt. Let's leave this place and get the show on the road to the Rikers'!

He had guessed wrong. The building on East 57th Street where they lived wasn't some tawdry white-brick job bustling with tenants in sweat clothes. An old Irish fellow at the entrance pointed to the end of the dimly lit lobby, from where his twin, after a series of false starts, conveyed Schmidt to the top floor. Walk straight in, he said. In fact, the elevator door opened directly on the apartment's rectangular foyer, which had white walls. On them, lit by ceiling spots, hung prints of cavernous buildings. Although the Irish twin, shifting from foot to foot, seemed determined not to leave until he had made sure that this was a guest, who would move on toward the noise of the party after blowing his nose, and not a respectable-looking burglar, Schmidt paused to examine the Rikers' art. It could serve as an instant and neutral subject of conversation. If only he had had a drink; why hadn't he ordered one at the club and signed on the chit a name of convenience—for instance Jack DeForrest's?

He was interrupted by the clatter of the elevator grill being dragged shut at last and the deep voice of a woman.

Do you like these? They are Piranesi's views of prisons. Some people find them hard to take.

They are fascinating. I am Albert Schmidt.

You had to be. Everyone else is here. And I am Renata, Jon's mother.

She saw that he was going to look at his watch and added, You are perfectly on time. I asked the others to come early, so that you would see us all at once, as in a photograph.

She was a large, erect woman dressed in a maroon skirt and a black-and-beige, rough-textured garment, which Schmidt supposed—because her jewelry was silver stuff with blue stones—must be an Indian poncho, worn over a long-sleeved white shirt. Her graying black hair was caught in a bun at the back of the head. Schmidt noted her large, severe brown eyes.

We are very glad you are here, she added, now come and meet your new family.

My husband, Myron.

Leah and Ronald Littman, my parents, from Washington. This is a special occasion; we usually spend Thanksgiving there.

My little sister, Suzie, and Bob Warren, her husband, and their twins, Marilyn and Meg.

Hello, what is this? No one had told Schmidt. A goy like him, only fat, and was there a secret smile of connivance when they shook hands? The girls were mousy, indistinguishable from each other, and myopic; they took after the father.

Jon's little brother, Seth.

And at last, the happy couple!

Indeed. Schmidt shook the hand proffered by Riker and kissed his daughter's cheek. Very nice, I've put on my father's suit and she her mother's, only Mary wouldn't have worn navy blue to this lunch. What goes on in that little head, why doesn't she hug me, hold my hand, stay at my side?

You'll have a drink, Albert?

The male Dr. Riker, a bit smaller than Renata and more in line with Schmidt's idea of a New York shrink, has stepped out of the photograph. Like Renata, he actually touched Schmidt, on the arm. Charlotte was busy talking to the grandparents. What does she call them? Leah and Ronald? Mrs. and Mrs.? Some funny made-up names?

Please call me Schmidtie, replied the grateful Schmidt. That goes for everybody here. Only people who try to sell municipal bonds to me over the telephone use Albert or Al. If it's not too much trouble, I would like a gin martini.

Clearly it was going to be trouble. Schmidt had observed the two respectable black ladies, one passing glasses of red and white wine and the other something that looked like little quiches. Dr. Myron Riker would have to make the drink himself. But was this a moment for altruism? God helps those who help themselves. Besides, couldn't Myron have sent Jon or Seth or Wasp Warren to get the martini, instead of meekly trotting off to wherever the makings were kept?

When Myron returned, he was bearing a shiny little silver tray on which stood a very small and shiny cocktail shaker and a martini glass. He poured the stuff. Little platelets of ice shimmered in the liquid. An olive lolled on the bottom of the glass. What a surprise. Schmidt told Myron it was the coldest and best martini he had ever drunk in someone's house.

Then have what's left in the shaker. There is time before lunch.

Time: this lunch would take at least two and a half hours, perhaps three. If he took a taxi straight to the bus—and why wouldn't he; Charlotte had made no suggestion about getting together afterward—he would catch the seven o'clock. Then he might have a hamburger and more martinis at O'Henry's. Late to bed and late to rise. There was nothing wrong with that in the case of a retired old guy. A bell of the thinnest crystal, like a fine wineglass one can squeeze and release, squeeze and release between one's fingers, had descended, separating him from the others and keeping them at an indeterminate and comfortable distance. It did not shatter when he sat down at table between Renata and Grandma Leah.

The latter, he was happy to notice, was absorbed in a conversation with her grandson Seth. His recollection was right; the boy also lived in Washington, and apparently spent a great deal of time at Leah's house. Did he house-sit when they were away, or was there perhaps an apartment for him in the back where he actually lived? Schmidt did not have the immediate inclination or the time to find an answer to the question. Renata's eyes were on his face. He smiled back at her across the crystal wall.

I am a little tipsy, he told her. Myron's martinis are very strong. I'll be all right as soon as I have had some of your turkey.

She smiled back.

They are deadly. He keeps the gin in the freezer and the vermouth in the fridge. Ice hardly melts in them. Besides, I imagine you are nervous.

Not anymore, but I was. Very nervous. I can't remember when I was last to a lunch where I knew no one. Probably never.

Now she laughed.

You certainly know Charlotte and Jon. He has spent so much time with you he has become a stranger in this house!

I wonder. I mean, do I know them in this avatar at all? I certainly don't know how to behave with them. Perhaps I should ask to be introduced. For instance by you.

It's so very sad Charlotte's mother isn't here. I do think women instinctively know their way around situations like this. She would have helped. I'm sorry you have had to cope with so much grief and this important change in Charlotte's life all at once.

You were kind to write. I remember your letter. It was very good. I suppose in your profession you have learned how to say things that most people can't say at all. I realize I haven't answered; I haven't answered any letters. I am afraid I never will.

It's quite unnecessary. Have some more of Myron's wine before they serve the champagne. I think he intends to make lots of toasts. And please stay after lunch to talk to me. Everybody else has plans; they are all going somewhere. We will be alone.

The turkey had been carved in the kitchen. One of the black ladies carried it around the table, and the other followed with a platter on which mashed potatoes speckled with what looked like fried onions predominated. Lucky Dr. Myron. Schmidt had never liked standing up at the head of the table, searching for the joint at which to sever the drumstick, waiting, filling individual orders, only dark, no only white, yes dark and skin, or probing with the long spoon for the last bits of stuffing, like an unsanitary curettage, or having to recommence before he had eaten what was on his own plate. A lifelong plot to rob him of the chance to taste the bird before it turned into cold leftovers, that's what it was. He noted the absence of the dreaded yams. Mary had considered them indispensable but never touched them herself. Wouldn't this amuse Renata? Schmidt told her about it in detail.

His enthusiasm for the lunch grew, even as the crystal wall was changing his voice so that it too seemed distant, heard from a place where he actually wasn't. He looked at Charlotte helping herself and called out, The pope's nose, sweetie, don't let the pope's nose get away.

It had always been necessary to save it for her; he rebuffed anyone else who dared to ask for it, and repressed the ogre inside who wanted it for himself. It was his favorite part of the turkey too. He had taught Charlotte to like it. For years, it was all she ate at the Thanksgiving meal until it was time for the sweets.

That's all right, Dad, you have it. Tastes change. All that fat is disgusting.

She turned to Jon for approval. Schmidt imagined that in reply he squeezed her thigh under the table. That was all right; he would take the despised pope's nose if it was still there when the platter reached him, and a double portion of the potatoes. In the meantime, he tasted the wine again, emptying his glass. It was better than what he was used to.

Afterward, he waited for Renata in the library, wondering whether that was where she received patients, the desk was so neat and somehow official looking, with only one photograph on it, probably taken at camp, of her sons in white shorts carrying a red canoe. Mary and he had never sent Charlotte to a real camp; they had felt it would spoil their own vacation. Besides, the best tennis, riding, and swimming were available right at home. Mary would have liked Charlotte to sail, and for several summers in a row he had duly offered to buy a day sailer they might keep in Sag Harbor. But nothing came of it in the end. Possibly, Mary sensed he was dragging his feet about adding yet another activity to Charlotte's already busy days of picnics and watersports. When is the child supposed to have her inner life, when will she get to read a book? he would ask when they discussed Charlotte's program. In the end he had his way; the child read quite enough all through those sunny vacations, school, and college.

Now she was making up for lost time: Jon and she had been the first to rise from the table, before coffee was served, in order to go for a run. That had to be the truth, why would anyone tell such a stupid lie? First eat turkey, but thank you no gravy, and puree of broccoli, then gallop around the Reservoir or perhaps some more ambitious course! Did Dr. & Dr. Riker also consider this an improbable, really intolerable breach of manners, or was it for them an example of freedom to lead one's life as one wishes that other young people attained only after years on the couch? He looked around the room for the couch and, sure enough, there was one to the left of the desk, disguised as a sofa with a back and arms, but one could lie down on it, perhaps comfortably, if the mountain of pillows was shifted around.

I think this lunch went pretty well, but I'm glad it's over!

He hadn't heard her come in. She headed for the sofa, re-arranged the pillows just the way he had imagined they should be, kicked off her shoes, and lay down, motioning him to an armchair.

Is this role reversal?

Aching feet and bad veins. You just can't see them, through the wool tights. I get tired standing up.

Me too, but it's my back rather than my legs.

My back is not so great either. How would you like to go into the dining room and make a scotch and soda with lots of ice for me and whatever suits you for yourself?

Don't you think I've drunk rather enough?

You seem quite sober, but do as you like. I need a drink.

He saw only scotch on the sideboard, but there was no other liquor he particularly wanted, certainly not more of the champagne Dr. Myron had so properly made to appear for the toasts. On reflection, what was wrong with having a drink with this lady on a Thanksgiving afternoon? He handed her the glass and sat down in his armchair, watching her massage her feet.

Are you of the view that I have sent everybody away by prearrangement?

Why would I think that? Anyway, I can't imagine that you arranged Charlotte and Jon's exit. You must have been just as surprised as I.

No, that wasn't my idea, but I knew they were going to do it. If Charlotte hadn't told me that they were going, I would have suggested that they find a pretext to leave you with me for a while.

And Myron and the others?

Let's see. In fact, I didn't arrange for us to be alone, but I did take advantage of how things were turning out. For instance, Myron thought he should go to see his mother. That's not a fair way to put it; he really wanted to go. She lives in a home for the elderly in Riverdale. Normally I would have gone with him. As for my parents, Seth invited them out; just imagine, they are going to see *Terminator 2*.

Really?

That's right; if I hadn't wanted to see you, I might have gone with them and let Myron make his visit by himself.

And the Warrens? The Warrens have only one wish: to get back to Philadelphia. But they would have stayed for an hour to keep me company if I had asked.

She had finished working on her feet, rearranged the pillows once again, and was sitting cross-legged facing him.

Well, I feel very flattered.

You see, something important is going on, and how it turns out, what effect it will have on Charlotte and Jon, depends to some degree on us.

On you and me? Why not Myron? Why not Jon and Charlotte?

Myron isn't having this conversation with you, that's why not Myron. He's off the hook. I thought it would be better if it was me. The kids—naturally, in the end, they will have to manage. I have in mind a particular moment, which is now, and a very particular responsibility you have for what is otherwise their business. You see, I am very fond of Charlotte.

Jon has brought her to see us quite often. We have no daughters. She and I sometimes have late lunch on Thursdays. I don't see patients that afternoon.

I am very glad to hear it. She is my only child. I tried to have lunch with her myself, two weeks ago, but she was too busy.

She has been working hard. I think, though, that she might have been nervous about seeing you. I wonder whether you realize the full extent of your authority.

Really!

He hadn't smoked since he had arrived at the Rikers' and now felt for his box of cigarillos. Would she mind? No she wouldn't. She got up, brought him an ashtray, and over his protest went to get more scotch.

My feet are all right now, she told him.

I am worried not so much about your feet as about the clarity of our minds. What are you trying to tell me?

Something that you already know, but prefer not to acknowledge, which is that Charlotte and Jon are terrified of you and of the weight of your disapproval.

How pleasant for a retired body like me to inspire dread in young grown-ups!

You think that you are being funny, but that's the precise truth. Why do you think Jewish mothers and witches are in business? To be scary and to punish. They say, or only think: You've neglected me, taken me for granted, invited those other people to your party but not me, or you have invited me too but only at the last minute. Just wait. I have the right spell for the occasion. Because it's always a spell. A pinprick puts the princess and the whole kingdom to sleep. Or they put on a face that's like Jesus Christ on the cross and the Mater Dolorosa rolled in one, fix you with a baleful stare, and say, See what you have done! And suddenly there is no more sunshine, nothing is fun. Schmidtie, you are toying with the thought of casting an evil spell.

She recrossed her legs. Whatever their condition might be inside the tights, they were well formed. He had finished his cigarillo. Should he now find a safe place for his sweating glass, bow, and thank her for the lunch and the chat? Was his dignity threatened if he stayed and, if so, was it worth saving? What would she say about him if he left, what would she say if he stayed? He lit another cigarillo, drew on it, and decided he might let Dr. Renata have some of her own medicine.

Not so long ago, he told her, while I was still a practicing lawyer, whenever I went out to dinner or lunch or when company called, I would make a point of leaving my small legal learning, and my lawyer's mannerisms and habits of speech, in some safe space. Let's say the umbrella stand or the coat closet. Not all lawyers make that effort, and I'm not sure I always succeeded, although I really tried. I know very little about the social habits of psychiatrists, but you have just talked to me the way I imagine you talk to your patients, not the way one speaks to a guest. I am a relatively patient man, but I am not your patient. I have not come here to consult you.

She smiled at him quite gaily, with her whole mouth and, for a change, curled her legs up under her. He wondered whether at her age such perfect white teeth could be real. If a new technique had been invented and it wasn't painful, he might want to try it.

Is that the longest nonlegal statement you have ever made? she inquired. I think I have got a real rise out of you.

As a matter of fact, I haven't quite finished; you interrupted, and I don't like that. If you are going to practice on me whatever therapy you think this is, I am going to practice a little bit of law. We'll break down the problem into smaller segments. First, the segment called Charlotte. Let's assume for the sake of the argument that I actually know something about her—perhaps even as much as you. After all, her mother and I did bring her up. So let's put her aside, or leave her for the very last, and deal with the segment called Jon Riker. You have just made the claim that I terrorize him. I put it to you that the claim is preposterous. He has always been one of my favorite associates. I don't mind telling you, in the privacy of this room, something he knows perfectly well even if you don't: he worked for me so much that he couldn't possibly have become a partner if he hadn't had my full support. I did support him. That was done out of deep respect for his value—and selflessly, too. It had already been agreed that he would veer off toward litigation. Nobody could accuse me of backing a candidate in order to have him stay in the firm and go on doing my work. If analogies amuse you, think of me rather as Jon's good fairy godmother: I gave your son what he wanted most!

Have you finished now?

No, but I've talked for so long that it's all right to break in.

That's exactly what Jon has told Myron and me: you made it happen. He was very grateful about it, and so were we—his entire family. We knew that Jon was bright and worked hard, but we also knew, because he said it over and over, that at Wood & King deserving to be made a partner is only the beginning. He was especially grateful that you treated him just the same, and supported him, after he began to go out with Charlotte.

As a matter of fact, I introduced them!

But that was unintentional; anyway, he didn't think you intended it to work out quite the way it did—Charlotte becoming his girlfriend. You see, all during those years when he worked for you he had the feeling that you relied on him and had confidence in his work but didn't especially like him. I mean, as a person. He thought that would begin to get in the way once he began to see a lot of Charlotte, even if you hadn't allowed it to matter before.

I see, said Schmidt. You mean that by going with Charlotte—if I may use their euphemism—he was doubling the stakes. The heart as well as chances of partnership put at risk! But why complain now? He's got the girl and the job. Isn't that enough? What else can he want?

To feel that you accept him, like him! You made no comment when I mentioned that, his feeling that you have no affection for him.

I liked him well enough to want him to be my partner, and I haven't refused him my daughter's hand—though I might add, entre nous, that he dispensed with the formality of asking for it. I repeat, isn't that enough? How voracious—after all, he doesn't want to marry me!

Was there something dreary about what he had just said? It had left him uncomfortable and dissatisfied.

You're an odd stickler for the truth. You know you have no affection for Jon, and so you are unwilling to bend even a tiny bit, not enough to hint for instance at the possibility that at bottom you do. Even though you are sitting here talking to his mother, and that's what she clearly wants to hear. And yet you seem to want Charlotte to act like a sweet, loving daughter! What was the second segment of the problem you were willing to examine?

Terror. Schmidtie as the totemic, terror-inspiring figure. That is also preposterous. Perhaps my classmates and I were scared of Dexter King when we were Jon's age. In fact, I didn't get around to calling him by his first name until I had been a partner for a year—maybe longer—even though he had told me, I don't know how many times, that it was the right thing to do. And to the day he died I wouldn't have sat down in his office without being asked. But today! The kids in the mail room occasionally called me Schmidtie to my face. And you should hear the accents! By the way, I have never pretended to enjoy it! And the way Jon and the other young partners talk back to Jack DeForrest and the couple of other relics of ancient times still left in the firm! I don't mean that there is anything wrong with giving a senior partner a hard time about the law, you are supposed to do that as soon as you arrive, or with expressing your opinion about whether one should tell a client this or that. I am talking about challenging seniors on matters of judgment that have to do with fairness within the firm, and expecting to prevail—for no reason except that you are young and will inherit! Actually, that's something I managed to get used to. Provided people are reasonably polite, having them challenge you all across the board is more stimulating than the old prep school cult of your elders.

I don't think that's it. Jon and the other young lawyers who worked with you weren't afraid of you because you were so senior, but because they thought they weren't as right as you, and you gave them the impression that you thought so too. The father figure who is right and has the last word—that's very scary. Also, most of them, Jon included, didn't think they were living up to your expectations. It's as though you wanted them to succeed but then were quickly disappointed.

Well, I'm gone, and that's one thing less for them to worry about! Anyway, since you have discussed all these things with Jon—by the way, isn't it odd that Charlotte has never talked to me about them?—you must know that my own practice had stopped growing. I was losing my value to the firm. That's another argument against the theory of terror.

Jon never saw it that way.

That's the nicest news I have heard in a long time. If only it were true. But, true or not, you have put me into such a cheerful mood that I must leave now, before you say anything that might spoil it!

On the contrary, you must stay. We really should reach out to each other.

"Reaching out" was not among expressions or activities Schmidt liked. He associated it with affirmative action, of which he disapproved, and justifications offered for hiring lawyers who didn't make the W & K grade. Therefore, he stood up to deliver what he thought might be his closing remarks.

Renata, he told her, you want to accomplish too much in one afternoon. Of course, I won't be a witch or some other sort of sinister presence at my only daughter's wedding or other family gatherings or at any other time! Have I acted today in a way that gives you any reason to think otherwise? I don't think so. On the other hand, Charlotte and Jon can't behave toward me like a pair of selfish brats. I am a lonely man, and I have suffered a dreadful loss—you can't measure it because you didn't know Mary. Those two have to treat me nicely—no more than that. They haven't; I won't go into details because they are petty. And they must make small, minimal allowances for the way I am. I know I am not all sweetness and light all the time, even though I really try to put up a good front. That I am sometimes sarcastic can't be news to either of them—or that my bark is worse than my bite.

Come, Schmidtie, sit down on the couch next to me. There is plenty of room.

How was he to disobey? The further rearrangement of her legs, which occurred as she turned toward the space he was to occupy, fascinated him, as did the grin that spread from ear to ear. When he sat down, she took his hand, not to shake it, but apparently because she meant to hold hands with him. Then, after a moment, she asked: What was your life with Mary really like?

He took his hand away and felt himself blush.

What kind of question is that, and why do you feel authorized to ask it? Has Charlotte been complaining about her home life?

Oh no. She has always conveyed the picture of an idyll—out of a stylish play. Two elegant and polite people, serious about their work, refusing nothing she asked for if it was "educational," very affectionate to her and friendly but distant with other people, and liking to be alone or with her.

Then I really don't understand your question. Charlotte seems to have given you an accurate if somewhat idealized account. We were a nice New York couple of our time.

It comes across though that you were rather stiff, maybe constrained, don't you think?

No, I don't. Busy, as you implied, and fond of our family life. We saw nothing wrong with the way we lived, and I don't now. And now I'm really going. Thanks once again for an extraordinary Thanksgiving.

Before he could stand up she took his hand again. Please don't be angry. I need to know you better. I need to know how you see your life. It's because I want to help you make things easier for yourself. You will be surprised how much easier that will make it for the children. That's all.

Am I to become a patient? I have never done this sort of thing, you know.

She laughed.

You couldn't be my patient, one doesn't do these things within the family. Anyway, I wouldn't recommend therapy for you: you are the wrong age, and you seem pretty well accustomed to the way you are—except for the effects of your loss, which will recede. To be in therapy, one needs to want to change. You don't, and why should you, if you can get over this rough patch?

Schmidt's mouth had become completely dry, as it always did whenever he felt himself pressed beyond the point where he could still control his irritation. There was a half-melted ice cube left in his glass. He tipped it into his mouth and chewed.

And your help, he asked, what might it consist of?

Companionship. Helping you to recognize certain kinds of trouble so you can stay out of the way. When I know you better, I may be able occasionally to give you a nudge, point you in a better direction.

Here she let go of his hand and gave him a poke in the ribs.

Like this. Don't worry about it.

The hand returned, warmer and very caressing.

I had a good life with Mary, Schmidt told Renata. I wish she were alive and could have outlived me. I don't know anything better one can say. As I said, Charlotte described the way we were accurately. We were every close. For one thing, from the beginning, we were orphans: well meaning, bright, and clinging hard to each other.

It was like this later as well? No great crises either after Charlotte was born?

Important ones? There might have been one, over a stupid indiscretion that Mary stumbled upon, but she didn't allow it to become anything. It left a hurt, but it was never looked at again or mentioned, even though it may have never quite healed. That's all.

A woman. And that's all? No other women?

No.

That was a lie. He let Renata go on playing with his hand. There had been the other world, where Mary never set foot, a world that consisted mostly of business trips. Schmidt arranging to avoid a meal with an associate or a client, or arranging to have the dinner end early. Then you could find him at the bar of his hotel, checking the place out, to make sure that the associate wasn't there too, in some corner or on a bar stool, hidden from view by an obese fellow drinker. Some evenings nothing happened. More often, he would manage to find a woman drinking alone. Women of all sorts: high-class bar girls, sluttish telephone operators, secret drunks, too chummy with the bartender, who might turn out to be anybody—an unmarried hairdresser, a librarian, the wife of a doctor. First an inane conversation, and then sex in his room that he would think about for months, while in bed with Mary. They brought a kind of excitement to sex that had been absent except during the time with Corinne. Why? He had never asked her for things that he did at once with those other women. But then, why hadn't she offered?

No, he continued, and there certainly weren't any crises about money or about Charlotte's upbringing or about our jobs. No midlife crises! We both liked our work and knew we were good at it. Of course, Mary had less tranquillity in her job. Power struggles in publishing houses are ferocious, and editors need to feel they have power. If they don't, they feel they can't publish their authors right.

And Mary?

What do you mean?

Did she have other men? Were you jealous? She must have been, after that indiscretion.

I'm not sure she was jealous. She probably thought she had taught me a lesson that would last me for life—and, in fact, in a rather good way, it did. I never gave her any reason to be jealous again.

That was true enough. Nothing ever happened after the encounters with those women. No presents, no letters, no phone calls. No diminution in Schmidt's ardor. Absolutely nothing to be jealous about.

But Mary? Did she have adventures?

Schmidt laughed. She had loosened her grip on his hand. He took advantage of it to stroke her forearm. He wondered if he dared to extend the motion a little higher, where he might encounter her breast.

Adventures in the other direction? I have always supposed that all sorts of things go on at the Frankfurt book fair and those booksellers' conventions that editors go to, or when a beautiful editor goes on a couple of weeks' book tour with an author. But Mary? She was so very fastidious—as well as serious. I don't think I could have imagined her participating in that sort of saturnalia! Or making up her mind quickly enough! I was always quite sure that after dinner she was really reading manuscripts in her hotel room, or catching up on sleep, or writing one of those marvelous letters to Charlotte.

That was another lie, though one a gentleman could not have avoided. He had, in fact, hoped that Mary was discreetly promiscuous in Frankfurt, Los Angeles, and Detroit, or wherever else the book trade chose to transact business and seek pleasure. Might not that make her, miraculously, into a good lay? Like his attempt to get her to touch herself? Except that she was so squeamish, quite beyond fastidiousness. It had been difficult for Schmidt to imagine her getting into just any bed with a man because he gave off the right sexual signals. There would not have been enough time for ceremony. But perhaps he was wrong. Perhaps she was like that with him, whereas other men could open her at once.

She patted approvingly the hand that was working over her elbow and grinned again.

It's all so intricate, she said. For instance, one has to take into account the excitement of being with a stranger. Also, there are sadistic fantasies that people who are married are often reluctant to act out with each other. Don't you think so?

I am sure you are right. Do you know that these are things

normally don't discuss, except possibly with one friend, a
man I have known most of my life? Why are we talking about
them?

I think it's because I have gotten you started and you find
that an intimate conversation with an analyst can be pleasant.
I doubt you have many occasions to talk freely—except for
that friend. We haven't gotten very far, because you haven't
been frank, but I should tell you that you interest me very
much.

How curious! I think I am the most conventional of men.

That may be interesting in itself. Is Jon right that you and
Charlotte have no family?

Essentially. Mary became an orphan when she was a little
girl. The aunt who brought her up is dead. My own father
died when I was in my early forties, and my mother much earlier. They each had cousins and maybe an uncle or two, but
they disliked them. There were no contacts with them. I
doubt any of them came to my father's funeral. On the other
hand, in a great big pink villa in West Palm Beach I have a
stepmother who is perfectly alive and claims to be hardly
older than me!

Jon has never mentioned her—or Charlotte either.

There is no reason they should. Charlotte doesn't remember her grandfather, and my dealings with Bonnie—that's my
stepmother's name—have been sporadic. After my father
died, I collected his clothes, which he left to me along with an
odd assortment of objects. Perhaps they were things she particularly disliked, perhaps there was another reason for the
choice. I haven't tried to think about it. We have written letters to each other—usually at Christmastime.

Schmidt paused and took away his hand. Renata dear, you might give me a tiny bit more whiskey. Actually, I don't mind talking about that story. It's so distant.

You pour it. I feel very languorous.

All right. Here it goes. You see, my father disinherited me, leaving absolutely everything to Bonnie, including furniture that had been in our family for a long time. Bonnie isn't someone I would have talked to Jon about. I doubt I even talked about her to Charlotte. She belongs to the world that existed when I was in law school, and when I started out as a young lawyer. I left it behind when I married Mary.

It must be sad to be disinherited!

It was and it wasn't. And this is a proper subject for us to discuss—family background, property, ghosts in the closet. It had to do with the quality of my childhood. My mother was a hypochondriac who had the misfortune of being in fact in bad health, so that the gaps between her migraines and backaches were filled by stays in the hospital, where one organ was removed after another: gallbladder, a part of a kidney, thyroid gland, you name it, and finally the usual female stuff. Even stronger than hypochondria was her sense of thrift. We lived in the Village and had Irish maids who did everything for the house. I can assure you that even when she was recovering from what turned out to be her last operation my mother wouldn't let the maid do the shopping, because she was afraid she would buy the more expensive grade of eggs or butter or potatoes, and that would have broken her heart. Then she would count the eggs to make sure that the maid didn't help herself to more than two a day! There wasn't any justification for this at all. My father was the head of a small and very successful admiralty law firm. In his case that really meant the sole owner, his partners were that in name only, really they were employees. Those were the days when the practice of admiralty law in New York was profitable. Thus we lived in a beautiful house on a nice street but in Dickensian penury. I went to a Jesuit school on Park Avenue that cost next to nothing, but gave one a pretty rigorous education. My father had lunch at the Downtown Association and dinner at whatever restaurant his shipowner clients favored. That was also the era of flamboyant shipowners: many Greeks, most of them related to one another, Norwegians, and even one Czech lady who made a fortune buying broken-down cargoes and then chartering them into the Korean War trade. Of course, my mother didn't control my father's bank account, so he was well dressed in the Wall Street lawyer style—well enough to cut a decent figure at the table of those magnates. My father and mother didn't go on vacations. My father thought that would have a demoralizing effect on the office. I was just beginning college when my mother died. Father took this event rather sentimentally, although they had fought all the time—over money. For instance, he collected Dutch pewter. Every piece he bought was a nail driven into her flesh. Anyway, I thought he would continue to live his perfectly regular life, except buying more frequently and more important pieces, when into the picture stepped Bonnie the Bimbo! She was the widow of one of his minor Greek shipowners, some sort of cousin by marriage of the Kulukundis clan—although she was perfectly American herself, from Nashville, with that unforgettable and unbearable accent—and he had done a will and maybe a trust for the husband. It's always a good deal to do a client's will in addition to the work for his business. Few things attach him to you more solidly than when he remembers that you will handle his estate. The husband died suddenly, my father became the executor or trustee, and one thing led to another. What a life he had with her! I used to think of my mother turning over in her grave like a chicken on a spit as the tap of the Schmidt fortune was opened to pay for gutting the house and redecorating at least twice, a butler imported from Hong Kong, a box at the opera, and on and on. Also my father gave up Brooks Brothers for the most expensive tailor in New York. That's where this number I am wearing came from. Luckily, until the last couple of years, when he put on some weight, we were the same size. And then he died, leaving, as aforesaid, to Bonnie everything he still had—which was a lot, as he kept on earning good money and had never spent it before. At the time, it felt like a kick in the rear end that I didn't need, but I got over it, and I must say I think Bonnie gave my father the happiest years of his life! Besides, I think he thought I had rejected him.

How?

His firm was one of those law practices that at the time the founder's son could inherit. Without quite saying it, my father rather assumed I would. When it turned out that I was a good student and got clerkships, first on the court of appeals and then on the Supreme Court, and later firms like Wood & King courted me, he couldn't, of course, tell me don't go there, come to work for me. That would have been ridiculous, and he knew it. I believe, though, he expected me to stay just long enough to get some solid experience at a big firm and then join him. But when that time came, I made no move, and he was too proud to ask. So nothing happened, except that, after I was made a partner, Dexter King told me about running into my father, some years earlier, at the Downtown Association, and how my father asked whether I was doing well. He is on the right track, Dexter replied, and I don't see what can derail him. Well, in law firm code language that means your boy will become a partner as soon as his turn comes, and normally that makes the boy's father offer to buy you a whiskey sour. Only my father instead turned his back on Dexter and walked off, very much to Dexter's amazement.

My dear Schmidtie, what a story! I want to hear more. Will you stay with us for some early cold turkey?

Actually, I want to kiss you.

I know, but it's a bad idea. We might not stop there. Besides, the others will be coming home soon.

You are right. It's just the way I suddenly felt. Like in the song, "New fancies are strange fancies. . . ." Thanks for the cold turkey. I think it would be better if I tried to catch my bus. And what do we do next, Doctor?

We become the best of friends. When will I see you? Will you come to the city to have lunch with me?

On one of those Thursdays? I don't know. I'll suggest to Charlotte that she and Jon invite you to the country. You should see the house while I still live in it. I am going to tell you something that must be a secret between us, because I haven't told Charlotte yet: I am going to give my life estate in the house to her as a wedding gift. That way she and Jon will have it to themselves.

Schmidtie, let's talk before you tell her that.

Perhaps we will, but my mind is quite made up. Never more made up than now.

A gale from the west was blowing through 57th Street. He walked leaning into it, fists in the pockets of his trousers. Third Avenue was dead. Taxis streaming toward the bridge had all lit their "Off Duty" signs. On Lexington Avenue, he found one and told the driver to go to 41st Street. A dirty-looking bus was waiting. He sat down next to a window, took *The Warden* out of his pocket, found his place, and began to read. Mr. Harding certainly knew how to make himself liked and how to live under the same roof with his family. Why are some people born with that gift and others not? He must ask Dr. Renata the next time they meet. And that serene celibacy! Then the bus started, and the driver turned off the overhead lights in the aisle. The reading light was too dim to continue. Schmidt turned it off, put the book in his lap, called the attendant and paid the fare so she wouldn't bother him later, and fell asleep.

He awakened unpleasantly, with a bad taste in his mouth. Something stank; it was the stench that woke him. He opened his eyes and saw that sitting next to him was a man as tall as he but much heavier, dressed in a threadbare tweed suit of the same shade as Schmidt's, soiled and too tight for his frame. Under it he wore a rough sweater that looked like army surplus, a grimy flannel shirt, and a salmon-pink tie, the knot of which was black with dirt. The man was slumbering with his mouth open. Down the side of his cleft chin ran a rivulet of saliva. That was, Schmidt supposed, because the mouth was toothless, like the mouths of the aged Kurds one had been seeing in newspaper photographs, although this man did not seem old, not much older than he. It was a good English or German face, except for that dreadful mouth, with eyes set deep under strong brows, a cocky nose, tiny well-formed ears, and a tough skull, the kind that, on a rough flight over the Pacific, when the captain walks through the cabin, would put the passengers at ease. The man's cane rested between his legs. He shifted in his seat and broke wind. It was expelled in ample bursts, followed by a liquid rumbling in the stomach. If one could judge by the delicate smile that floated briefly on the man's face, rather like a baby's, after it has been burped, he felt relief. The cloacal odor was unbearable, but different from the stench that had interrupted Schmidt's sleep and continued to nauseate him. Was the man hiding a piece of carrion in his pocket, had he a suppurating wound on his feet or somewhere under his clothes? It seemed impossible that an accumulation of dirt and sweat alone accounted for such fetor. And why, with the bus almost empty, had the man moved over to sit next to him, instead of spreading out over two seats?

It was clear to Schmidt that he had to get away. How to do it was less clear. The man's thick legs occupied the entire space in front of him, and Schmidt did not think he could step over them. He would have to shake the man and ask him to move over. That's what he did. The man broke wind again, and inquired, Your bowels acting up or your bladder?

It seemed to Schmidt that he winked as he said these words.

Neither. Please get up for a moment. I'd just like to get by you.

Hoity-toity, aren't you? Isn't that something: he would

just like to get by me! What's the matter, doesn't he like sitting with me?

He shook with laughter, and spread himself more comfortably in the seat, putting his gloved hands—the gloves were of knitted cotton thread, of a sort Schmidt hadn't seen in years, that Charlotte had worn with her riding clothes—on the handle of his cane. He gave Schmidt another wink; this time there was no doubt about it.

Sir, I don't know you and I don't want to talk to you. I just want to leave this seat. Will you please get your legs out of the way!

The man pursed his mouth. He he he!

The way he laughed, or perhaps it was his mouth, reminded Schmidt queerly of the first judge before whom he had ever appeared, on a routine unopposed motion to ask for permission to amend an answer to a complaint. The judge denied it. He he he. And then he said, Haven't you heard me, young fellow? Sit down! That had been an absurd ruling, and it took considerable labor to overturn it, but what was he to do now? Remain in the stench for another hour, with this mad hobo sneering at him? Ring for the attendant, an adolescent girl sitting next to the driver, and try to get the driver to mediate?

Let me out, he told the man. I can't wait. I've got to go to the can this very minute.

That's better. Now let's try saying please.

Please.

The man stood up in the aisle. As Schmidt squeezed past him, the man caught him in a long embrace and kissed him near the ear. Yeah, I like you when you're polite, just like my brother, he whispered.

In the chemical toilet Schmidt washed his hands and face. As he made his way back toward the front of the bus, he saw that the man's eyes were closed. The driver was a big black, listening to a West Indian talk show on a radio stuck in his shirt pocket. The row immediately behind him was empty, and that's where Schmidt sat down. *The Warden* was somewhere on the ground near his previous seat. He wasn't going back there to search for a pocket book. When the bus stopped in Southampton, he dashed out, found his car in the jitney parking lot, and locked himself in. Only then did he look back. The man may have stayed aboard. He was nowhere in sight. Schmidt waited for his heart to stop pounding, started the motor, and pulled out of the parking lot onto the highway. Then, in the beam of his headlights, he saw the man energetically walking east on the side of the road, swinging his cane and nodding his head with great satisfaction.

V

ALL NEXT MORNING, Schmidt waited for Charlotte to call him. Surely she would want to tell him she was glad the first encounter with the Rikers had gone well. Would she say, I was proud of you, Dad, you looked so nice in that old suit? Then he would mention the conversation with Renata about a weekend visit when the Rikers might see the house. Schmidt had contempt for people who find it easy to say, left and right, come to dinner soon, you must visit us at the beach, let's see a movie together, and then let the subject drop. He had invited Renata. That had created a piece of unfinished business to which he would attend promptly, for instance when he wrote or telephoned to thank her for the holiday lunch. His normal preference was for writing, typically on one of the postcards he collected for the day he might want to make a sly allusion to this or that event, but a telephone call appeared more friendly. It was his intention to be friendly toward that woman; he had been thinking about her. He assumed that Charlotte's office was closed on the Friday after Thanksgiving, but she might have gone to work anyway, like young lawyers at W & K. He imagined her for a moment in her sweat suit and running shoes, carrying her papers, yogurt, and banana in the neat little backpack that seemed to accompany her everywhere. But, in any event, she and Jon would have slept later than usual. It wasn't reasonable to expect that she would call before eleven. On the other hand, could she be waiting to hear from him, thinking he might want to say how pleasant the lunch had been? That would be a good thing to do, like stroking her hair or cheek, like his efforts to succeed with the Rikers. At a quarter past the hour, he dialed her direct line at the office. Six disconsolate rings, and he was switched to a recording: Rhinebeck Associates was closed; press 1 and dial the appropriate extension or the first four letters of the name of the person you are trying to reach and leave a voice mail message. No, he wouldn't record a cheerful fatherly statement that Charlotte might or might not listen to before Monday. Instead, he tried her number at home. Jon's voice, speaking very slowly, told him he could speak as long as he liked. What the hell; turning red in the face, Schmidt informed them that he had telephoned. They had gone out! A more pleasant explanation occurred to him. Charlotte and Jon were still asleep; that could be why the message had come on right away.

He found the senior Rikers' number in the directory. It would have been the last straw if they had been unlisted. A voice he didn't recognize, the secretary's, he supposed—why would psychoanalysts have a nurse?—instructed him to state his name and telephone number. Dr. Myron Riker or Dr. Renata Riker would be in touch, as soon as they could. All right, he liked that formula. Albert Schmidt, calling to say what a wonderful time he had at Thanksgiving lunch. He would call again or write unless Dr. Riker or Dr. Riker called him first. It had been a dumb move destined to fail: In all of Manhattan, was there one shrink who answered the telephone? There had to be another number, real and unlisted, that rang elsewhere in the apartment.

Noon. A small, rapid rain had begun to fall. Why not break the rule against daytime drinking? Nobody would know or care. He poured himself a bourbon as big as the Ritz, added ice cubes, took the receiver off the kitchen phone, found a volume of Anaïs Nin he read on such occasions, and, glass and book in hand, went to bed.

VI

SCHMIDT'S FATHER had not shown much concern about his only son's upbringing or education. Had anyone asked him the reason, it was a toss-up whether he would have answered that he was far too busy or that it seemed to him the boy was doing just fine. He did, however, as soon as Schmidt had learned to write, order him to keep a journal.

A man is responsible for what he does with his time, he said. Unless you get it down, it will be lost. Each day, make a record of what you did, and how long it took you.

Many years later, thinking about those words when his father was already dead, Schmidt came to the conclusion that, at least subconsciously, the old man must have meant something like time sheets, the attendance to which is a daily chore of every practicing lawyer who expects to be paid for his work. Thus, transposing, to take into account that you are a schoolboy, you enter: Meals, one hour and five minutes; cleansing of your person, seven minutes; attending school (transportation included), approximately eight hours, etc. Certainly, there was no diary or journal among the papers Schmidt and the executor of the estate reviewed. The record of the father's deeds was in his firm's ledger books and in the bills sent to clients. For professional services and advice rendered in connection with the arrest and mortgage sale in Panama City of *The Iphigenia*, and similar adventures.

As long as Schmidt had lived at home, until he went to college, the current volume of his diary, always a spiral school notebook with beige cardboard covers, his father having neglected to offer, even at the outset, a more enticing object, reposed in the bottom drawer of his dresser, in plain view, to the right of his underpants. The notebooks he had already filled were stacked on a shelf in the closet. He expected his diary to be read. In any case, there would have been no point in trying to hide it. His mother had a flair for uncovering evidence of sinful activity and regularly searched his possessions. She had no shame about it. Therefore, during those years, Schmidt's daily entries were exercises in hypocrisy or style, the former written to appease his mother by the flaunting of pious sentiments and appeals to her vanity, the latter intended to enable him to answer yes when the old man asked, out of the blue, at dinner, whether the son's records were up-to-date, consisting of laconic but precise and increasingly polished descriptions of what a model boy in Schmidt's circumstances might be expected to accomplish or see during the particular day. Had he been obliged to lie, had a respectable number of pages not been scribbled on, his mother would have contradicted him. It would not have occurred to the father to inquire how she knew, or to Schmidt that he might protest against the spying.

Soon after his mother died, Schmidt got rid of those notebooks of humiliation. They filled several big shopping bags that he placed in a neighbor's trash can on the sidewalk of Grove Street. Along with them, he threw out a smaller bag into which he had stuffed photographs of himself as child and adolescent, framed ones that she had kept in her bedroom and others taken from her albums and boxes of odds and ends; letters he had written to her from camp; and the birthday and Christmas poems over the composition of which he had labored, each dedicated "To my darling mother with love," and copied, before presentation, with a calligrapher's pen, on sheets of cream-colored paper that was supposed to look like parchment.

In the second semester of his freshman year, at the insistence of Gil Blackman, who was taking, by special dispensation, a course on symbolist poets normally closed to undergraduates, Schmidt read Baudelaire's *Mon coeur mis à nu* and a volume of excerpts from Kafka's diaries and returned to writing in his own diary with something like gratitude to his father for the habit he had been forced to acquire. Schmidt was intelligent enough to know he would never write anything like those texts, but they showed him that a journal could be a way of trying out certain thoughts, perhaps even getting at his own truth. With years, the need to confess became less strong. He worked at his diary sporadically, in the main to set the record straight—not quite the record his father had had in mind—or at least to give his side of the story.

Alone in the house after Mary died, he found that keeping a diary was also a pleasant pastime that cost nothing, a more dignified way of breaking the oppressive silence that surrounded him than talking to himself. He became quite diligent. And, to the extent that any of us understand the forces by which we are buffeted, what he wrote down at that time was far from inaccurate.

Sunday, 12/1/91

When I woke up from my nap yesterday, it was already dark. I took a bath. Then, very wide awake, I went down to the kitchen, and made a cup of tea. That's when I saw that the telephone was still off the hook. Had she called, had anyone called? I hung up. Suddenly, it rang. Charlotte, of course, her voice like a little girl's, the voice she uses with me when she wants to be especially nice. She says all the things I might have expected about the lunch and avoids being triumphant about the Riker apartment, the good taste, how cultivated they are, etc. I ask about issuing the invitation for a weekend in the country. She holds a quick consultation, hand over the receiver, with Jon and tells me that's perfect. I should invite them. Please avoid the weekend before Christmas: she and Jon have things they must do in the city. That makes Charlotte think of Christmas itself. Of course, they will have to spend it with the Rikers, it's very important to the family. I contain myself and don't say how droll that they should care, and so forth, or that, in the order of importance given to that holiday, my Christmas might rank ahead of theirs. On the contrary, the noises I make are noncommittal but pleasant. Instantly, Charlotte says that Jon wants to speak to me. All right.

Schmidtie, will you spend Christmas with us? We have it in Washington, with the grandparents, except that I haven't been since I met Charlotte. They really want you.

I tell him the truth: it's more than I can do. (Not the whole truth, because I don't add: even if I wanted to.) I can't imagine traveling to celebrate Christmas without Mary, not to a large family gathering, not this year. And I ask him not to worry about me, I won't lock myself in my room to brood. Possibly, I will go abroad—to someplace without Christmas. This idea just popped into my head. It has merit, if I can think of where to go.

Charlotte again. They have picked a date—the first Saturday in June. A June wedding. Will that be all right? Once again, I weep. She notices right away. I say she mustn't pay attention, I can't help being sentimental. It will be a beautiful, romantic wedding with the garden at its very best. A sea of fresh bloom. Probably it's not a moment too early to reserve the caterer and everything else that goes with it.

This is just as good a moment as any to speak about the house. My heart is in the right place, no trace of resentment, so why not get it over with? She hears me out, without interrupting, and says, Why is this necessary? I mean it's a very generous present, but from my point of view it won't change anything for the better, why can't we remain just as we are?

She is a smart girl. I say the house is too big for me (not true, I like big houses) and it depresses me (true enough, but what house wouldn't?).

Another whispered, muffled conference between Charlotte and Jon. She says they will call back.

I make another cup of tea. This time, I put rum in it.

The next conversation begins with Jon. He wants to know the financial implications. I tell him they are simple: Charlotte will own the house and almost everything that's in it now, but once I move out they will have to pay the taxes and upkeep. He wonders if they can afford it—especially as they plan to buy an apartment in the city. I say that's a fair question, and they should think it through and tell me. Just in case he doesn't understand the gift and estate tax aspects and, therefore, doesn't realize how generous this wedding present will be, I explain them to him. He too is smart. By the time you have finished, he asks me, won't we all be worse off? We don't need a country house of our own. Forget about the life estate, it's just a technicality. We'll come and go just as we do now. In time we'll help with the expenses.

I tell him they are both terrific. He must let me know about their cash flow. And I say to myself I must really try to figure out how necessary it is for me to go through with this.

That's done. Of course, I won't put on them a burden that's too heavy, but I wonder whether my plan, although born from self-destructive and spiteful feelings, is not, in fact, the best for all of us. With me as the resident janitor/owner/father/censor—or in whatever other order one lists those roles—will they, will I, have a good time? Mary would have made it all right: she and I would have had our life to lead so that I could let Charlotte and Jon lead theirs without it being such an effort for everybody. Which is the real sacrifice, to leave or to stay?

I have some more tea and rum, and begin to feel hungry. Not a fruit or vegetable in the house. Only my dear sardines and Swiss cheese.

The telephone again. This time, Renata Riker. How sweet of me. Next weekend is perfect. Perhaps the children will drive them.

Ciao!

I put on my blue blazer, because it's Saturday and I am tired of puttering about in a sweater, and drive to O'Henry's. The place is crowded. I have a bourbon and then another at the bar, standing behind a barrier of unidentified locals two rows thick. Finally, the owner decides to seat me. I follow, my eyes fixed on the back of his jacket, so as to avoid greetings and the like. The table is one of Carrie's, but it's a big boy who brings the menu. He has brown and yellow hair smoothed down with some sort of goo and a large ring in his earlobe. Two smaller rings pierce the top of the auricle cruelly. They are so thick light must show through the holes when he takes them off. Carrie's off, he observes, she worked all day on Thanksgiving.

I must be a subject of discussions, more probably jokes, among the help in this place. Why else would he assume that I am interested, or that I know her name?

Wednesday, 12/4/91

Two more meals out. With Carrie. First time the owner, and yesterday, the second time, the waitress who seats guests when he isn't there or doesn't feel like taking the trouble, leads me to one of Carrie's tables, without being asked. Is that normal, if one comes relatively often and always alone?

I feel a bit foolish about the seat assignment and my response, which is this mixture of embarrassment and satisfaction. Embarrassment, because I seem to have become a habitué, like the Weird Sisters who take on an amused air when I appear but make no move to invite me to their table. According to my way of seeing others, I am a figure of fun: an old fellow with nothing better to do than to converse at a bar and grill with a beautiful waitress almost too young to be his daughter! Satisfaction—bordering on pride—because the waitress acts as though she were glad to see me, almost as glad as I am to see her. Of course, I take into account her professional obligations. Being a good girl, she takes them seriously, I suppose. Waitresses are supposed to make customers feel welcome.

There is something to it, all the same, that goes beyond the professional aspect. For instance, she seems genuinely fond of chatting with me. Probably, she likes my paying attention to what she says—I have always had the reputation of being a good listener, but usually it's just an *appearance* of listening while my mind is a thousand miles away. More important, yesterday evening, when I was in such distress, she came to my aid. I suppose it was nothing for a street-smart kid raised in Brooklyn or the Bronx, it's shameful that I have forgotten which it is, but she did protect and comfort me like a true friend.

Here is what happened: I looked up from the table, because she had just brought coffee, and there, on the sidewalk, pressed against the plate glass, not more than fifteen feet away, staring at me, stood the man. He wore the same suit, perhaps with one more layer of sweater under the jacket, so that the buttons were pulling and the seams were ready to split, and a little knitted beet-red ski cap pulled over his ears. As soon as he saw that I had seen him, he smiled—a wide, entirely toothless grin—and winked. Mean, small eyes. My face must have remained immobile. The grin disappeared immediately. He puckered his lips, instead, and nodded, to show disappointment at the lack of a friendly response. Then, quite laboriously, he lifted his right arm and gave me the finger. In place of the equitation gloves, he was wearing mittens made of navy-blue wool, of a kind I have seen only in films, worn by nineteenth-century beggars or grave diggers, that cover the hands and fingers, but only to the middle joint, leaving exposed the nails, long, caked with dirt, and broken. Terror? Revulsion? When I managed to speak to Carrie, my voice was a croak as hoarse as hers. Look, I uttered, look at him, look!

It's him again, she replied. Don't pay any attention. Attention is what they're after.

Then she made an angry gesture with her fist, shooing him away.

Incredible to relate, the man let his arm drop and moved off, with apparent reluctance but defeated, looking back over his shoulder at me, or perhaps really at Carrie, mumbling something. Then his step quickened. Thrusting his cane at an invisible opponent, he crossed the street and disappeared into the darkness of the parking lot opposite the restaurant. My hands lay flat on the table. I had no feeling in them except extreme cold. It may be that Carrie saw that I was shivering. She put her hands over mine and whispered, You need warming up. I'll get you some fresh hot coffee.

We did not speak afterward because she was running back and forth to the kitchen and the cash register, filling orders, bringing checks, taking away dishes. When I paid, some fifteen minutes later, she asked whether my car was in the parking lot, and when I said yes, she told me she would take me to it.

We went out of the restaurant into the night air like a father and daughter, my loden coat over her shoulder. She saw in the dark like a cat, and led me straight to my Saab. I asked when she had seen the man before. Sometimes these crazies and winos come from the city on the bus and wander around here, was the answer. She sounded uneasy and evasive. Why?

When I was in the car, before I closed the door, she punched me in the arm and said, Hey come back soon, will you?

Friday, 12/6/91

Bad dreams all night. After breakfast, I called the police, told the operator I have been supporting their benevolent association for the past thirty years, and asked to speak to someone in charge. A Sergeant Smith came to the telephone—once I pointed it out to him, he seemed to appreciate the affinity of our names. I told him about the man and the interest he was taking in me, and said I was worried, because I live alone in a large house outside the village and because, in fact, the man might seek me out anywhere. Smith asked me to describe him in detail and having written it all down said it sounds like one of those loonies released by mental hospitals because of a shortage of funds or space.

I suppose that is the case.

Then he told me that with a description like that the guy was bound to be picked up by one of the cruisers. They could charge him, but with the courts being the way they are, they would, more likely, just make sure he "departs the area" and doesn't ever feel like coming back again.

He added that he would make it one of his personal projects, and gave me a telephone number at which I could reach him directly. I thanked him quite effusively.

Later, when I went for a walk on the beach—as usual not a soul there, brilliant sunlight, high waves ending in bursts of foam, sand reduced to a narrow strip, bizarre forms buried there, back in the twenties and thirties, I think, to serve as a barrier against the winter ocean waves, cement cylinders with rusty loops of cable embedded in them, segments of pipe, and piles of compacted metal, protruding dangerously from the surf, all of it completely futile and perhaps aggravating the erosion—I realized that the conversation with Sergeant Smith had not left me pleased with myself. These nice-looking local cops, so polite and understanding with the likes of me, must be totally brutal with the likes of the man. Here I was, with my waterproof shoes, wool socks, corduroy trousers, pigskin gloves lined with cashmere, and an old but expensive parka designed to be light as a feather and yet keep one warm in the bitterest gale, freshly washed and shaved, and so healthy and fit despite my old codger face and the number of years I have lived. The man had disgusted and embarrassed me, and frightened me as well, but there had been no other harm. What right had I to let loose on him Sergeant Smith and his men, with their clubs and boots, and long black flashlights?

Reread yesterday's entry in this book.

Voice 1: What if Carrie gets it into her head that she is the object of "unwanted attentions" and lets me—and all her colleagues at the restaurant as well—know it? Gives me the back of her hand; I have seen, with the man, that she knows how. Disgrace. End of those pointless, melancholy, but not unpleasant evenings. And if she welcomes my attentions, what then? She won't. She isn't a dissatisfied housewife filled with booze looking for furtive sex with a traveling salesman. There are enough good-looking boys here, of her age and her kind, to satisfy her needs.

Voice 2: It may be that she is drawn to me more than I think. I make her laugh. That's always important. With a respectable old guy like me, she doesn't need to ask herself whether I have AIDS or whatever else she can catch from some character like the one with goo on his head and rings in his ear; I am unlikely to be violent. To her generation, sex is no big deal. So why not fuck me in my nice clean bed? Under that T-shirt with "O'Henry's" written on it, probably a lavender bra. Breasts neat and hard like burial mounds. Tiny waist. Stomach. A narrow stretch of black fur. She's ready, soaking through her tights. When those are peeled off, legs of an antelope. No polish on her toenails; feet sore, perhaps a little swollen, she stands on them all day. That's where I start, kissing the soles of her feet and then the toes, working my way to the thighs, which she keeps closed at first, and then, as I reach the furry place, she opens, pushing at my face. Insistent, raucous cooing: Wait for me, take me, now!

Voice of Experience: You are too serious or too stuffy (you choose) for a one-night stand with Carrie, and what else could it be? If she likes you, it's because you seem gallant. Don't step out of that role and play the fool. Give her a little Christmas present—a pin or a nice scarf—and have fun at the restaurant when you want to get away from canned tuna.

Monday, 12/9/91
The weekend is over; therefore, just as one might expect, I am back in perfect health.

Since they were arriving on Friday in time for dinner, I got Mrs. Wolff to wait on table and wash the dishes. What will happen when she retires? No one else here will serve a meal that starts after nine. The idea of Charlotte and Renata making a fuss about how I must move to the living room with Jon and Myron while they clean up was intolerable. Mrs. W. agreed to help with Saturday night dinner and Sunday lunch as well. Saturday lunch was a meal I thought we could have in the kitchen, with a free-for-all at the sink afterward. In the same spirit of keeping cooperative efforts to a minimum, I did the shopping for the entire weekend. I made a beef stew for the first evening, so I could feed them as soon as they were ready. Champagne and oysters on the half shell, which I picked up just as the fish shop was closing, to start. For Saturday and Sunday, I got stuff I was sure Charlotte could cook; she might think that was what she ought to be doing. Flowers in the corner guest room, flowers in Charlotte and Jon's bedroom, French soap in all bathrooms, linen hand towels in profusion unmatched since the end of Martha's reign, lights ablaze throughout the house. It looked quite grand; I could imagine Renata deciding I can put on a show even if I have lived an emotionally deprived life. What the hell, it's only time and money.

Queasy moment, when I recognized that sort of excitement that goes with being ready and waiting for guests who matter—how else can I characterize the Riker visit?—and thought of Mary. I was doing all the things that she taught me or that we had learned together. We had been a good couple. People would tell us that, and also, with tiresome frequency, that we looked so well together, as though someone had entered us in a dog show they were judging—but it really was true.

Thanks to Mrs. W., I could stay out of the kitchen and concentrate on making martinis for Myron in the silver shaker I hardly ever use because it leaks. Never mind: I wrapped yet another starched hand towel around it. When I offered Myron an olive, he commented on my having rinsed and dried them, thereby rising once again in my esteem. For my part, I noticed that Charlotte was drinking soda water and was pale as a sheet, with tiny lines beginning to show at the corners of her eyes, and that Jon got himself a Diet Coke from the fridge and had put on weight. In the corner of the Chesterfield sofa, wrapped in a gray jersey dress and a russet shawl, her Indian warrior profile turned toward the fire, Dr. Renata looked like a million dollars. I put the stool on which I like to sit next to Charlotte's armchair and listened to them talk: traffic leaving the city, new construction out here (it turns out the Dr. & Dr. occasionally visit a fellow shrink in Springs whom I vaguely know, so this is not terra incognita), program for the weekend (they have been told I haven't invited anyone to meet them and I think suddenly I should have, lest one of the four feels slighted; if I am lucky, perhaps the shrink from Springs and his wife are free and will come on a few hours' notice), and other agreeable nonsense.

Dinner is served. I had the beautiful Renata on my right and Charlotte on my left, which meant that the two Riker males sat next to each other. Riker the father could have been on my left, which would have put Charlotte and Jon next to each other, but that solution hadn't occurred to me, and, anyway, with its leaves out, the table is round, so that the conversation could be general. I began to pay attention when it turned to the house. It's even more beautiful than Jon had led

Father Riker to suppose. Renata agreed. Father Riker continued: It's the most magnificent wedding present. I can't
imagine how Schmidtie can bear to leave it for another place.

I stole a glance at the beneficiaries of my largesse. They
looked uncharacteristically demure, one might say, sitting
there with downcast eyes. Communication about my plan
had taken place, and the financial problem had found its solution. Of course! Dr. & Dr. must have said they would help
with the apartment, or some variation on that theme. It
might have been nice to tell me in advance that my offer had
been accepted, but never mind. No greater proof of a child's
love, Mary used to say, than when the little snake takes you
for granted. Therefore, I raise my glass to their happiness under this roof and to the grandchildren who will be wrecking
the place, perhaps even enjoying the colonial fort with its
palisade Mary had installed for Charlotte in the shade of the
red beeches that Charlotte had never much used. (Immediately I wished I had omitted that piece of family history, but
it rankled in Mary's heart and it rankles in mine.)

In all, I had had one martini, one glass of champagne, and
less than a whole glass of burgundy, so it couldn't have been
the liquor. My eyes began to burn, even though I didn't feel
hot; in fact, I felt rather cold. I could tell that I had turned
red, red enough for Charlotte to ask whether I was well. I told
her not to worry, but that I wasn't quite sure. Of course, from
that point on, they were watching me: my eyes, my color
(from red I had, according to Charlotte, turned light green),
became the subject of intensive commentary. By the time
Mrs. Wolff had served the cheese, I was quite weak and
sweating, which is something that happens to me only rarely.

Myron got up, put his hand on my forehead, and then took my pulse—I wouldn't have thought that shrinks knew how—and said, You are running a high fever. Why don't you go to bed? I'll come up to listen to your lungs when we have finished dinner

He did. It was rather odd to have him in my bedroom, pressing his ear to my chest and back, as the poor man hadn't brought a stethoscope, going knock-knock, but it was also, in equal measure, sweet to abandon myself to these ministrations. There was nothing he could hear. He told me to stay in bed and take lots of aspirin; the flu would pass, perhaps overnight.

Strange night, full of obsessive dreams, cut by hours of sleeplessness, trips to the bathroom, and indecent thoughts that may have been dreams floating just below the level of consciousness about those two couples, one across the hall (my daughter in bed with Jon), the other to the right, down the corridor (Renata in bed with Myron). Meanwhile, perhaps because I had been working so hard, my fingers and also my toes had been worn down, perhaps atrophied, until they were like little knobs. Quite impossible to take hold of any object, and I didn't dare try to walk. I woke, definitively I thought, around eight, heard the rest of the house still asleep, dragged myself once more to the bathroom, stared at my wild face in the mirror, shaved, took a bath, and found a thermometer. 104! Remembering that baths raise one's temperature, I lay down and let ten minutes pass. 103.

Another sleep. No dreams. I found my body was covered with a secretion more like oil than sweat. 103.5. It's nice to know the earlier reading wasn't a fluke. Another bath and extensive cleaning of teeth. Then I put on fresh pajamas, sprayed myself with toilet water, remade my bed, got back into it, and thought about bad luck, and also how death and, one hopes, the flu dissolve all obligations. But I had really wanted to do well, and it seemed that this was the last effort I would make in this house, except to give the wedding and clear out my personal possessions.

The house was full of noises, but I could identify only a few. The growl of the orange juice squeezer, car wheels on the gravel, which meant Charlotte or Jon was going to get the paper. Still full of good intentions, I got up and opened the door to make clear that it was all right to come in.

I must have fallen asleep again. Back to the bathroom, and new pajamas out of my inexhaustible stock. Because my teeth were chattering, which told me something was going on, I didn't bother with the thermometer. Three pillows propping me up, I sat there glaring, until I dozed off, like another Gregor Samsa. Sound of steps on the floorboards, a presence in the room? I opened my eyes. It was Dr. Renata; the noise was that of the rocker. In the place of wilted vegetables, she had brought me orange juice and a pot of tea.

I can't imagine you want to eat, she told me, but perhaps you do, something like a yogurt. We've all had lunch. The children and Myron have gone to walk in some woods near Sag Harbor. Let me feel your head.

Big hand with a turquoise ring on my forehead, which was once again greasy.

You need more aspirin, she decided, and, when that was done, she said, Let's talk if you are up to it.

Why did you stay in the house, I asked her.

To take care of you! was the reply. Charlotte was going to stay, but I wanted her to go on the walk. She needs the fresh air, and it's no fun for a big boy like Jon to go hiking with his mother and father while his fiancée . . .

Looks after her father. I completed the sentence for her.

I wonder about this grudge against Charlotte. Remember, I made her go with Jon and Myron. She would have stayed with you.

That's right.

I wiped some of the grease off my face and drank another cup of tea. The tramway running back and forth inside my head was turning into a big Mack truck.

Renata, I said, you have me at a disadvantage. I am sick, I feel weak, I look disgusting. I haven't the strength for a family therapy session. If you want to stay with me, please tell me a nice story or read a book to yourself. Otherwise, please go for a walk on the beach. I will be fine by myself, with this tea you brought me. Believe me, I don't care whether it's hot or cold!

She moved over to the side of my bed and once again put her hand on my forehead, keeping it there for a couple of minutes. I was glad I had shaved, because when she took her hand away it brushed against my cheek.

No therapy, Schmidtie, she said, but don't be such a drag. It's true you are feverish, but that's no reason not to have a conversation. Here she stretched—rather contentedly, I thought. Think of all those nineteenth-century consumptives. In your present condition you may be quite interesting.

For instance, she continued, you have really handled very well not wanting to live with them in this house—you surprised me. How come? After such an unpromising start.

Her voice goes up a little at the end of declaratory sentences, turning them into questions without a question mark. Jewish accent, or the way everybody in New York talks now? I would like to ask Charlotte. Meanwhile Dr. R. had quietly taken my hand and was caressing it in a very soothing way. It's nice that she is set in her ways. Not returning the pressure, I pretended I didn't notice. Illness has its privileges.

Reply: I love my daughter. (I keep all note of pathos out of my voice. It helps to be the last of the Wasps.)

And you didn't want to make her a poisoned gift.

That lilt again. I nodded my throbbing head.

And Jon? How does he fit into your view of the future?

As my daughter's husband and potentially the father of her children—my grandchildren. I hope a good husband and a good father. A man is not required to love his son-in-law.

But it's a great happiness when you do! We love Charlotte!

It's clear that you and Myron are particularly kind. That's your reward.

All of a sudden, she leaned down over me, and kissed me on the lips, passing her tongue briefly along my front teeth, which, unprepared for this favor, I had kept in their normal closed position. Then she sat up, took both my hands, and said, You wanted to kiss me and now you have!

Thank you, but I am hot and cold and disgusting. There will have to be a return engagement. (In fact, against my better judgment, against common sense, I would have liked to continue, but was cautious enough to know I should leave each move up to her.)

That may be too complicated and too dangerous! You did love your wife, didn't you.

Very much.

But it's not true that you were very faithful.

Again that lilt. I said, You didn't really expect me to tell you all my sins the first day we met!

I think you were unfaithful to her every time you got a chance. How did you feel about that? Is that being a good husband?

Not every time, far from it, only when I felt an irresistible urge and the circumstances were right. You do realize you are extracting a confession from a sick and enfeebled man, don't you?

Of course. So how did it feel?

Like a breach of a contract. One promises to love, to live together loyally, and to forsake all others. But I thought my breaches were minor. She didn't know, I didn't love her any less because of them, and I was discreet. No one could start being sorry for Mary. What about you? What about Myron? Are you always faithful to each other?

She laughed. If she isn't repelled by my condition or afraid of catching my flu, why doesn't she kiss me again? I was glad that she had taken my hand back into her good graces.

Myron is a mystery. I don't think he has much temperament. He would tell me if he had someone. It would be the end of his being the injured party, but life would be simpler. I've had a lover for many years.

Really?

I was genuinely astonished.

He was a patient, but it only happened when the therapy was over. She laughed. The therapy was very successful—until recently. He is seeing another analyst. A man.

And Myron knows? And your sons?

Of course. By now, Charlotte, too, I imagine.

You still sleep with Myron?

When he wants to.

Suddenly she fell on me. It was like an attack. Her hands raced down my body. Just as abruptly, she pulled away. There was a silence. I was waiting for her.

You are lovely, Schmidtie, she told me. This won't happen again. We will go back to being proper and good, like the father of the bride and the mother of the groom.

I only did it, she added, because of an intuition. It's as though you were somehow doomed, disintegrating before my eyes.

That's unpleasant, I said. Will you watch over me, will you help? Then I told her about the man. After all, I might get to be just like him. We are alike, except that I am thin and very clean.

She took a moment before replying, No, that's not quite it. I will watch, if I am there. I don't know that there is any way I can help.

And what, I called as she was leaving the room, what if your psychiatric sixth sense and your damned intuition are wrong and I keep going, just as I am?

Why, I suppose that will mean we will all live happily ever after!

Thursday, 12/12/91

Just before they all left for the city, Charlotte came to see me. I was still in bed, feeling less definably sick but very tired, unable to stay awake for more than an hour at a time. She said she wished she could stay to look after me, but urgent work at the office, etc., wouldn't allow it. Then she told me the Rikers had been very generous. They were going to pay that part of the price of the apartment that couldn't be financed, and that was why Jon decided they could afford to take over this place after all.

I can hardly think of a more irritating way she could have described the situation. In one or two sentences, she managed to make much of what the Rikers were doing—less than five hundred thousand, I suppose, but how is one to know since the apartment in question hasn't been found—and deprecate my gift. Worse, the business about being able to afford to take over this place "after all" sounded as though they were doing me a favor, relieving me of an onerous obligation!

I didn't respond, and I am glad I didn't, not just because I want to keep peace but because, if one looks at the thing from a certain angle, there is an ugly grain of truth in what her remarks suggested—a grain of truth the existence of which nevertheless did not, in my opinion, justify her speaking to me as she did. It is this: I have a selfish motive in this transaction—to avoid the duty I would feel to treat my married daughter and her husband as co-owners with me of this house. The Rikers have no such motive. They are very simply helping their son, who is on his way to becoming rich but hasn't got there yet. When I think of how much money he will be making if the firm doesn't fall apart, I am tempted to advise the Rikers to make Jon a loan, not a gift, but that would be against Charlotte's interest. But maybe it is a loan. It is also true that I have no legal duty, in case I were not to give Charlotte my life estate in this place, to treat her as a co-owner. She isn't, not while I am alive. I could, if only I knew how, act more naturally, and say that while I am alive I am the owner, with the rights and obligations of such, and you and Jon, my dears, will have to wait your turn.

I did, on the other hand, ask why I hadn't been told, by letter or a phone call, that they had decided to accept my offer. Charlotte seemed disconcerted by the question. I guess we thought we'd tell you when we got here, was her answer. Then Myron spoke up before we ever got a chance.

So be it.

Christmas festivities were next on her agenda.

Did I know where I would be going?

No, not yet.

Probably they would be unable to squeeze in another weekend in the country. Could I come to the city, have dinner, and exchange Christmas presents? Is the day before I leave on my vacation convenient?

In order to be cooperative, I said yes. The truth is that I hadn't given any thought to presents, and still don't know where I might go.

So much for that.

Renata's bedside manner needs work. She is too heavy to be throwing herself on top of me. Might have injured one of my vital organs. I didn't like those massive breasts or the stiffness of the undergarments.

She likes connivance laced with tension. That's what the conversation after Thanksgiving lunch must have been about. When I was sick, there was a new element: something like a bid for domination. The kiss, the revelation that she is available and is being used outside the marriage. She is counting on the delayed aphrodisiac effect. I think she wants to be the Sphinx in the Sahara of my affections.

I looked at myself in the bathroom mirror after writing

these words and noted that I need a haircut. It's been at least five weeks. There is a barber in Sag Harbor; perhaps I should try him instead of commuting to New York for the dubious pleasure of hearing Carlo plan his next vacation while he snips away. To think that in all the years I have been going to him that man still hasn't learned to keep my shirt collar dry when he washes my hair! The advantage is that the result of his work is totally predictable.

How many more of these cycles of maintenance?

Monthly haircut, weekly clipping of the fingernails and toenails, daily shave and hair wash, daily or twice daily bath, depending on whether I have been out of the house; shirts, underwear, socks, and handkerchiefs thrown into the hamper and returned in disorder to my chest of drawers every Friday; each week, a visit to the cleaner in the shopping mall. Hand over two pairs of no longer fresh khaki trousers I have rolled into a bundle; receive their proud comrades hanging stiffly from wire hangers inside plastic cocoons; pay a certain number of dollars. The nice lady I deal with has early Parkinson's—each week I pretend I don't notice.

On the other hand, I will never again need to order a dinner jacket or an overcoat. The ones I have will see me through. Their remaining useful life is longer than mine.

VII

T HE INVITATION is extended over the telephone by Mr. Gilbert Blackman's assistant, new on the job or for other reasons unknown to Schmidt, although, having heard her speak, he might have sworn to Sergeant Smith that he could describe her in all relevant detail: medium height, a trifle on the heavy side, baby fat in all likelihood; ash-blond hair cut in a pageboy; gray eyes; blond fuzz on cheeks and upper lip; black crew-neck sweater with short sleeves, Black Watch kilt, pale stockings with seams straight as a rail, and black calf pumps. Except that he was all wrong. The Boston debutante Schmidt had beheld in his mind's eye—a graduate, in that order, of Miss Porter's, Smith College, and Katharine Gibbs's starchy establishment—who had spent some time working as a movie mogul's social secretary because the oaf who hadn't as yet managed to give her an orgasm thought they should wait to get married until he got his diploma from the Harvard Law School, indeed could have been, as a matter of generations, the mother of Mr. Blackman's employee. But she wasn't. According to our information, the daughter of the Boston debutante so well known to Schmidt teaches aerobic dancing on the Upper West Side and lives with an African-American photographer. Gil's current assistant is a brunette of Greek extraction, alone among her siblings, every one of them a college graduate, to have acquired a well-bred voice and perfect diction. When she makes the telephone call, she wears a red leather miniskirt, so short it makes it rather awkward to sit down. She prefers knitted silk to cashmere and has no immediate marriage prospects, among other reasons because—unbeknownst to Schmidt, months having passed since he and Gil last exchanged confidences of that nature at lunch—Mr. Blackman regularly bangs her on the sofa in the sanctum sanctorum accessible only through a discreet door in the office, graced by a Miró, where Mr. Blackman conducts the common run of his business. No matter: the vision induced great affability in the nostalgic Mr. Schmidt. Wordlessly, he forgave the slight (Gil could have come to the telephone himself; he knows very well I no longer have a secretary), and agreed to have dinner at eight in the country on the following Saturday. How lovely, rejoiced the perfect voice. Gil and Elaine will be so glad; I believe it will be just you and them.

Thus at five before the hour, in order to be neither early nor unduly late, in his better blue blazer, too stylish for O'Henry's but exactly right for the Blackmans', equipped with presents (CDs for the parents and the elder, presumably absent daughters, and a cologne spray for Lilly, in Schmidt's opinion sexually advanced and much maligned), Schmidt stepped into his ice-cold car. Under a moon so fine and bright it could have shone over the palace of Osman Pasha, he drove to Georgica. There stood Gil's cottage. Not a car in sight—

neither on the circular drive nor among the giant azaleas where a guest fearful of blocking others and indifferent to the welfare of the lawn might have parked. They would, in fact, be alone. Schmidt sniffed the greenery wired to the brass knocker, rang the doorbell, and entered. In the hall, under a majestic tree, packages had accumulated. He added his shopping bag. Was this a new extravagance of the Wandering Jew, to hang a wreath and dress the tree during Advent each time he pitched his tent for the night, or were the Blackmans actually planning to spend Christmas in Wainscott? Schmidt directed his steps to the library. Ho, ho, ho, he called out, here comes Schmidtie, the ruddy-nosed reindeer!

Gil rose from his wing chair and opened his arms. A huge, silent embrace—Schmidt felt a contraction inside his chest, as though his heart too had been squeezed. They had, after all, remained friends. When he took a step backward, away from Gil, his heart moved again. Gil had on a thick silky cardigan, beautiful as Joseph's coat of many colors. It was the sort of garment that Schmidt knew Gil would not have bought for himself. Elaine had given it to him. Here was proof she was still in love, physically. She wanted her husband to be gorgeous. Schmidt imagined the sweater he might have received from Mary: the best kind of lamb's wool, burgundy or dark green, to go with his tweed coat, and probably crew-necked, so that he could on occasion wear it without a necktie. There was nothing wrong with the rustic approach to decorating one's husband; in truth, Schmidt thought it quite appropriate in his own case. He might have added that it had never occurred to him that he was a glamorous object of desire. Nevertheless, as he turned to kiss Elaine on the cheek, he wondered how much of that was in the eye of the be-holder: What would it have been like to be married to a Jewess? He might ask Gil about that. Gil had drunk from both wells.

The exotic lady in question hugged Schmidt in turn. It's so wonderful about Charlotte, she whispered. I don't know the boy, do I? They'll be so happy. If only Mary could have seen it!

The Blackmans were having champagne—silver bucket, large silver tray, tulip glasses. A mound of dark gray caviar on a crystal plate showed signs of recent erosion. Schmidt put his back to the fire, asked for a martini, and watched Elaine load the caviar on rounds of black pumpernickel.

Is lovely Lilly here?

She's at her father's, sleeping over, Elaine told him. It was perfect scheduling. The juvenile delinquent he screws is visiting her parents in Scranton, so he has time for his daughter, and I don't have to worry about Lilly being embarrassed by the way they carry on.

You see the symmetry? Gil had returned with a martini in a silver goblet. He handed it to Schmidt together with a little linen napkin and a piece of bread brimming over with caviar.

Gil continued: Our juvenile delinquent leaves her mom's home where she lives with the man who was crazy enough about her mom to abandon his own daughters and their mom, and goes to visit her real pop. In the meantime, the unrelated juvenile delinquent her pop is screwing, who could be his daughter, goes to visit her own mom and pop. If we only knew about the pop in Scranton—is this really his daugh-ter?—we could extend the frieze.

You are revolting. Lilly isn't a juvenile delinquent.

Neither is Judy! She is a rising rock artist who works very hard. I wish we could say as much for dear Lilly.

Now, now, said Schmidt. Time out. Is there more martini in that silver shaker? Have you taken the family silver out of the vault just for me? Or does the decoration mean you plan to spend Christmas here?

Elaine made a sniffing noise that Schmidt thought might be real.

You tell Gil he is a brute. He used to listen to what you say. Maybe he still does. The tree is for Lilly. She is having a party tomorrow afternoon for the kids from the stable.

Halsey's! Mary and Charlotte used to do that until Charlotte decided riding took up too much time.

What a nuisance: Schmidt's own eyes filled up with tears. He blew his nose elaborately, drank half of his second martini, and ate another wallop of caviar. Angry at the tremor in his voice, he announced: I have a problem with this Christmas.

Of course, said Gil, it must be very tough. Why don't you spend it with us? We are going to Venice, just a few couples. We'll be at the Monaco. If you decide quickly, I bet I can still get a room for you—or you and Lilly can share.

That's the only condition on which I would go. I'd like to have you and Elaine as my parents-in-law. But it's more complicated than that. I don't think Venice is the right idea, although I am really very grateful.

Tell us over dinner. I am going to put the food on the table.

In fact, it was a small Oriental, an almost entirely round, elderly woman, shifting about in powder-blue felt slippers, who served the dinner. Elaine spoke to her with emphasis; either she was deaf or there was a question about how well she understood. The food was a succession of Chinese dishes of the kind Schmidt remembered eating before Hunan and Szechuan restaurants invaded New York, and afterward every shopping mall—peas, pea pods, and water chestnuts swimming in white sauces among mushrooms and alternating chunks of chicken and shrimp. It had a comforting taste. He ate with pleasure, hungrily, using his fork and knife, observing the Blackmans click their ivory chopsticks. These were linked at the top by thin silver chains—a new refinement, so far as Schmidt was concerned. The wine was fruity and strong. He was drinking it too fast, and Elaine kept his glass full.

A little Merlot that goes with anything, I get it directly from the Sonoma Valley producer, Gil informed him; would Schmidt like to be included for a couple of cases in the next order? Thereupon, he resumed needling Elaine about the education of teenage girls, Lilly in particular. Unless they had talent—and he challenged Elaine and Schmidt to point to a single case of a talent that lay in hiding, waiting to be discovered—they should not be allowed to fool themselves into thinking they were special. The proper question was: How could they make themselves useful and financially independent?

It occurred to Schmidt that Gil had not applied this theory with full rigor to his own daughters. But it was not for him to bring that up. He was to be a buffer state. That was why they were having dinner à trois. Therefore, taking another gulp of wine, he asked, Who else is going to be at the Monaco?

Then you will come with us, cried Elaine. It will be so much fun! We even have another lawyer!

She named a partner in the most profitable firm in New York, the husband of one of her cousins, a man Schmidt disliked but didn't know, although they had been at law school at the same time; a writer and his wife who also wrote, both of whom had been published by Mary; and a man whose name Schmidt recognized as being that of a movie producer. I don't know whom Fred will bring, she added, but I hope it will be Alice. She is such a good sport!

I don't think I can. You see, I've made all kinds of nice overtures to the parents of Charlotte's fiancé, and they have asked me to spend Christmas with them—in Washington, of all places! I said I'm not up to it this year, which is quite true, and everybody—the parents, Charlotte, and Jon—will take it badly if instead I go off on a party in Venice. Besides, I'm not sure I am up to Venice either.

It was Gil's turn to be practical.

Then what will you do, old friend? he asked.

I don't know. To put an end to the discussion, I told them I would go away to someplace that has no associations with Christmas. The trouble is I can't think where that would be. And it's kind of late. Christmas is practically here. Perhaps I will just stay here and pretend I am somewhere else—let's say Kyoto!

That won't work. They'll ask for your telephone number, they'll want you to call them, they'll expect presents from Kyoto when you return.

That was the practical side of Elaine.

I think you are right.

Kyoto is not a bad idea, said Gil. Of course, it will be cold and humid and the gardens won't seem like much—except the Moss Temple, which is best in the winter. I shot some scenes there one January. Why don't you go to a place like Bali? You will be in a marvelous hotel, you will have the beach, and you will get a real rest.

And have all those couples all around me, enjoying the best years of their lives?

He's right, said Elaine. It would be like going alone on a cruise in the Caribbean.

How do you know? You've never been on a cruise. That's just where people go to find a lover. Bali's the thing. There must be lots of men who go alone to study the topless Balinese, and women too. I don't mean only lesbians; women who don't mind being near men who have been put in the right frame of mind.

You are really disgusting. I know what Schmidtie should do. Let's send him to our Amazon island.

What's that?

Gil, you tell him about it.

That's exactly the place for you, and I think it can be done. We went there in the summer, which is not the right season, three or four years ago, after my film opened in Rio. You remember Marisa, the Brazilian who played the mute whom Jackson finally marries?

Certainly.

Her family arranged it, when we told them we were exhausted and needed a place to be alone and rest. It was the best thing we have ever done. We flew to Manaus from Rio, and there we chartered a tiny plane that could land on a tiny clearing in the jungle on an island in the middle of the Amazon, about an hour west of Manaus. The island itself is the size of your hand and the river is very wide; I think the shore was almost two miles away, on either side. At one end of the island, near the landing strip, there is a village of caboclos—that's the word for Indians of mixed blood who have more or less joined the twentieth century. They live by fishing and are obviously very poor, but there are a couple of television sets in the village and so forth. Toward the other end of the island, completely surrounded by jungle vegetation, is the guest house. It's owned by some Brazilian company that runs it like a club for invited guests—usually not more than two couples. But I think you could have it all for yourself, as we did, if it hasn't been booked. An amazing structure: imagine an octagonal house, made entirely of native Amazon woods and very airy. The walls don't quite reach either the roof or the ground—no nails, indeed no metal components in the construction, except in the bathrooms and in the kitchen. Caboclo servants, very silent, moving like polite shadows. You only see them when you want something, and they seem to know it without being called. And rather wonderful food. Strange fruit juices and jellies that are supposed to prolong your life and do other things for you that are even better, flat bread, and river fish. For a couple of days, we had chops, that's really what they were, carved from a fish like a huge river monster. An absolute delicacy! To drink, there is beer and *pinga*—a Brazilian rum with the kick of a buffalo. If you want anything else, you will have to bring it.

Did they speak English? Or is speaking Portuguese another one of your attainments?

You don't need to speak. The other thing is that you won't have to stay in the house all day and all evening reading and listening to the parrots and the monkeys. We had a guide who met us on the island and acted as the majordomo as well as guide. He told the caboclos what to do. He is German—in fact I wonder if his name wasn't Herr Schmidt!

My Doppelgänger.

Gil, his name was Lang, and you never called him Herr.

That was just a nice idea. The man's name is something else; more like Oskar Lang. He is a biology student from Hamburg, who came to Manaus right after the war. He intended to study Amazon fish—actually, he says *studien* instead of study—but in the midst of *studien* he got hooked up with an Indian woman and never left, except for funerals, when his mother and then his father died. He married his Indian. She became a nurse in Manaus and he became a river guide, working for people doing documentary films and scientific expeditions. He is quite an expert on fish.

And breasts! He kept on pointing out to Gil that white women's breasts fall as they get older—here he would look at me—while his Indian woman has boobs that stayed small and hard. Like *mein* fist only nice, so nice and small, was how he put it!

That's true. He showed us a photo with boobs he had taken of her in one of those round backyard pools made of blue plastic, right behind his house in Manaus. Anyway, Schmidt—I mean Lang—had a comfortable long rowboat with an outboard motor. He also had an assistant, the most beautiful young Indian boy you can imagine, who paddled when we went out in the canoe instead. And what eyesight that boy had! He would say something very quietly to Lang and point and, there, in absolutely impenetrable foliage or hidden in the reeds near the riverbank was just the bird we had said to Lang the day before we especially wanted to look at. Every morning, Lang and he took us out on these nature trips or to visit another caboclo village, which was more primitive, on an island nearby, and once to a village that was pure Indian and pure Lévi-Strauss. That was probably the most remarkable experience we had during our stay. A place of complete serenity: huts on stilts, women grinding food in wooden bowls, naked children dozing in the dust under the huts, and then the arrival of the men in canoes filled to the rim with fish. The women met them at the edge of the river, and the men threw them the catch, still jumping. They didn't have to ask for the fish—we couldn't see any connection between the givers and the takers. It was distributed like manna. Then, at night, Lang would take us out to look at alligators. We would drift near the bank. Suddenly, he would turn on his flashlight and there would be those burning red eyes. The whole bank seemed to come alive!

Remember when the Indian boy caught one?

Yes, that was quite a trick. Lang put the boy on shore, and we pushed off and drifted a little. Then the boy gave a sort of whistle, Lang turned on his lamp, and in the beam we saw the boy on the bank holding up an alligator by the gills. He had crept up on him from behind. Why the other alligators didn't eat him is beyond me. We never understood it, because Lang showed us they can move really fast on land. It's a weird, terrifying kind of sprint.

It all sounds quite splendid, but do you think it's for me?

Alone? I have never had a powerful interest in nature—bird-watching or anything like it.

This is different. It's not like sneaking around in the brambles surrounded by Yalies with binoculars and skin cancer on their noses. Nature is quite simply there: overpoweringly beautiful and omnipresent. You are in it. Besides, we were there in the bad season, when there really are no flowers, but you will have amazing orchids in the trees, other blossoms covering the water as far as you can see. But if you want company, come to Venice with us. We would really like that.

Venice is out of the question. Let me think about the island.

Think fast. I would hate to find it had been reserved for someone else.

The woman in felt slippers served coffee in the library—that is, served it to Schmidt. Both Blackmans drank chamomile and both sat on the sofa facing the fire, which was fit to roast an ox. Felt Slippers must have added logs to it during dinner. The room was so warm that Schmidt didn't worry about blocking the fireplace. He stood again with his back to the fire.

This stuff isn't decaffeinated? he asked.

No, we would have warned you.

Then I would like some more.

If he couldn't sleep, he would take a pill. It was nice of Gil to remember his addiction to coffee. He should reciprocate by drinking an unreasonable amount of it. With a new and insistent feeling of benevolence, Schmidt surveyed the neat bookshelves, the Fairfield Porter watercolor of Gil done in the garden behind the house where Gil had lived when he was still married to Ann, the predictable but sound arrangement of the furniture, and Gil and Elaine themselves. Couldn't consolation be drawn from this scene, regardless of his actual distance from it? Keep envy at bay. The small aches in his neck and shoulders, and also in his left ankle, which, twisted so often, became sore as soon as the cold weather began, were melting away. He eyed the bottles on the silver tray on the coffee table and the snifters and was about to ask for a brandy when he realized that neither Blackman had spoken for some minutes. That must mean they thought the evening should end.

Beautiful Elaine, he said. Thank you! I had better return to my Schloss.

Forgive me. I know my eyes are closing. It must be Gil's all-purpose Merlot.

Nonsense! It's the bliss of having given your old pal the first home-cooked meal he has had in a week—one he hasn't cooked himself.

He stooped to be embraced by two arms in black angora and kissed her. One would not have thought it looking at her across the dinner table: the cheek felt rough. Rigorous diet, too much sun all year-round, not enough face cream under the powder and the rouge, or just the ordinary death march of the cells? For the third time that evening, a fist busied itself with Schmidt's heart. Until the end, he had marveled at the softness of Mary's skin, even when she had lost so much weight that it had become puckered around her mouth and on the neck, like a child making a monkey face.

Wait, said Gil. I am coming with you. I don't feel sleepy at all and I can tell you want a drink. We'll have it at your house.

The Ottoman moon was hidden. Schmidt drove west faster than was usual for him on country roads, keeping Gil's Jaguar in his rearview mirror. It had gotten even colder. Puddles he hadn't noticed on his way to the Blackmans' had turned into shiny mirrors of ice. Whenever Route 27 was visible at a crossing, he would see the headlights of a car hurtling this way or that. Nothing else; along the polite, clean roads south of the highway, the houses had been deserted, the thermostats turned down, the alarm systems set. Why shouldn't he spend the ten thousand dollars or more and give the Amazon a try? He would be lonely but warm, and perhaps not that lonely. It might be a nice change to doze over a drink in his room, or in the salon if there was one, knowing that well-meaning brown persons with eyes like worlds of sadness were but a few feet away, busy with his dinner. There would be candles or some sort of lamp on the table. He could read while he was eating: *Almayer's Folly*, or some other suitable Conrad in paperback. Probably, the humidity there made books curl; no need to expose his good edition to it. Long Island air was bad enough.

He slowed down for the sharp left turn into the driveway to his house and crept along on the gravel. When the front of the house came into view, he braked so suddenly that Gil's bumper touched the rear of his car. As always when he went out in the evening, Schmidt had turned on the lamps on both sides of the front door and the reflectors on the front porch. In the harsh light he saw a large figure, like a melting snowman, squatting on top of the steps. Its exposed buttocks were fat and exceedingly white. One arm was raised, perhaps to shade the face against the glare. Very slowly, tugging at its clothes, the figure straightened itself. Then, as though to signal satisfaction with the result, it made a little bow in the direction of Schmidt's car, dashed like a startled pig to the end of the porch, vaulted over the balustrade, became a shadow jogging toward the back lawn, and disappeared behind the honeysuckle hedge. There could be no mistake: it was the man.

Gun the motor, make a U-turn around Gil's car, and to hell with the grass, spend the night at the Blackmans' or at a motel?

Gil was already striding toward the house, flashlight in one hand and some sort of stick in the other. All right, let it be. Schmidt turned off the ignition, and got out, holding on to the door to steady himself. He caught up with Gil.

Gil, that's a lunatic. I've seen him before. I don't want to deal with it. Let's get away. We'll call the police on your car phone or from your house.

We can't just leave your house because we've seen a marauder. How do you know he hasn't broken in?

I told you: he's a nut, not a burglar. A big, unpleasant nut.

That's all right. I can take care of him.

Gil held up the object that looked like a stick.

A crowbar! Are you mad too?

I keep one under the car seat, just in case. It steadies the nerves. Come on, Schmidtie, we'll check the doors and windows and, if nothing is broken, we'll have our drink. I don't feel like chasing that guy around the pond either.

The moon had reappeared, so bright one could have read the newspaper. A house well put away for the winter: not a dead leaf or broken branch to be seen, garden hoses and wheelbarrows stored, storm windows intact. Schmidt looked at the house as though it were a stranger's, ready to congratulate the old fellow who lived in it, and ask about his yardman. They circled back to the front door. He felt no surprise. On the doormat, still steaming, lay the fruit of the white buttocks.

We should kill the bastard, whispered Gil.

Getting him back to the loony bin would do it for me. I'll tell you something shameful: I'm glad you are here. Go on into the house, and light the fire in the living room. The liquor is on the sideboard. I'll get rid of this.

He flushed it down the toilet off the kitchen and put the snow shovel back in the garage. Then he washed his hands. His face was green, as though he had just vomited. Perhaps the light in that bathroom was also too harsh. He could change it for a soft, pink bulb. The other solution was to do nothing. Why not leave it for Jon Riker to worry about?

That's taken care of, he told Gil. Really, no worse than dog shit. You might have thought it would bring back fond memories—like picking up your dog's mess from the middle of the front lawn, while everybody else is eating lunch on the porch, but somehow the effect on me was different.

That's because malice is so uniquely human.

Debasement, too.

Look, I really want to hear what you know about this guy, because what happened isn't funny, but not right this minute. In fact, I asked to come here to talk about me.

That was pretty clear.

I am in a strange situation. I'm involved with this girl—she is all of twenty-four, in fact her birthday was last week—

and I don't know what to do about it. It's not the usual thing. First of all, it wasn't my idea. She engineered it all by herself, from the unexpected pass she made to the daily sex when I am in New York. Second, she is really beautiful. Third, she isn't after anything—you know, getting to have a part in some television show, presents, whatever. I can't even take her out to lunch or dinner! Where would we go without being noticed? Fourth, she may even be intelligent; anyway, she doesn't bore me. And fifth, the sex is irresistible. It isn't so much what she does—though she does plenty—it's her unbelievable enthusiasm. She makes me feel I am some kind of god of love, capable of magical feats. This would be very nice if it weren't for Elaine. You saw me give her a hard time at dinner. But that's an act. I love her. She loves me. We have a good marriage.

I know.

A marriage with good sex. We haven't stopped. It's not one of those once-a-month arrangements you read about in women's magazines—if such things do in fact exist. I've always wondered. Unless we are tired or I am drunk, we make love. Another curious fact is that the thing with the girl hasn't had a bad effect on the thing with Elaine.

Perhaps you think about the girl when you do it.

You're wrong. That breaks your concentration and stops you dead in your tracks! I believe it's something very healthy: the girl has made me more interested in the activity. I feel better about my old carcass. That must be the reason.

Then what's wrong? It sounds quite ideal. Or does she want you to divorce Elaine?

She says she knows I'm too old for her. Of course, I've told her that I will never leave Elaine. I don't just love Elaine—I like our life together. The girl is certainly smart enough to understand that.

She may not believe you. Anyway, there seems to be a category of women who don't mind living with men who are old enough to be their fathers. Particularly when they are glamorous and rich, like you. There are lots of examples.

Sure, but usually they're older than my girl or a little crazy.

Is she the latter?

I don't think so. I think she is just a nice, oversexed kid.

Then I ask again, what's wrong?

The duplicity. I don't have an unmixed reputation as far as fidelity is concerned, but I don't deserve it. You might say that I've only been unfaithful to Elaine in moments of distraction. Never in a way that made me shut her off from what I do and think about every day. If only I could bring the girl to the house to be the number-two wife!

Elaine might like that.

She'd hate it. So would Lilly—and Nina and Lisa. You know that those two are crazy about Elaine. There would be a solid front against me!

Like the Maginot Line, right? Then maybe the only solution is to stop. If the girl is so intelligent, and you have explained everything to her, she should understand. You could even introduce her to somebody more suitable—for instance, a younger me!

But I don't want to stop! That's like saying I should tear up a flower bed. If I put the problem of duplicity aside, which I can't, I've got something happening to me that's quite marvelous. I've been transformed into a brand-new man, admired and desired for some qualities I can't even see, and this by a girl who is like a daydream, except that she is absolutely real! You know the normal me: important and self-important, days cut up in thirty-minute segments of appointments with other men like me, weekends here or on the Coast, and vacations planned by Elaine months in advance, like that Christmas trip we're making with the usual idiots, intermittent orgies of spending money and paying bills, and every eighteen months or so the ritual fit of nerves about a film I know is going to turn out pretty much all right. Do you think it's easy to give up this new thing that's grown up in my life? Could such a thing—so unpolluted by my permanent self—happen again?

Ah, the mirage of fugitive youth!

That's another problem. How long can I keep it up, this sort of stuff—I mean physically? And what happens when I slow down?

That will take a while, especially if you're not in New York all the time. By the way, are you jealous? I mean, do you care whether you are the only one?

I don't dare to be. She has asked me a slightly different question, whether I wanted her to be faithful. I said that would be an unfair request, since I am not faithful to her. She was so genuinely shocked that I had to explain it was only with Elaine!

Schmidt found it difficult to comment on this revelation. A moment of thoughtful silence followed, interrupted by Gil.

Look, what about this guy? Are you going to call the police?

Perhaps tomorrow. I feel too tired. There is no rush; by

now he might be anywhere, including, of course, my back-yard. There isn't much I can tell you. I met him, if that's what you want to call it, on the bus. He sat down next to me and stank. I don't think I could bear to touch him. I believe he sensed my revulsion and used it to terrorize me. This is an abstract way of putting it, but it's as good as any other. I saw him a second time, through the window of O'Henry's, and had the same feeling of panic. What was the meaning of tonight? A coincidence? Was he looking for a house with a front door that was unlocked, happened to check mine out, and took a shit on my doormat out of frustration? Is he fol-lowing me around because he knows he can scare me? What-ever it is, I don't like it.

I don't either. Let me know what you decide to do.

After Gil left, Schmidt had another, indecently large, drink of brandy. It was not the first time that having listened to one of his friend's tales of woe he wished he had the same sort of problems to contend with. The visit from the man, on the other hand, was right up his own alley. Shame and paral-ysis! Was he expected to call the police and ask Sergeant Smith to rescue him from a bum defecating on his doorstep? Wouldn't it be more decorous to get a crowbar, like Gil, or the ax handle he already owned, and brain the fellow when he pulled his next stunt? But his nerve would fail; he was un-manned by that strange hobo; it was the effect, which he had never seen, of a snake on a bird. Two birds with one stone: there was something wrong with that pun that brandy pre-vented him from identifying, but it was all the same. The Amazon island would put plenty of distance between him, the man, and all pretense of Christmas cheer.

Nothing.

Perhaps on Sunday the man too sleeps late. Perhaps he is at mass.

When Blue Felt Slippers answers the telephone at Gil's house, the party is in full swing. Schmidt insists, and spells his name; eventually, Mr. Blackman comes to the telephone. Yes, he wants very much to go to the island, the sooner the better. No, he hasn't called the police. He has thrown down his gauntlet to the man and has felt no fear. Gil and Elaine mustn't worry.

IX

It's very hot, but the air is so clear that Schmidt can see the trees on the distant bank of the river as clearly as if he were looking through binoculars. In fact, he has forgotten to bring them, which is stupid, because the birds are as amazing and varied as Gil—or was it Elaine?—had told him. Instead, from time to time, he borrows the guide's, feels squeamish about putting them against his eyes, but doesn't want to offend that observant and sensitive man by wiping them first. He has told the guide and the Indian boy to take the morning off; he will move a chair to the landing and read in the sun. It might be nice to get some color in his face before he goes home. They spend so much time on jungle paths, and, when they go out in the boat, drifting near the riverbank, in the shade of the trees, that he is almost as pale as when he first arrived.

In fact, the book—*Nostromo*, since he decided that if he were going to South America he might as well test his theory that Conrad had fixed in it completely and forever the essence of that continent—lies in his lap open to the page where he began almost an hour ago. The reason is that

Schmidt has been overcome by intense, rather stupid happiness. It permeates his body. He feels good all over; were someone to ask his blessing, he would like to give it. He could also sing, perform uncommon acts of charity, tell a small child stories of creation. Nature is beautiful and good—even though under the surface of the opaque, tobacco-colored water, fish are devouring each other, alligators asleep in the mud among the reeds will awaken to pangs of great hunger and spring on their prey, and the barefoot, brown boys and girls tirelessly playing soccer in the village perhaps half a mile away with a bundle of rags tied with a string will never get to kick a leather ball or learn to read. Schmidt is in harmony with nature. For the moment, all that matters is that and his gratitude. It is so very splendid to be alive!

When the evening falls, he writes to Charlotte. His stay is almost over. Probably, there is no sensible way to mail a letter from the island at this point. He might as well do it at the Manaus airport, on his way home, if he is going to mail it at all.

There is a confession he owes her: The way those years when she was a child and then a big girl sped by, he has trouble constructing a narrative of what happened between him and her. Nothing very bad, of that he is sure. When she was little, and then at Brearley and at Harvard, she was always a model daughter, a source of such pride, and he cannot think of a time when he withheld his approval, any mean act of which he was guilty, or anything even halfway sensible she wanted that he did not try to make sure she would have. But what did they do together that had more substance than the time he put in watching over her at the beach, driving her to all those lessons, or sitting beside her at the movies? The rare visits to a museum in the city? A couple of performances of *The Nutcracker*? Taking her and her roommates out to dinner in Boston, when he visited her at college with Mary, or during the few trips he had made alone, as a lark, when Mary was away at a sales conference? Had he and Charlotte ever had a real talk, either when she was little or as grown-ups? Was there something he had taught her about life that was worth mentioning? Incorrigible, he adds he isn't sure he knows such things. Perhaps that is why he has so little to say to her now, except how much he loves her and, of course, when they fight. Had Mary done better, and if so, how had she managed it? If she did, it was some quality she possessed and he, Schmidt, lacks. Would Mary have felt she had more in common with her daughter?

There is a violent downpour in the afternoon. No nature trip. He hasn't uttered a word all day, except *obrigado*, to thank the servants. Having reread what he wrote, he tears it up and says, out loud, Even if this stuff is true it's no excuse for the way she behaves. Good manners are the one thing she might have learned from me.

X

H E HAD SENT under the cover of envelopes, because the only address where he knew he could reach her was O'Henry's, postcards of the restored opera house in Manaus, Indians spearfishing from canoes and lounging in their hammocks, and birds of the Amazon. Before leaving, he had deposited her Christmas present with the bartender: bright red leather gloves lined with wool. Therefore, her being so utterly business-like the evening of his return, Schmidt having rushed to the restaurant for dinner, really just in order to see her, as he acknowledged to himself—she greeted him and took his order without a word about the four-week absence, the gloves, or his having written—surprised Schmidt. He had expected connivance, a sign that would distinguish him, but there was nothing, not even one of her languid smiles. It would have been easy, so it seemed to him, to make a teasing remark about his strange tan; his one serious session in the sun made him turn the color of copper, with just a touch of verdigris. But as he chewed his way through the dinner, it seemed to him that she was paying less attention to him than ever, less than was due an habitué, who also happened to be a local notable. He was reminded of the times when Mary, Charlotte, and he would return to the city after the Christmas vacation and discover that out of the entire staff of their building—as numerous as the progeny the Lord had promised to Abraham, had been his invariable joke—only the cross-eyed and wizened Ukrainian handyman would thank them for the substantial gift of cash that had been distributed, before their departure, by the super, his colleagues apparently considering manifestations of gratitude to be acts beneath their dignity.

Immediately, he was furious at himself: What right had he to put Carrie in that context? She had always thanked him nicely for her tip. Those silly extraneous attentions must have been quite simply unwelcome, perceived by her as the hesitant, almost leering advances of an old bore sick with loneliness. He skipped the second and third espresso and the after-dinner drink. When she brought the check, he found that in his wallet he had the twenties and tens he needed to pay and leave a gratuity, correct as the figures worked out, although somewhat less generous than usual, without asking for change. He waved goodbye and stalked out.

The overnight flight from Rio de Janeiro to New York had left him tired—he had rejected, as too complicated, the solution of avoiding it by using the Salvador–Miami connection—and he had intended to go directly to bed. But he felt dissatisfied and agitated. His skin itched. The accumulated mail was on the kitchen table. He hesitated between brandy and whiskey, poured a large whiskey and soda because he was thirsty, brought over a wastebasket for the junk mail, and sat down to sort it.

Mostly it was junk. He put aside the *New Yorkers* and the *New York Review of Books* and the bills—electricity, gas and heating oil, his two credit cards, the club, and the yardman; really, it was nothing, when compared to the time when he had a real household. Was he spending less money than he had expected? Mrs. Cooney could have told him right away; she had liked reconciling his bank statements, a task that required the use of felt-tip pens of various colors for doodling and underlining and offered her the opportunity to volunteer acerbic comments about Mary's and his expenses. Actually, the balance that appeared in his checkbook was substantial; he hoped it was correct. He had not continued Mrs. Cooney's labors of verification after leaving Wood & King and her providential care. This was no time to begin, especially as he would have to go back to where she had left off. There were also several communications from W & K. All but two went directly the way of the junk mail; Schmidt was not interested in the firm's monthly news bulletin, the memoranda to all lawyers in the office and selected clients on the more striking developments affecting executive compensation, or the questionnaire about partners' preferences as to the date on which the dinner for most recently retired partners (Schmidt among them) might be held at the Metropolitan Museum. His current intention was not to attend. He put on top of the reports from his investment adviser a notification from the accounting department that his retirement benefit for January 1992 had been duly deposited. The other letter, signed by Jack DeForrest, he read over twice: It told him that the firm had amended, by a unanimous vote of active partners (so Riker had voted yes), the pension plan to continue his payments at the current level, but, in the interest of fairness to younger partners and taking into account the welfare of the firm, only until the January 1 nearest his sixty-seventh, rather than seventieth, birthday. He would, of course, appreciate the favorable contrast with the normal payment period of only five years following retirement.

Nice, thought Schmidt. That's when they think I can stop eating. It's OK with me; perhaps I won't even be around to notice.

This news called for another large drink. Schmidt had bought in Manaus some moist, dark, and rather sweet tasting cigars. He cut the end off one of them with the carving knife and lit it with great care. A neat circle of ash began to form. It lengthened faultlessly. Schmidt poured more whiskey into his glass. It struck him as strange that so many of his contemporaries had decided to give up smoking, alcohol, and coffee—and, of course, cheese, eggs, and red meat as well. Had they information about the advantages, perhaps even pleasures, of longevity, of which he had remained ignorant? He must inquire of DeForrest. At least he answered his telephone; Schmidt wouldn't have to leave the question with his secretary, to be answered by some assistant. Unless there was such a secret, it seemed reasonable to stick to his agreeable, life-shortening habits, perhaps even to acquire new ones. He wondered what they might be and to whom he might put that question. Perhaps Gil, if he wasn't away. He might do it at the same time he reported to Gil on the Amazon island and, no doubt, received a report on the idyll with the girl.

Abruptly, money and the need to avoid the calamity of a too-long life made him think of Charlotte. He had not called her upon arrival. He could still do it; they never went to bed before eleven. On the other hand, she hadn't telephoned either, although when he saw her and Jon in New York he had told her the date of his return and had mentioned it again in the postcard he wrote to her from Brazil. It was possible, of course, that she made a mistake entering it in her calendar, or that she hadn't put it down and had forgotten, or that his card had gone astray or was taking more than three weeks to reach her. Sooner or later he would have to call, there was no rule that said she had to be the first to call when he came back from vacation, he didn't want to create an unnecessary awkwardness, and it would be nice to know what plans they had for weekends. From the contents of the refrigerator it was clear that they had been around, in all likelihood with friends, as neither of them, to his knowledge, ate margarine, drank prune juice, or saved half-finished bottles of Coors. But he hadn't found any note from them on the pad of paper on the kitchen counter or in any of the other likely places where he had looked. More whiskey, heartache, and the beginning of another cigar: the telephone call would wait until the morning. It had gotten late; that, and not his feelings, prevented him from dialing their number. In the morning, he would leave a message on the answering machine.

He took the *New York Review* and moved from the kitchen table to his rocking chair. He leafed through the magazine until he reached an article about women that seemed to span the period from the Renaissance through the nineteenth century. The author was an Italian professor called Craveri, whose name he did not recall having seen before. What a well-managed life she must have led to know so much! He imagined perfect index cards with notes on everything she had read, filed in color-coded folders. Or did this lady have perfect recall, might she be one of those people who can rattle off the dates of the Council of Trent and name the day of the week when Napoleon and Alexander met on the river raft? And such orderly exposition! Schmidt had never filed anything. His notes, taken on yellow pads, accumulated in stacks and were of questionable utility when he was still working on the problem to which they related, because he remembered what was in them. Afterward, when he had finished, they had no value: to put them in order would have taken too much time, and where should he keep them? In his own office or in the firm's central files? The question would be answered by tossing them vengefully into one of those boxes for papers to be shredded that the mail-room staff occasionally brought around. Thus during his last days at the firm he had erased his personal record of his work, month by month, year by year, disposing of the leftovers in an orgy of self-mutilation that astonished even Mrs. Cooney, whose knowledge of his work habits was unsurpassed. Isn't there anything you want sent to the country? she kept asking, not even your correspondence? No, he had replied, what difference does it make what I wrote in '83 to the Southern Trust Company about fraudulent conveyances? The statute of limitations on my negligence has run out, and if it hasn't, and the firm is sued, the boys will find what they need in the central files. Mementos of closings followed to the trash the rich blue-and-maroon-bound volumes of transaction documents: tombstone ads laid to rest in Lucite, miniatures of products associated with various borrowers, his name on tarnished strips of fake brass glued to the base on which they were displayed—among them airplanes, oil tankers, trucks, and earth-moving equipment, and one large black telephone, and framed photographs of him signing opinions or, more often, hovering behind some borrower's president, ostensibly to make sure that potentate wrote his name in the right place. Unlike many of his partners, he had not used these articles as paperweights or displayed them on his window ledge. On his good days, when he knew that a principal involved in the transaction was due at his office, he would rummage in his closet and, if he could find it, put the appropriate toy in a place of honor on the coffee table or lean the photograph against the bound volumes on his bookshelf. Really, it was like the system Mary and he had for dealing with paintings they bought from artists who were friends or, far more dangerous, paintings that artists had given to them: there was a nail from which they would hang the work in question (usually it was Mary who remembered it had to be done) just before its creator came for a meal or for the weekend. Otherwise, since artists, like pigs in search of truffles, immediately head for the place where they last saw whatever work of theirs one had acquired, it was necessary to invent a theory of migration: the painting or drawing wasn't there because, depending on the circumstances of the visit, it was in the country, in the city, at the framer's because it had buckled, or, in extreme circumstances, at Schmidtie's office. A high-wire act, given the investigative skills of most artists.

Craveri's article took an unexpected turn; he had been reading about peasant women in England gathering animal turd for use as fuel in the kitchen fireplace—an activity he had never heard of—when the author, without transition, launched into an anecdote about the hour at which the prime minister wanted dinner served. The chef was in the wrong. Disraeli insisted that the sweets had begun to melt before they reached the table. There was more to it, but he couldn't find it on the page. He rubbed his eyes. Where was his cigar? Not in the ashtray, not at the edge of the end table where he sometimes balanced it. He stood up abruptly, frightened that the thing was burning somewhere. The cigar rolled from his lap to the floor. It had gone out. He brushed off the ashes, re-lit the cigar, and carried the whiskey glass to the sink. The running water made him realize he badly needed to go to the bathroom. When he came back to the kitchen, he saw it was past one in the morning.

He was tired, and yet once again so wide awake that, if he went on reading downstairs, he knew there would be no going to sleep without a strong pill. It would be better to read in bed. He got a glass of soda water for the night and was beginning to turn out the lights when he heard a series of rapid knocks at the front door and then the doorbell. The man? Burglars of more than usual impudence? In a passage off the kitchen that served as a mud room stood an ax handle he had bought years before intending to use it on the pair of unknown black dogs that had taken to rooting in the flower beds next to the back porch and clawing at the porch itself, presumably to get at a rabbit burrow underneath it. As if forewarned by the purchase, the dogs stopped their visits. He grasped the weapon, strode to the front hall, and turned on the outside light. Peering through one of the narrow windows at the side of the door, he saw a figure he had not expected: it was Carrie, in the same red ski parka and black tights she had worn when he and Gil saw her on the sidewalk outside O'Henry's. Her hands were bare. She was rubbing them together. When he opened to let her in he realized that the night had become very cold.

Come in quick, he told her. You must be freezing.

I am.

She wanted to keep her parka on until she warmed up. This is quite a place, she said. You weren't asleep? I was going to drive off if you didn't come to the door right away.

And then, seeing the ax handle, she made a hoarse giggling sound that was like a flashback to the nights he had spent listening to jazz on 52nd Street, and added, You were going to whack me!

Not you. The intruder. I will give you a drink.

She refused his offer of whiskey or coffee. She wanted a glass of milk. He told her he hadn't any; having returned that very day, he hadn't done his shopping. They settled for tea. She followed him into the kitchen and watched while he fussed with the kettle and teapot, her head, always somehow too heavy for that delicate long neck, pressed against her shoulder and fist as though she were going to snuggle it under a huge wing, her whole body leaning against the arm of the rocking chair. Schmidt thought that was what she must look like when she went home after those long hours of work to that apartment in Sag Harbor—he wondered whether in reality it could be more than a furnished room—and that he mustn't allow himself anything like those feelings of excessive and proprietary compassion that regularly overcame him each time a dog, without an owner in sight, followed him from the beach to the car and yelped, wagging his tail and rubbing his face against his knee, as though an adoption deal had just been consummated. This was a complicated young person, apparently quite able to take care of herself, who happened to work as a waitress. The advice he had given himself to be cautious remained valid.

Would you like to have your tea here? he asked her. I think I will have a cup too, and a whiskey as well, although I have already had several.

Can we go to the living room? I'd like to see this house. This is quite a place, she repeated.

My wife inherited it years ago, from an old aunt.

He thought that might make living in such a house more acceptable, much less a symbol of incalculable riches. On both sides of O'Henry's there were store windows of real estate brokers with photographs of properties for sale, usually with the asking price. This child would have a fairly accurate idea of how much the house was worth on the market.

And then he added, In fact this place doesn't really belong to me. I am just entitled to live here. When I die it will automatically become my daughter's. But, as she is getting married quite soon, I plan to give up my squatter's rights and move to a much smaller place. Then she and her husband will have this house without an old fellow getting in their way.

That's too bad!

Not really. It may be a nice change.

The Polish brigade had been hard at work. The living room had a disorderly but unlived-in appearance.

Now that you have seen the salon, he said to Carrie, let's try the library. It should be more cozy. There may even be wood in the fireplace.

After he had put down the tray and lit the fire, while they were still standing, she gave him a little punch on the shoulder, the same as in the parking lot.

You haven't asked me why I'm here. Aren't you surprised?

I hadn't even thought. I guess that's because I'm glad to see you. Of course, I was surprised. That's why I was carrying that stick.

Oh, yeah. I'm not even dressed up, or anything. I came over from work.

Of course.

When he asked her to sit down, she remarked that the fire was so warm she might as well take off her parka, and threw it into a corner of the room. The garment she was wearing over her tights turned out to be a man's shirt. She lowered herself carefully into the middle of the sofa that faced the fire, pulled off her sneakers, and massaged and wiggled her toes. Then, with a little moan, she stretched out her legs.

You mind if I put my feet on the coffee table? she asked. It sure feels good to get off them. You just going to stand there?

She continued to wiggle her toes while he poured her more tea. Definitely, the sofa was to be avoided. He moved one of the spare dining room chairs over to the coffee table where he could sit facing her, with his back to the fire.

I'll tell you why I came even if you're not curious. It's because I acted sore this evening. Did you notice?

Certainly. Was there a reason for it?

The way you came in. You didn't care about seeing me. Like you didn't greet me. Just hello, here I am, bring me a drink. You could have given me a hug or told me what it was like where you were. But there was nothing. Like I was a machine. Or a waitress in a drive-in. You hurt my feelings.

I am terribly sorry. If you want to know, I thought you were treating me coldly—from the moment I saw you! Usually, you say something friendly, and come over to chat, but this evening you didn't. That's why I didn't try to tell you about my trip. I figured you didn't want to be bothered.

Am I supposed to believe that?

It's the truth. Don't you know I'm your friend? I wrote postcards to you. I left a Christmas present for you.

She interrupted. Yeah, you took it over to the restaurant on my day off!

I am sorry. That was stupid of me. It was my last day in Bridgehampton and I didn't know where to find you.

You could have asked at the restaurant!

I didn't think you would like that.

Why? I'm not ashamed of you. You're ashamed of me! You didn't write your name on the package. I figured out why you put your postcards in envelopes. It was so that nobody would know you were writing to me.

Carrie, I used envelopes because that's more private and friendly. Also, it gives one more room to write.

All I know is you don't want anybody to think you like me.

She emptied her cup. As though she were withdrawing from the world, she drew her legs under her on the sofa and looked at him cheerlessly.

I don't want to embarrass you, that's all. It seems to me that a beautiful, young girl like you would hate to have people tease her on account of an old man.

If you liked me, you would let me worry about that.

Can't you tell that I like you quite a lot? Why else would I go to O'Henry's so often? It's not for the cuisine.

Should he leave his chair and sit down on the sofa, keeping

prudently to the corner? Repeat with Carrie the dumb show of the hour or more he had spent holding hands with Renata? Attempt a more daring scene? They could, for instance, look at photographs of the Grand Canyon. There was no reason why the book he had used with Corinne wouldn't be on the same bookshelf, in its old place. It occurred to him, simultaneously, that ruses were unnecessary, that he wasn't sure he wanted to succeed, and that his breath must be awful. He stood up, poked aimlessly at the fire, and added a log.

Hey, Schmidtie, you really mean it?

Was it possible to fall in love with a girl's voice?

She moved like a cat. The unforeseen embrace—she got up on her toes to reach his mouth and held him by both ears—and the weight of her body caught Schmidt off guard. He steadied himself, put his arms around her, and very tentatively stroked the back of her head. It was miraculous that the hair, indeed the head, he had studied so attentively, and in such secret, should be so available. He ventured to touch her tiny, tightly formed ears. When she ended the kiss she ran her tongue over his hand and then remained pressed against him, her head quiet and obedient in the hollow of his chest.

After a while, she whispered, You want to sit down on the couch?

She grabbed his erection and squeezed hard.

He's nice. Too bad that's all you're getting tonight.

But on the sofa—Let's sit quietly side by side, I want you to talk to me, she told him—she took hold of him again right away, while rebuffing, with her free hand, the caress Schmidt attempted, in part, at least, out of the feeling that he should reciprocate.

I said, no monkey business. You're going to talk to me.

He found that difficult. It was like using the one foreign language he had learned and forgotten, his high school French. Each word had to be looked for, found, and mouthed. What came out sounded like someone else speaking. The subject of the assignment had seemed evident: he began to describe to her how the strangeness of Brazil had struck him, at the same time as the intensity of the heat and light, as soon as he found himself in the open air in Manaus, intent on following the driver who had met him inside the terminal building—until then, when he wasn't on a plane, he had had the impression of sleepwalking in the air-conditioned chaos of the Rio, Saõ Paulo, and Brasilia airports. That wasn't, though, what she wanted.

You can talk about that some other time, she told him, increasing the pressure. I want to hear how come you like me.

Because of your long neck, your big eyes, and your hair. And because you're always hoarse. But you'll have to work on your voice a little if you are really going to be an actress.

You don't like my voice. It's Puerto Rican and not fancy.

That's not true. It's your secret charm. I'd like to save it on my ears, like on a tape, so I could hear it when you're not there.

Liar! If you wanted to hear me talk you would come to the restaurant more often. What else do you like?

The pain of controlling himself had become as great as the pleasure, but Schmidt thought that if she took her hand away nothing could stop him. She would laugh at him if he used another word. He must say it. It couldn't be helped.

Squeeze my dick hard, Carrie, as hard as you can.

A ring of iron. Now he could go on forever. If she would only touch his balls.

You're not telling me why you like me.

Because you work such long hours, because sometimes you look tired, because of your skin, and your feet, and your mouth. I haven't seen your breasts. I think they are small and hard.

You're wrong. I've got big tits. And you think I'm uneducated and dumb. And now you think I'm a whore.

No, Carrie, I think you are wonderful and crazy.

I like you because you're crazy. Are you in love with me?

Not yet. Perhaps. I don't know.

I'm going to make you. Stop closing your eyes.

Tug and release, tug and release. He stopped trying to speak. When the wet came, he felt it spread as though it were somewhere far away.

That's something! You've been storing it up.

I am sorry.

Don't be dumb. I know what I'm doing.

And, after a pause, sniffing the air, You smell like a mushroom. Schmidtie, the mushroom soup!

She put her tongue in his mouth. Then she pushed him away, stood up on the sofa, leapt from it onto the armchair, picked up her sneakers and parka and put them on as though she were trying to see how fast it could be done, and said, Got to go. You want to walk on the beach tomorrow? It's going to be a nice day. I'll pick you up at eleven.

XI

THERE WAS NO REASON she should be on time; it was, after all, her day off, and he hated to think of how late she had stayed with him. Still, when she hadn't showed up by eleven-thirty, be began to think he was a fool not to have asked for her telephone number. Without much conviction, he looked in the telephone directory and then tried information. No such listing. It was possible that he had got the spelling of her name wildly wrong. The Poles would be arriving any minute. He wasn't sure he liked the idea of their seeing Carrie come to the house: they had been Mary's cleaning women for years, and now, for all practical purposes, except that it was he who wrote their check, they were Charlotte's. Getting them started on Carrie—he could imagine the questions, sly looks, and perhaps comments—made him uncomfortable. He decided to take his car out and drive just a little way down the road and wait for her there. The only disadvantage was that she might call and not get an answer. Momentarily he wished he had an answering machine on which to compose a message for her. If he waited a bit longer, until the Poles arrived, he could ask Mrs. Nowak, who had no sense of humor and seemed to be less nosy than the others, to tell Carrie that he was waiting at the beach, but he didn't like that either, because, while he was making the arrangement, she might arrive, and then the fat would hit the fire. He was going to the beach with a young working girl. He had no doubt about his cleaning ladies' sense of social categories.

To hell with it. The thermometer read twenty. It would be colder at the beach and windy. He put on his old Abercrombie & Fitch hooded arctic weather garment that could really keep one comfortable in any kind of gale and his fur gloves, got the Saab out of the garage, and crunched his way down the drive and onto the road. The first car bearing Poles passed him, and then the second. They waved cheerily at each other. Then at a respectable distance from the house, he pulled over to the side, lit a cigarillo, and turned on the radio. The Southampton College radio station jazz program he liked was still on. If it hadn't been for the irritating uncertainty about when she was coming, if, indeed she had not decided to stand him up altogether, he would have been ready to say that he had nothing to complain about. Looked at another way, being stood up didn't seem like an affair of state. He doubted Carrie took appointments of any sort as seriously as he. Something might have come up. She might not have heard the alarm clock. It couldn't be because she felt offended or angry. There was no reason. Besides, there was a mysteriously self-contained quality about her visit—like the Raven's, only after midnight. Perhaps it was better that it should not have an immediate sequel. The memory of Carrie's visit was so vivid that, without giving it any thought, he began to masturbate discreetly under his coat.

He was thus engaged, eyes concentrated on the dashboard radio dial, when he heard a tapping on the car window. There she was, making a funny face at him, dressed like the night before except for one unpleasant detail. She was wearing a red ski hat just like the man's. It was a good idea to cover her head, but why with that horrid object?

She kissed Schmidt on the cheek and then on the mouth. He wondered at how natural that seemed.

You're not mad because I'm late? There was a line at the laundromat. This is the only day I can do my washing. Can I drive your car? You go and put mine into your driveway.

Sure.

And then, because it had suddenly occurred to him that, when it came to things she was likely to do, it would be better not to let her know what annoyed him and what didn't, he added, I'm not mad at all. I rather enjoy waiting. It's like finding time you didn't think you had.

I hate it. Don't ever try to be late for me.

When they were finally together in the Saab heading for the beach, she asked, What were these two other cars in your driveway? They don't look like cars you would own.

They are the Polish cleaning ladies'. There are so many of them, and they are so fat, they can't fit in one car. Not like you.

What were the ground rules? He forced himself to take a grotesque liberty—feeling the inside of her thighs, as though to check whether they were really there. To his surprise, she didn't tell him to stop being fresh—those were the words he had expected to hear—or take her hand off the wheel to slap his hand or brush it away. Instead, she pulled on his wrist until his hand was high between her legs, higher than he had dared to go, and then brought her thighs together very tight.

She looked at him nicely. It belongs to me, she said, and they can belong to you. You want to keep them? Do you like them?

They're marvelous.

She began to rock and wiggle a little in her seat, so that his hand rubbed against her.

Hey, Schmidtie, that feels good. You're making me wet. And me, do you like me?

What kind of question is that?

I don't know. Are you in love with me? Come on, tell me.

Her hand made a foray under his parka, between his legs.

Your little guy sure is in love with me, he doesn't get tired. How about you? You're not in love with me at all, not even a little bit?

I don't know. Probably, I won't be able to help it.

A huge north wind that carried grains of sand as sharp on the face as needles was forcing the surf back on itself, transforming the ocean into a luminous, blue-green, wrinkled, and silent plain. During the winter storms the beach had shrunk some more. The only flat place to walk was at the very edge of the water. There the sand was very hard, almost frozen. Patches of wet, where the tide had pushed farther, were covered by frozen brown foam. They were following Schmidt's routine, heading east. She put her left hand in his pocket. He took his glove off, and held her hand, his thumb inserted into her glove so he could feel her palm.

Do you come here often? he asked.

Yeah, last summer, if I had time before the dinner service.

Or on my day off, when there was a party. I don't have a sticker for this beach, so I'd go over there. She gestured over her shoulder toward Peter's Pond.

He thought he knew the half trucks, the coolers of beer, the charcoal fire, the rough voices, and handymen in tank shirts with wispy beards and tattoos on their biceps. A truck stereo would be turned on full blast, or they would have set up black boxes containing an elaborate sound system. Furtive, disapproving stares cast by all the proper Schmidts finishing their evening walk, ready for the first white wine and soda of the evening, noses wrinkled at the thought of the townies' debris. After the last of the hot dogs and corn had been eaten—maybe they no longer bothered, just brought pizza—did they screw by the side of the trucks or in the dune? Did they swap? Was that a part of the deal? Had he passed by during that summer of Mary's agony, Charlotte's arm resting on his, when Carrie was on a party?

Now that I'm retired, I walk here every day, he told her. In the summer, I like the swimming.

Are you kidding? In these waves? You wouldn't get me near them. Anyway, I never learned to swim in college. I took dancing instead.

Pity painted over the ugly pictures before Schmidt's eyes.

I'll teach you, he said squeezing the hand in his pocket. It's not hard at all.

You think you'll get me to go into these waves?

You can't teach people to swim in the ocean. We'll do it in my pool, on your days off, or any day if you have a little time.

I heard you say you were giving your house to your daughter and moving out.

That plan had gone out of Schmidt's head. It seemed possible that he was forgetting everything except the warmth of that hand, which responded to every pressure and invented games of its own.

Let's turn back, he said, you'll start getting cold. You're right about my giving up the house, but I think I'll move to another house with a pool. It will just be a much smaller place. There should be lots of them on the market. I'll have to start looking pretty soon. Perhaps you'll help me.

How will your daughter feel about that, I mean having me visit houses with you? You haven't told me her name. What's she like?

Charlotte. It was the name of my wife's mother. She died when my wife was a child, and my wife was brought up by the aunt who I told you left her this house. Charlotte: she is tall, a bit taller than you, very blond, and I think quite beautiful. She looks like—Joan of Arc! Have you seen Joan of Arc in a picture? She was the virgin warrior who saved France from the English in the fifteenth century. Then the English burned her on the stake, and she became a saint. Of course, Charlotte isn't a virgin; she's been living for years with the guy she is going to marry, and she's not very warlike, although I believe she plays a mean game of squash.

You love her a lot, Carrie said glumly. Is she older than me? Her fingers disentangled themselves from Schmidt's.

He reclaimed the territory gently, the way he used to take Charlotte's hand when she was a child.

Of course, I do. She's my only daughter, my only child, my entire family. She must be older than you. She'll be twenty-seven this August.

I'm twenty. Then she laughed: I bet she has a good job. Did you get it for her?

No, she did it on her own. Lots of people would say it's a good job, but I'm not sure I think so. She is in public relations. Her kind of public relations means explaining to the public why tobacco companies are really a misunderstood group of good guys manufacturing a fine, useful product, or how Citibank never sleeps. It's fun and games.

You smoke.

Sure. I've got nothing against fun and games, but they aren't very useful—except to people who play them. You don't like your job very much, and it's hard, but you get something done. You bring real food and drink to people, you collect real money, and you take away real dirty dishes. The other stuff is expensive make-believe. Charlotte wouldn't agree, but, in my opinion, her education is wasted on it.

I'm not going to wait on tables all my life either, I can promise you that, and I'll finish my education. I bet she went to a good school.

Schmidt nodded his head.

It'll blow her mind. You with a Puerto Rican waitress seven years younger than her!

Any woman would be hard for her to take. Her mother died last April. Charlotte has never known me to be with anyone else. But we can see each other just as much as you will like, without rubbing her nose in it, and if you are my friend I'll want you to look at any house where I might want to live.

Don't worry, I'm your friend.

In the car, after she had finished checking out the Saab's dashboard and the full range of adjustments that could be made electronically to its seats and climate, she punched him in the arm and said, If you really want to buy a house, you'd better take me when the real estate agent isn't there. You wouldn't want them to turn you down!

Then when he asked whether she wanted to go out to lunch—he had in mind the hotel in Sag Harbor that in the winter served lunch until late and where, because it was expensive, she was unlikely to be known and would, therefore, avoid any embarrassment—she told him he had to be crazy. She didn't want to eat.

Let's go to your house, Schmidtie. Quick, while you still live in it.

She began to undress as soon as they were in the door, throwing her clothes left and right, so that except for her tights she was naked when she ran ahead of him up the stairs. Frantic, catching her by the shoulders, trying to kiss her shoulder, he pushed her in the direction of the bedroom.

The bed astonished her: Hey, that's really something! Two queens put together? We can have a party! Then to test it, she jumped on it, up and down, as if on a trampoline.

Just king-size.

OK King, don't you want to pull off my tights? I'm all clean for you. No, wait, I'll undress you first. Look at that, your little man isn't here. What's the matter? He must be shy.

She had scattered his clothes on the floor, on the chest of drawers, stopping him each time he attempted, yielding to habit and feeling foolish about it, to hang them over the back of a chair. When he had finally removed her tights and the pantyhose she wore under them, and she lay quietly on the bed, her arms folded under her head, he realized Carrie had existed only in his imagination. He knew, of course, her hair, face, and neck, her hands and gestures, and her *voice*. But for the first time he was seeing—and soon would be able to touch as long as he could bear it—the triumphant limbs of Diana the Huntress, between them the tight triangle of hair, a sliver really with red bumps on its sides that told him she shaved it to wear the skimpiest of string bikinis, the pristine valley of her stomach, her belly button, so small and perfect it moved you to tears, and her breasts that were like sacred hillocks. The tabernacle! He would pry open her legs. But she wanted him to be able to see. Before he had touched her, she raised her knees and her pelvis.

She asked very softly, Are you ready, darling?

There was an interval between unconsciousness and waking during which he was certain only of his disorientation. It was turning dark outside. He must have slept very hard. Then he saw the outline of her body under the covers. She was lying on her stomach, her head almost touching his shoulder, as though she had sought it, her feet in the far corner of the bed. Cautiously, he touched her hair and played with its tangles. Affection, and desire for her proximity—he was astonished by how happy he was to have her less than an arm's length away and to find her so fantastically available. Here was an aspect of unemployment and nearly total loneliness he had not previously examined, let alone apprehended: they set one free! He need not worry about how long this girl would sleep, or what she might want to do after she awakened. There was Charlotte's wedding reception to be held in June and the need, which was turning into a wish, to move to another house. Other than that, he had no engagements or appointments. His quotidian future—whatever its term—stretched before him uncharted.

During their last embrace, she had moaned, Do you like it, darling, it's only for you. He was buried under the black avalanche of her hair, to detach his mouth from the nape of her neck was inconceivable, so he kept thrusting into her, only harder. She moaned again: Yeah, now I really belong to you.

When it was over, she had asked: Did you like it? Schmidtie, talk to me, you know it's just you, say you liked it. Tell me why you liked it.

He thought he was returning from a distance that could not be measured. Perhaps he had dozed off. The question would be repeated until he had answered. Therefore, he replied: It's what you said, you said you belong to me.

My darling.

Nobody had ever called him that. Certainly not his father. Not his mother—until she died he had been Schmidtie or sometimes Bebop, the nickname of his Baltimore godfather, the man to be counted on at Christmas for a postcard of an Eastern Shore oysterman and a check for ten dollars; not Mary, whose terms of endearment, used distractedly on Charlotte, every other child she addressed, her editorial assistant, and himself, had been sweetie and its variants sweetness, sweetie pie, and sweets; not Corinne or any of the women of his one-night stands. But this girl, with her hoarse voice and rough diction, had; she had called him darling three times, and it didn't seem an automatic pattern of her speech—such as her relentless, Do you like me? It was enough to make one believe in the remission of sin and life eternal.

The telephone rang. He looked at Carrie: no reaction.

That was another miracle: the sleep of a young girl. He took the receiver off the hook, and, not allowing himself to listen to his daughter, said, Just a moment, please, I'd like to talk to you from the kitchen.

Lights on in the kitchen and a glass of cold tap water. He brought the telephone to the table and sat down. Must remember to hang up the bedroom telephone when I finish.

Dad, where have you been? I have tried you twice, and you haven't answered.

In Brazil until yesterday, and today at home in the morning and, in the early afternoon, at the beach. If you want to know, just now I was taking one of my senior citizen naps!

I'm sorry. You got back yesterday, but you didn't call?

It's a long overnight trip, baby; I was tired. At first, while I was puttering around, I thought I might hear from you, then I went out to get a bite to eat, and then it was late.

I lost your postcard with all the dates, so I wasn't sure when you were coming home. Did you have a good time?

Perfect. I think I wrote to you about it.

You did. I got that postcard too. Dad, we were out at the house with people from the firm a couple of times while you were away—associates working with Jon—so I don't think we'll see you this weekend or, probably, the next.

Right.

By the way, Renata thinks we should start planning for the wedding. She was asking whether you have done anything, whether you feel up to it, you know, or want her to help, or just have her do it for us.

Which way to the air-raid shelter? Schmidt asked himself. The next thing I know, the grandparents will also want to get into the act.

He answered by a question of his own: Do you still want to be married in June, at the house, and have the reception here?

I guess so, sure, if you're up to it, that's what Renata really meant.

Let's leave the beautiful Renata out of this for a moment. The question is what Miss Charlotte would like.

I'm just worried it will be a lot of work for you. And our friends are mostly in New York. Have you thought where we could put them up?

In fact, I have. I presume that almost all of them are grown-ups. That makes it quite easy to put them in hotels and motels. I thought I'd reserve in advance, starting now, blocks of rooms at different prices—some for the weekend, and some just for Saturday night. We can have a few people here and maybe have one or two couples stay at the Blackmans'. Your mom would have asked the Bernsteins or the Howards, but I haven't been seeing them. Maybe I'll ask anyway.

Here Schmidt's voice broke.

You see, Dad, that's the problem! You get all worked up.

No, it's just when I think how Mom might have done things. I'm all right now, really. There is another idea I had that might work for some guests: a nice, comfortable bus leaving from Manhattan around three and returning after the party. That assumes you would get married at six.

That is clever! And you could handle the food, and all that stuff?

No parents can "handle" such a big party. I'll find the name of the caterer who did the Parsons' wedding. Weren't you there? Mom and I thought it was lovely. He'll do it all, except the orchestra. That's something I'd rather leave up to you, unless you are willing to dance to Peter Duchin or Lester Lanin. What I really need is the number—more or less how many guests you'd like to have. I know that two hundred fifty is no problem. That's how many Martha had when Mom and I got married.

Hmmmm.

There's another thing—you see, I've really been thinking. You might want to wear Mom's dress. It would need to be taken in or let out here and there, but basically it should fit, and it's right here waiting for you.

Oh. Do you think so? I don't know.

Speaking of apparel, Schmidt had not bothered to put on his bathrobe. It rather amused him to take his ease naked in the warm weather or when the house was nicely heated. It was so cold outside that, luckily, in anticipation of Carrie's visit, he had set the bedroom thermostat and the one that controlled the downstairs at a toasty seventy-two degrees. Carrie! He wished she had gone on sleeping until this conversation was over. Nevertheless, Schmidt's spirits lifted when he saw her, so freshly and thoroughly explored, drooping like an orchid, lithe as a foal, tiptoe into the kitchen. The white terry-cloth peignoir was ridiculously long. "Hesperus entreats thy light, / Goddess excellently bright!" To make sure she remained as silent as the moon, he put his index finger to his lips. In reply, she made the face—part Bronx cheer and part other elements unknown to him—that he had already seen her make at his car window. Then pouting, her own finger at her lips, she plunked herself down in his lap, put her arms around him, and began to lick the inside of the ear that was not pressed against the telephone receiver.

There is no special hurry, he told his daughter. If you decide not to wear it, you should be able to find a very elegant white suit or a short white dress. I'll help you look, if you like. A long dress other than Mom's is out of the question, since this won't be a church wedding.

She snickered. It sure won't be that! By the way, we're going to have a very nice rabbi.

A rabbi!

Leah and Ronald expect it. That's what Renata said.

Leah and Ronald?

Jon's grandparents, Dad! Remember? You know, you've met them.

Of course, I'm very sorry.

He can't actually marry us, because there isn't time for me to convert, but he'll say some prayers and bless the marriage.

Schmidt didn't wince, so exquisite were the sensations procured by what Carrie's tongue was doing to his ear and her fingers to his right nipple.

Instead, he inquired: Will there be equal time for the true church?

Which one is that, Dad? Do you know any ministers? When was the last time you went to church?

To your mother's service. David Haskell—that's the name of the priest. I certainly know him.

And before that?

Charlotte, you know perfectly well that neither your mother nor I were churchgoers. That's not the point.

Will you explain the point then?

The novocaine was wearing off. He nudged Carrie off his lap.

Not before you explain to me what you meant by your remark about conversion.

Just what I said. There isn't time between now and June.
There will be time later and maybe I'll convert. There must
be more to being a Jew than your kind of Episcopalian. At
least it would be genuine!

Genuine! Have they got you on some sort of pills, baby?
Otherwise, why not a Hare Krishna? Do you actually plan to
light candles and go to the ritual bath? I bet dear Renata
doesn't. Is this what we brought you up for?

Dad, you hit the nail right on the head! That's exactly right,
Mom brought me up to admire the Jewish tradition and to
think your Jew baiting is disgusting. Just listen to yourself:
one mention of the word rabbi and the real Albert Schmidt
Esquire comes out of the closet! Then it's goodbye caterers
and nice short white dress: not for the daughter who's marrying a Jew and wants to bring a rabbi onto her father's lawn!

That grace, those simple good manners, must have come to
Carrie naturally. Or had they been taught by Mr. Gorchuk,
revealed as Muscovite prince or the son of tsarist general?
Schmidt observed with grateful admiration that she seemed
to have gone stone deaf, and anyway was off at the far side of
the kitchen, fixing him what looked like a bourbon on ice.
Bare feet, noiseless steps. She had found the round little
silver tray and brought the drink on it. Then, squatting on
her haunches, she hugged his legs. Like a cat, she rubbed her
head against his knees.

You don't think, Dad, that anyone is fooled? At Wood &
King it was a standard joke: Schmidt's last stand against
Zion! That's why they never let you near the management of

the firm. Half the firm would have walked out the door! Ask Mr. DeForrest. Ask some of your other pals over there. They'll tell you they didn't want an anti-Semite to be presiding partner.

The effect of one hundred proof bourbon on an empty stomach was fabulous.

Jack DeForrest? he asked. That notorious defender of Israel? Nick Browning? Or maybe Lew Brenner, our honorary Wasp? Are they casting the first stone? No, it's Jon Riker. I guess I must have thought the Riker family arrived on the *Mayflower* when I pushed him for partnership.

Dad, it's *everybody*. Sure, you helped Jon make it, but you held your nose doing it. Remember your clients? Was there a single Jew among them? Or your friends? And don't tell me about Gil Blackman!

If you want to do Jew counting, sweetie pie, you are welcome. It's not my habit. You might even start by all the Jews your mother and I have had to dinner and lunch, both here and at Fifth Avenue, for the weekend, and out at parties. Really!

Those were Mom's friends, not yours!

There you are right, Charlotte. I have no friends.

Except the fancy Gil Blackman!

Yes, my old college roommate, who wasn't all that fancy when he and I first met. All right, baby. I think you have told me quite enough. Please say to Renata I'm quite able to manage, and say hello to Jon and the rest of his family. I'd like you to write within the week, with the number of guests, if you want me to give the wedding here. If you have something else in mind, you work it out, and I'll pay for it.

There was a beginning of a reply—he didn't want to hear it and raised his voice: Don't dare to apologize. Ever. We will simply get on with our lives.

After the click, the face at his knee looked up. Man, that was wild!

Yes. I am sorry you heard it.

That's OK.

The face began an upward journey toward his center, paused while Carrie opened her peignoir, lingered until it was satisfied.

I want it. What are you waiting for?

She pushed his hands away from her breasts, let the peignoir fall to the floor, and, arms stretched out, leaned over the kitchen table.

Hold me hard.

Later, panting: Do you like that? You can come, Schmidtie.

I don't want to. I like it too much.

She too was hungry, but she didn't want to go out to dinner. Give me your car keys, I'll get us some pizza real quick. You like it with everything?

She had found a shabby blue Brooks Brothers shirt in his chest of drawers and was wearing it and his old tennis sweater over her leotard top. As she was leaving, she pulled out of the pocket of her parka the red gloves that were his Christmas present and put them on. He said he hadn't noticed them before.

I didn't want to spoil them in sand, she replied. I wore my old ones. These are so fancy!

He listened to her gun the Saab's motor, producing a rich

growl, like the recordings of the Daytona track the pre-med across the hall from Gil and him used to play in their freshman year, and put on a pair of pants and a sweater. A candlelit dinner for two in the kitchen! The lightness of being was swell. Before setting the table, Schmidt inspected its edge, hoping for a smudge of Carrie. No dice. He got the Georgian candlesticks—thank God, no tarnish—a starched white tablecloth, and napkins. Were salt and pepper required? Perhaps pepper, in the silver grinder. He supposed he might as well give the silver pieces to Charlotte. The new house wouldn't have a butler's pantry or a deep drawer to hold the Shreve Crump and Low silver chest and the other dignified doodads at rest in their flannel shrouds. He'd take his wine with him. Meanwhile, to celebrate, he would drink quite a lot of it, beginning with the burgundies he had laid down the year of Charlotte's birth. A bottle of that quality with pizza! Nothing like it could have happened before.

Yes, I do like it, he told Carrie, and took a big bite. I like it a lot.

In fact, it was good—with a thick, chewy crust, cheese and tomato sauce an inch deep, and lots of pepperoni, olives, anchovies, and little canned mushrooms—reminding Schmidt of the pizzas he used to eat years ago in the restaurant on 72nd Street that, according to the bartender, belonged outright to the Mafia, not just a question of protection money. The owner, who looked like Vittorio Gassman, was just a front. The Mafia also owned the house in Babylon with the round pool, a photo of which was Scotch-taped to the mirror over the bar; only the wife in Bermuda shorts and the little boy were really his. Schmidt had reset the table, because she wanted to sit next to him; across the table, facing him, was too far away.

You should eat at home more. You wouldn't believe it. What you get at O'Henry's isn't worth a third of what you pay. Especially the liquor. The way you drink that's important.

I know. But when I go there I get to see you.

Now you don't need to. I'll come to see you.

She took his hand and kissed it.

You'll give me a key, and if you're in bed I'll sneak in and wake you up. No—I'll just wake up your little guy. I guess I know how to do that!

If you aren't careful, you'll wear me out. Don't forget I'm an old man.

I'm kidding you. We'll just sleep holding hands. Hey, I want to ask you a question. You think it's OK to get in bed with a guy and not do anything—I mean maybe just kiss? Not even fool around?

Of course. That's how married couples are—much of the time.

I don't mean when people stop fucking. I mean with you right now I feel like I want you to put it in all the time. There are other times I'm closed down, like I'm tired. Then I just want to be quiet.

He nodded his head.

You want chocolate-chip ice cream? I got a quart. Hey, I've still got your change in my pocket. I'll put it on the counter by the toaster.

Then when they were eating the ice cream, she asked,

You're not going to be mad if we don't do anything tonight?
Maybe just watch the TV in bed and neck? Promise?

Of course. If we're friends, we can't just make love all the
time. We have to do other things together—read, listen to
music, do nothing. That way there is a chance you won't get
tired of me and bored!

Oh shut up! You're nuts. Schmidtie, look at me. I need to
know. Are you asking me to be faithful to you?

What a strange question! Why do you ask?

It was a strange question, but all at once it occurred to
Schmidt that it wasn't unprecedented. Hadn't Gil's Greek-
American put something like that to Gil? Was it a part of the
mating ritual among the ethnics?

I need to know. I want to know if you'll go crazy when you
find out I fuck someone else.

I don't think I'll like it, Schmidt answered. How could I?

Oh, Schmidtie, you are asking me to be faithful.

He had no Elaine to worry about. But he also didn't have
Gil's high opinion of his own person. It was all eerily just as
he had foreseen, just as uncomfortable and troubling. How
could he allow such a rule to be established—what would he
give her in return. His sexual ministrations? Enlightened
conversation? Evenings out with a gent who would be naturally mistaken for her father if she didn't have that olive skin
and kinky hair? Little presents? Big presents—cash, college
tuition? Of course, his love! But what was the new language
of love? If being in love was the same as having a crush, no
problem! He could tell Carrie that during their nap he had
fallen in love. Maybe that was all the assurance she needed, a
sign that they were at some level above casual sex, and being

faithful meant nothing but the opposite of promiscuity. But he thought that her feelings were much more delicate and complex. It wasn't right to play with words. Therefore, he told her, as tenderly as was within his power, that she had become very dear to him and that he wanted her, but only for as long as she really wanted to have him, as long as she wanted it to last.

Carrie, he concluded, you've got to understand, I want to be fair. If I want your good, your happiness, and I do want them very much, I can't ask for something that could stop you from finding the right guy—someone very nice and of the right age, not a broken-down senior citizen!

Well-intentioned pomposity. Schmidt didn't like it. It didn't play well with Carrie either.

Yeah, I got it. You like the way I do sex, but you're not in love with me. That's what I understand.

She looked sad. Then her face brightened. She moved to sit in his lap. You're not going to get mad at me? she asked.

How could I?

I don't know. There's a guy in Sag Harbor—Bryan—I've kind of been with him since I got this job. If I tell him about you, he'll go nuts. I don't know. Run around the room, beat his head on the wall, break things. It's crazy.

She laughed and put her tongue in Schmidt's ear.

The news went through Schmidt like an icicle.

This way, I won't tell him, OK?

He put his hand under her turtleneck, into the cup of her bra. The nipple stiffened immediately. He began alternately to squeeze it quite hard and then reward it by a gentler caress. Nothing mattered. He had to keep her body. She had said she belonged to him.

And this Bryan doesn't mind if you stay out all day and spend the night with me? You are going to stay?

He squeezed, with all his strength.

God, Schmidtie, keep doing that, you're making me wet, now rub. Rub hard!

And then she shrieked.

The videocassettes he had didn't interest her. Ice hockey was all right. She used his toothbrush and said they should both wear pajamas to bed. When they lay down, she made him lie on his side of the bed. He had told her one didn't have to be always doing it; now he could prove it. They were going to watch the game. Carpe diem. Schmidt stretched his leg toward her so that his toes touched hers. That was apparently all right.

And Bryan? he asked her. He really doesn't mind if you disappear for a whole night?

He was from Quogue; his parents had moved away to Florida. His sister, who still lived there, was married to a doctor. She had made it through college. Bryan hadn't. He was doing carpentry and house watching for summer people with a buddy. The buddy had a house in Springs, where he lived with his girlfriend, the red-haired waitress at O'Henry's. Bryan lodged with them. That was how Carrie met him. She hadn't moved in with them because the buddy was rough and had tried some funny stuff with her on the beach.

Bryan needs me, she told Schmidt. Like he'll be in my room, waiting, when I get back from work. Sometimes he wants to play around, but mostly we have beers and smoke. That's why I asked you about going with a guy and not having sex.

But you do have sex!

Yeah, when he wants to. It's like I told you. We hang out. He's not the love of my life. I just don't want him to go crazy

She slid over and whispered: Don't look like that, darling. You can do anything you want with me, always. I told you I belong to you. And I'll be faithful to you. I want to be. Just be very careful at the restaurant, promise? And, please, don't get mad about Bryan!

He wanted to have her full attention. When the hockey game was over, very cautiously, as though he were stepping out of a car barefoot onto the surface of a parking lot that was baking hot and covered with shards of glass, he put the question: The love of your life, who is he?

She laughed and with her toes tickled the foot he had left touching her.

It's you, you dummy.

Then, seriously: I was kidding. It was a long time ago. I wasn't even fifteen. An old guy, like you. He broke me in. Man, I really loved him.

How did it happen?

It was real weird. I had this boyfriend, a Jewish kid. Was he cute! We used to go to the chemistry lab after school. He had the key, because he was like the best student and was always working on special projects. So after he locked the door we'd lay on the floor and fool around. It was pretty wild, but I wouldn't let him fuck me. I was real scared of getting pregnant. My father would have killed me.

Schmidt noted her hand working under the covers. The memory was exciting her.

One day we're in the lab and Frank has me on the floor

with my legs spread as far as they can go and my T-shirt off when the door opens and the lights turn on. Guess what: Mr. Wilson walks in right on top of us. He was the chemistry teacher. So he had a key too. Was I scared! He could have got us both thrown out of the school. Instead, he's very polite, says he is sorry, and leaves, locking the door. Frank was afraid he'd bother me and ask me to do stuff, but nothing happens. He just says, Hello, Carrie, when he sees me in the corridor and smiles and then the school year is over. I told you my father worked for the Board of Education? One day during the vacation I'm on Livingston Street, so I go to see him, and when I'm leaving Mr. Wilson gets into the elevator with me. I almost died!

Meanwhile he looks at me real cool like he's taking my clothes off and says, Let's have a cup of coffee or a Coke. We sit down in this booth in the luncheonette and he tells me what a good student Frank is, and what a nice guy, and asks if I'm serious about him. I say I don't know. Then he tells me how girls should be careful and how it's too bad to learn about love on a dirty floor. Believe me, it was unreal!

I believe you.

You can't believe it! This old man, maybe even a couple of years older than you, but nice looking—he looked a lot like you but bigger, not fat just big—he's talking to me about birth control, and how a guy doesn't need to come inside the girl if he's careful and crazy stuff like that; only, the way he talks about it it's real beautiful, and he tells me he used to be a professor at some university. Then something happened and he had to be away for a couple of years. When he got back, his job was gone, and that's why he's teaching high school.

So I finish my ice cream and he finishes his coffee and he kind of winked at me and said it's time to go home. By this time, I was acting pretty fresh, and I asked if he had to go back to his wife and kid. He just laughed and laughed! No, he says, there are too many girls in the world. Wasn't that a cute line? He lived just a couple of blocks away, so I said I would walk him home, and I kept kind of bumping into him on purpose, to tease him. So suddenly he grabbed me by the elbow and said very quiet: You've got some cunt. I saw it. I want to fuck you. It was like I was melting. I tell you, Schmidtie, I thought I couldn't get up the stairs I wanted it so bad.

That man raped you. In New York, one goes to jail for abusing a fourteen-year-old girl!

You've got it wrong, Schmidtie. He didn't rape me and he didn't abuse me. He was my great love. You're just jealous.

I'm sorry, said Schmidt. That's how it struck me. And then what happened?

He was freaking out a lot. I didn't do stuff with him. At first he wanted me to, but when I said no he never asked again. Then he freaked out real bad. He almost died. They took him away, then they let him out, and they took him away again. He'd go nuts. It was like a routine.

And you kept on seeing him.

At first. It got pretty heavy. Then, when I was a senior, he was away a whole year. He lost his apartment and everything. Sometimes he just wandered around from place to place. There is a kind of little park at Brooklyn College. He'd sit on a bench and wait for me. Shit, Schmidtie, leave me alone. He became a homeless bum! He'd ask me to go with him under the boardwalk at Far Rockaway and I couldn't because he smelled!

She cried very hard. At first she would push him away each time he tried to stroke her head or arm. Then he remembered he had a bar of chocolate in the refrigerator and got it for her. She ate it like an unhappy little girl and went to sleep holding on to him.

She was the first to wake up, although it was past nine in the morning. They had breakfast. She told Schmidt she wouldn't go back to Sag Harbor before work; there was nothing she needed to do, and she could go to work as she was. The kitchen was full of sun. He asked her to sit with him in the window seat.

You're not mad at me? she asked. I mean how I acted like a baby?

You felt terrible, that's all.

And you still like me? Now that you know about Mr. Wilson? You're not disgusted? You will want to sleep with me?

It's not your fault what happened to him. I'll tell you a secret: I think I am beginning to love you.

And Bryan?

He had forgotten about Bryan; his mind was occupied by the new fact, by the man.

It doesn't matter, he replied.

XII

A WEEK LATER the telephone rang. Hello, hello, said the vibrant voice. Renata here. Naturally, thought Schmidt, Thursday morning, the day when Dr. R. Riker attends to family business. Too bad Carrie is still here. Perhaps she will sleep through this.

Schmidtie, we've got so much to talk about I'll get right to the point. Will you come into the city and have lunch with me?

Today? answered Schmidt, thinking he'd play dumb.

Yes, if at all possible. It's the only time I'm free during a weekday. I'm sorry I'm asking at the last minute. I tried to reach you yesterday evening, but you didn't answer. Won't you drive in, or take the bus?

Is it really necessary? Couldn't we talk on the telephone?

You know that's not the same. Besides, wouldn't you like to see me?

Not particularly, thought Schmidt, you meddling witch. The audible answer was, Can you doubt it, dear?

He asked her to meet him at his club. As he knew that, in the end, he would pick up the check, it might as well be there or McDonald's. Club food would do for him, and Dr. Renata had better watch her weight. One might say he was doing her a favor. Besides, he would get to shake the hand of Julio, the Puerto Rican hall porter, whom he missed—come to think of it, perhaps he was one of Carrie's uncles, the scout presciently dispatched by a tribe ready to invade—and pick up some cigars. Satisfaction with the meanness of these witticisms masked for a moment the sick feeling in Schmidt's gut, like mint toothpaste after you have been retching.

It was a short moment. Then the thoughts that had been going round and round in his head returned.

Why wouldn't his daughter deal with him face-to-face? What had he done to her during all those years when he thought he loved her and she loved him? That Charlotte should have been told the vile canard about his reputation for anti-Semitism was unbearable. Believing it was even worse. Who would have put such a lie into circulation? It could only be Jon Riker, closeted with his fiancée. If that was what he had done, he was a blackguard, worse than a traitor, a man whose handshake must be refused.

And it had to be a lie. He could not think of a single act in his career at Wood & King on which such an assertion could be based. Certainly not on his treatment of associates who had worked for him or of the other Jews in the firm, partners or associates, or on his role in recruiting lawyers. On the contrary, he had used his prestige as an alumnus who had been an officer of the *Harvard Law Review* to cajole a large number of its Jewish members into coming to work at the firm. Some of them were Semitic types straight out of a Nazi propaganda cartoon, including his favorite, the best associate he had ever worked with, who eventually left W & K for a professorship at Harvard. That one used to wear a yarmulke to the office! Then what could it be? Not anything he had said. He had never told jokes about Jews—in fact, he didn't tell jokes of any kind, because the few times he had tried no one had laughed.

The stuff about clients was hogwash, too. Poor Charlotte should know better but probably didn't; no one seemed to have a historical perspective. At the time when his relationships with insurance companies and other great American financial institutions that directed business to W & K were cemented, there were in their management all told maybe five Jews who made decisions about investments and hiring law firms, and certainly no Jews in yarmulkes, or blacks, or Puerto Ricans, or women, or, so far as he knew, homosexuals. These people were white male Protestants—usually with the same background as his own. He didn't especially like them for that. Too many were tedious, slow-witted boors, but one took one's clients as one found them, and said thank you!

And friends! They had had Jewish friends. Of course, they had met most of them through Mary. He had done his best with them, and it was they, along with everybody else out of Mary's world, who dropped him when she died, not the other way around. The same was true of the homosexuals who used to come so regularly to lunch and dinner. Mary got to know them, because homosexuals work in publishing houses and write. But Dad, are you telling me that blacks and Puerto Ricans don't write? No, Charlotte dear, of course they do. But in publishing they aren't easy to find; it's like looking for a needle in a haystack. And your mom hadn't had the good fortune to publish Wright, Baldwin, or Morrison, who might not have wanted to be friends with Mr. and Mrs. Albert Schmidt even if she had! He used to think he had Jewish friends of his own too, at his firm. If Mr. Riker or whoever else was telling tales about him was to be believed, that had been an illusion. It follows that you've got it right, Charlotte: there is no one left who counts, no one except the unmentionable Gil Blackman!

Righteously indignant, Schmidt nevertheless continued the examination of his conscience. Do you like Jews, or blacks, or Puerto Ricans, or homosexuals? En bloc, no. Were you pleased to hear that Charlotte was going to marry that upstanding, bright, and very successful Jewish boy? No, I wasn't. And was it because he is a Jew? Not exclusively. But you would have swallowed hard and cheered up pretty quickly if he had been a nerd with a name—unchanged and unanglicized—like Mr. Jonathan White? Most probably. And it wouldn't have been quite such an adventure to visit Mr. White's doctor parents in their Manhattan apartment at Thanksgiving? Not really. Thank you, Mr. Schmidt. One more question: Would you prefer it if Carrie weren't a lower-class, Puerto Rican waitress? I love her skin and her kinky hair. I am afraid you haven't answered the question. In her case, the devil take the rest.

His mood darkened.

Have you the right, Mr. Schmidt, to withhold your affection from your daughter's fiancé because he is a Jew—yes, I know, you don't need to repeat it, principally for that reason? Yes, every right. Who has the right to pry into my emotions? I don't sit in judgment on the feelings of Dr. & Dr. Riker or those adorable grandparents. It's enough for me if they behave decently. What is there to blame in my actions?

Schmidt thought that was a pretty good answer, but he was not content.

He found Renata in the waiting room reserved for guests. Black knitted suit that looked like real Chanel, black patent-leather pumps, black leather pocketbook on a gold chain, and opaque black stockings of an alarming brilliance—whatever this occasion was, she had clearly dressed for it. Wasted effort. She might as well have worn a burlap bag. But how was she to know that at most four hours earlier Schmidt had risen from Aurora's couch?

Let's go up to the dining room, he told her. They don't take reservations here. The early bird catches the worm! We can do our drinking at table.

Once installed, he cut short her exclamations over the grace of the building and how rested he looked. Practice makes perfect: Hadn't he spent more years than he could count chairing meetings and getting straight to the point? What was the issue on the agenda, and what did she want to do about it?

Schmidtie, she said, I'll be very frank. I think Charlotte shouldn't have talked to you the way she did. There were things she wanted to say, and she didn't know how to say them. She was overwrought. That makes people with her psychological makeup become aggressive. You were very restrained. I was proud of you.

Thank you! I assume then that Charlotte gave you a detailed report about our conversation. It's quite admirable how you find so much time to devote to a father and daughter who aren't your patients!

Now Schmidtie, you are being sarcastic. Is that necessary?

No. It's a reflection of my overwrought feelings.

Exactly. And one of your feelings is that I am to blame for Charlotte's confusion and aggressions.

To some extent. Of course, you didn't bring her up. I believe that upbringing is important. That means my poor Mary and I have to shoulder most of the blame. Or do you think it's Charlotte's nature, something in her genes? We gave her the genes too.

I don't think that being so unable to deal with conflict, having so much trouble saying to her father something he doesn't want to hear, is genetic.

All right, we're back to upbringing. Early childhood experiences. And where does that take us?

To how we straighten this mess out! Right now you and Charlotte and Jon are under dreadful stress. The relationship among you should be unblocked.

If Charlotte talked to you about our conversation in detail—remember, I asked you—then you know that I told her what she should do next. I rather intend to take it from there myself.

Take it from there—in which direction? Suppose what she writes to you isn't what you would like to hear. Does a chasm open between you?

There is such a chasm already. I'll figure out what I should do when I see her letter. Perhaps it's already in the mail. You would know. Is that why you wanted to see me?

Charlotte didn't just talk to me about your conversation. She gave me a tape of it. Here it is. It's for you. I have a copy. I played it again, just before coming here.

He pushed the cassette back toward her. They were seated at a corner table. Portraits of the distinguished New Yorkers who had been presidents of the club hung on the four walls of the room. He had no forebears among them, yet he looked at these intelligent and quirky faces hoping for sustenance, perhaps a sign he could decipher. Those of the club's elders who had not allowed the cold to interfere with their routine were either downstairs, finishing their martinis, or had tottered into the dining room next door, reserved for members unencumbered by guests, perhaps with one more drink in hand. They would be talking about things one talks about at lunch: the likelihood of Macy's filing for bankruptcy, George Bush's sagging political fortunes, the sex drive of the governor of Arkansas. Whenever the door between the two rooms opened, he heard the roar of those jolly voices. Could he rise from his chair, rush into their midst, and seek tribal wisdom or sanctuary? Help, help, I am under attack by a shrink in a black suit whose son the lawyer is marrying my daughter! There were two members, who were shrinks themselves, sitting at separate tables near him entertaining guests. They'd tackle him and send for an ambulance. It was no use.

Therefore he asked: Isn't that illegal, taping a telephone conversation without asking for permission?

Jon doesn't think so. You know she only did it because they realized she would be too upset to remember clearly what was said.

I'll have that bastard disbarred! Thrown out of the firm!

Ha! Ha! You're dreaming, pal, he said to himself as soon as the words left his mouth. Will Jack DeForrest and his team of bean counters take measures against a bankruptcy litigator, just as they are salivating over filing after filing in the bankruptcy court? Kill the goose about to lay golden eggs. And over what? Ungentlemanly conduct? Since when are bankruptcy lawyers supposed to be wimps? Too bad that Schmidt can't keep peace with his own daughter. Always had been rigid, not good at adapting to new circumstances.

He observed that Renata was putting away her lipstick and was about to attack a second macaroon. He begged her pardon. She returned a kindly smile.

All right, he said. Do let's get to the point. What do they want?

Dear Schmidtie. Could we have some more coffee? In one of these wonderful French *café filtre* machines? I haven't seen one of those in years.

They have sort of disappeared.

He caught the attention of a waiter.

You see, Schmidtie, Charlotte is afraid of you and doesn't want to hurt your feelings. Believe me, she doesn't. I know. And Jon reveres you. Don't interrupt. That's true. There is, of course, always the Oedipal aspect in these situations. That's what makes communication among you so difficult. The point is really quite simple. In the lives of young people there comes a moment when they enter into a new alliance— marriage! Suddenly, their allegiance is no longer the same. The change can be very startling. In the case of Charlotte, she really wants to become a part of our family, whatever that implies. It has a great deal to do with the death of Mary, there being no cousins, aunts, or uncles on your side, and the way we have welcomed her into our family. Do you see?

Yes, I do. You are Naomi and she is Ruth the Moabite.

Really, Schmidtie, how can you. Ruth's husband was dead!

A minor detail. The point of that story is that Ruth was in love with her mother-in-law. Is that what's happening here? Have you bewitched my daughter? Put her under hypnosis?

Schmidtie, please stop. Jon loves her, and Charlotte, as I have tried to tell you, is deeply drawn to our family. Nothing could be happier or more normal. The consequence is annoying for you: Charlotte has rethought certain things. She no longer thinks that having the wedding in Bridgehampton is a good idea. Apparently, you have both drifted away from people there, so that practically all the guests would be imported! That does seem odd.

And the house? Doesn't she want to be married on the lawn of her parents' house, the house where she spent all her summers, all her vacations?

Of course she loves the house. It's so beautiful. But the house has become something of a problem for both of you. It's also a problem financially for Jon—but it's more a matter of lifestyle; he isn't sure he sees himself and Charlotte living in that sort of place in the Hamptons. Your wanting to give the house to Charlotte has made it all much more pressing— perhaps even oppressive. Jon has a different idea. We hope you won't be put off by it—you've been so amazingly generous!

Aha, thought Schmidt. In heavy fog, I am to drive my car off a cliff. They collect double-indemnity insurance money and everything else I have, and sell the house. That must be it.

I suppose I should hear about it. Am I to hear about it from you? They are too busy or too timid to speak to me, I suppose.

Schmidtie, they don't want to fight with you. That's all. The idea Jon had about the house is this—he says it has some tax benefits: Instead of giving the house to Charlotte and paying such a huge gift tax and then moving, why don't you buy her part of it? That way they will have some capital, and you get to have the house. You can still leave it to Charlotte in your will.

Well, that's quite a proposal! What do they do with that capital? I suppose it pays for the apartment, and they no longer need to borrow from you and Myron—unless you were planning to make a gift.

She sidestepped the nature of the Riker-to-Riker transaction.

It depends on the value of the house. Jon said he doesn't know whether you have already had it appraised. Yes, they would use the money for the apartment, but there is something they might do in addition. We have always rented in the summer, but now we are looking at a property upstate, near Claverack. Do you know where that is?

Yes.

There is an adorable little farmhouse adjacent to it. They thought it might be exactly right for them. There are skiing areas nearby they would enjoy.

Schmidt nodded and lit a cigarillo.

Schmidtie, you do understand the tax business, don't you? Jon explained it, but it has gone out of my head.

Those are details. The real question is whether I can afford to keep the house once I have given away or spent all that cash. I had counted on buying a small house that wouldn't be so expensive to run. I am fairly certain I will do what Jon and,

I assume, Charlotte want. Let me think about it for a day or two.

You are a very good and generous man. If the house is too big, couldn't you sell it after you have bought Charlotte out?

That isn't exactly what Mary had in mind. I do have to think about it. Do I give the answer to you?

They'll be thrilled to speak to you, Schmidtie.

I am sure. What about the wedding? I take it they are still getting married—to each other—somewhere!

That's not funny. I don't think you realize how much they are in love. They would like to have a wedding in New York. Not in a hotel, of course, and our apartment is really too small. They were thinking of one of those nice new places downtown.

I don't know anything about them. I'll stay out of it then. That should make everyone's life simpler. You are the lady who has been listening to the tape. Didn't I say something about that?

You said very generously that you would pay for the wedding even if it wasn't in Bridgehampton.

And so I will. You may reassure Charlotte.

But we'll be more than happy to chip in—after all, it's going to be a modern party!

Thanks. That will not be necessary. The new plan may end up saving me money. Don't go yet, he added, seeing that she was putting the disdained cassette in her pocketbook. You have already told me so much, but there is one thing more. I was quite surprised by Charlotte's remarks about my bad reputation at Wood & King. It's odd that no one has warned me. I can't square them with some of the things that you have

said, how Jon and his contemporaries hold me in such high regard. I realized that you were exaggerating, but were you saying the exact opposite of the truth?

I was hoping that you had put what Charlotte had said on
that subject out of your mind.

How could I?

The dining room had emptied. She looked around and
asked, Don't the waiters all wish we would leave?

Doubtless.

He was going to add something like, Don't worry about it,
they aren't supposed to make members uncomfortable if a
conversation is prolonged, when he thought of Carrie, and
how fatigue showed in her eyes and in the way that from one
moment to the next her head would seem to droop.

Instead he said: Good try, but I won't let you get away.
Let's go downstairs, to the reading room.

More coffee? he asked when they sat down again. You
might want to have a brandy. I shouldn't, since I'm going to
drive back.

Thank you, Schmidtie. Nothing at all. I think you should
recognize that these remarks were what I described as
Charlotte's aggressive behavior. She knew your feelings were
going to be hurt by what she and Jon had decided about the
wedding and the house, that made her feel guilty and unhappy, and the only solution was to attack, to hurt your feelings even more. You handed her the opening, when she spoke
about the rabbi and perhaps converting. That's all.

I don't understand. Are you saying that the aggression
consisted of telling me the truth or of telling me a lie? Did
she make up what she told me?

Not entirely. She knows you turned on Jon because he is Jewish.

Suddenly, Schmidt felt very tired. Sleep, he needed to sleep, if only for a few minutes.

He wanted to say, I didn't exactly turn on him, and, I wasn't unhappy only because he is a Jew, but what was the use of splitting hairs?

Renata, I am sorry that I didn't respond more gracefully.

The first time we met I told you that you were under very great stress. It had to affect your behavior. But I can tell you do have strong anti-Semitic feelings. Perhaps you should examine them. Jews aren't that bad. On the average they aren't worse than other people.

They are different.

Don't let that frighten you.

Before she got into the taxi he had hailed for her at the corner of the street, she gave him her cheek to kiss and said, Oh Schmidtie, I had hoped we would be such good friends. Is that still possible? Don't answer now, when you are angry.

He returned to the club before going to the garage and went to the toilet. Face slightly flushed, otherwise recognizable. He washed with cold water and rinsed his mouth with Listerine. The cigars were waiting on the bench in the hall. Julio could be counted on; he was a real friend; Gil Blackman was another. Smart and cynical and he'd known Gil forever. He asked Julio to connect him with Gil's office. An English voice, like Wendy Hiller's in *I Know Where I'm Going*, informed him that Mr. and Mrs. Blackman were at their home in Long Island. Oh ho! Could she connect him there?

You've returned from paradise, you old rascal, called out the robust maestro. When am I going to see you?

I was hoping to come to your office right now. I'm in the city. But as you're out there, I'll drive back this afternoon.

Then have dinner with me. What a relief! The mummy's here on a visit. Elaine and she will be able to eat together on trays in front of the TV. A girls' night in! Ha! Ha! Around seven-thirty at O'Henry's? Yes, the earlier the better! I can't wait to get away. Ciao!

The mummy was Elaine's mother. According to Gil, she was still unreconciled to the misalliance between her own daughter, the lineal descendant of the world's foremost manufacturers of work clothes, and an interloper whose grandfather had been born in Odessa. The insult had penetrated deep under the skin that surgery had made as impervious to the passage of time as the limestone facade of her mansion on Pacific Heights. Would her problem respond to treatment by Dr. Renata? Schmidt feared it might be too late.

The Saab on cruise control, resolutely in the far left lane of the expressway, snaking past slower traffic, Schmidt reviewed what had been demanded and offered. Purchase of Charlotte's remainder in the house? One and a half million, he figured. That was a lot of cash, but he would manage it. He might, in fact, take Dr. Renata's advice: sell the house and move into a place that wasn't like a hemorrhage of hundred-dollar bills. If not right away, then sometime later. "Dust inbreathed was a house—the wall, the wainscot and the mouse." He wouldn't be selling the Schmidts' ancestral homestead. Someone must have sold that long ago. This house was nothing except his life with Mary, which was over, and memories of Charlotte's childhood, which was over too. Charlotte was going against Mary's wishes, not he. There was no need for him to play the martyr. If he didn't sell the house, those two would do it as soon as he died and the estate was settled.

Carrie winked at him. When he had left the house in the morning, she was still a shape under the covers like a very large cat. If she weren't in her waitress clothes, she would have on the same pink flannel shirt with a red-and-blue flower pattern she wore last night, when she appeared in the bedroom so soundlessly that he kept on reading until he heard her speak: Who's come here to play with Schmidtie? He looked up—a Halloween witch's mask. Scared you, didn't I?

Hey, you're early tonight. The usual drink?

Yes, please. Very cold.

He told her that he was waiting for Gil Blackman, the man with whom she had seen him have such a long lunch.

Yeah, that guy. I'll leave the table set for two. Enjoy. Whenever you're ready.

You're going to come tonight? He put the question in a voice that was very low, without being a whisper.

No answer. Panic in Schmidt's heart. Stop, you old fool. She has told you she doesn't want it every night. Leave some air between you and her. If you don't, you will lose her respect.

She brought his martini and put it before him on a square cocktail napkin. Not a word. The napkin had on it "O'Henry's" in large red letters and below it the telephone number. When he lifted the glass, in the space between them he saw what she had written in red ink. He associated that sort of neat, almost square script with girls who had gone to very good schools, but, having paid all those checks she had brought, he knew it was also Carrie's. The message said: "C loves S."

Enter Mr. Blackman. Long, belted shearling coat, under it black trousers, black cashmere turtleneck. Resplendent hair cut shorter than usual. Yes, Mr. Blackman will have a martini. Just like his friend, Mr. Schmidt. Straight up, with an olive. And very cold!

Nice!

His eyes are fixed on Carrie, her head to the side, on her way to the bar to fetch him the drink.

Really, not half bad. Some sort of Latino. Isn't that the girl who spoke to you on the sidewalk, the last time we had lunch in this place?

Yes, she works here.

A stupid answer, but Gil does not say, Really! He asks instead about the Amazon. Did it turn out to be everything he and Elaine had said?

And more!

And did the other Schmidt take you around in his boat?

Yes, only he claimed his name is Oskar Kurz. Perhaps he has changed it!

Otherwise the same man? Squaw wife with small breasts? Yes? Then he has changed it or he has delusions! He thinks he is somewhere up the Congo! Ha! Ha! Ha!

What about Venice?

Let's order dinner first.

Gil flirts with Carrie about Manhattan chowder and broiled breast of free-range chicken. Amusing to see the enemy across a small table. The restaurant is teeming with them: men who look rich and talk fast. Yes, but they have wives. Carrie wouldn't like the problems. Don't kid yourself, Schmidtie, Gil is a problem solver. Perhaps the thing to do is to tell him about Carrie. That's different from not being careful in the restaurant.

It was Venice as usual in the winter. *Acqua alta*, fog so thick it stopped the vaporettos for a few hours, and a couple days that were just plain gray and humid. The rooms at the Monaco are too small—even the good ones! Elaine caught a cold and blew her nose all night. I could have murdered her.

I'm glad you didn't. And your merry band of revelers?

Tiresome. Isn't there something inane about going on holiday with people you see all the time, at all the same places, in New York and on the Coast? It's beyond comprehension why I do it. I wouldn't mind taking a trip with you—you're the silent type and there is only one of you. The pure hell of booking tables for six in a restaurant, and forcing the other five to be there at more or less the same time! There is always someone coming from some inconvenient other direction— say, the Gesuiti! Naturally, he or she gets lost and is one and a half hours late. I went through this twice a day, every day. Never again!

He stopped to examine the wine bottle. This stuff is dreadful. Do you mind if I order another bottle?

Carrie was nowhere in sight.

I should have said the financing for my film was falling through, Gil continued, and I must stay in New York until the end of the year to hold it together. Then I might have been able to send Elaine and Lilly to Venice with Fred and Alice and stay in New York myself.

It can't have been so bad!

Yes, it was and still is. Believe me. I don't mean just Venice.

Carrie was clearing the table next to them. Gil gave her an ingratiating smile and named the wine he wanted. That task accomplished, he went back to looking glum.

Schmidt was surprised to find that the inevitability of hearing more about Gil's sorrows wasn't all that irritating.

What is really the matter? He tried to look concerned.

It has finally happened: my youth is dead. Gone. Finished. The me I used to know is dead.

Gil, what are you talking about?

My girl. Katerina. The one I told you about. She has left me. While I was in Venice, she went to Jamaica. You know Periklis Papachristou?

I don't think so.

Yes, you do. You've seen him at our apartment. P.P., for power play. He's an agent. Anyway, he rented a house on Round Hill grounds and invited some people. He invited Katerina too, as a fellow Greek. She met this other guy there, also a Greek. He's some sort of thirty-year-old stockbroker, divorced, no kids, who had been going around with Bianca Jagger. He laid Katerina the first evening and left her black and blue. Of course, she loved it. Moved in with this jerk as soon as they came back. She wouldn't have gone to Jamaica if I had been in New York!

Isn't she the one who asked you if you wanted her to be faithful? You should have said yes.

Fuck you, Schmidt! How could I? I told you I couldn't let her think I was going to leave Elaine.

I remember. Well, this solves the problem of lying to Elaine. Seriously, what could you expect? To keep laying her, in perpetuity, on your office couch? Things like that don't last.

Yes, they do. No, you're right, they don't. Not with a wife

like Elaine. I would have had to take Katerina with me on trips and so forth. Like Tom Roberts! He lives with his wife in New York, the one who looks like an old Gypsy, and goes out with her to dinner and parties, but travels everywhere with his secretary. Out of town, she is Mrs. Roberts! But Elaine would never accept that.

You see.

I don't see anything, except that you have zero sympathy for me.

They had finished the bottle of number-two wine, and Gil asked Carrie to bring one more. This time he inquired about her name.

When she told me about the jerk—in detail, that's why I know about their first night together—she said, You know, I really loved you. If you weren't so old, we could have worked it out. It's better for me to be with someone my age. That was so unanswerable. I had never thought I was "old." After all, I'm in good condition, I've never done better work, women like me. I thought I was older, not old. But after she said that, I had to remember what we thought at her age of people who were the age we are now, and that really flattened me out. If you can believe it, she actually thought I was sixty-five. Of course, it made no difference to her at all when I pointed out that I was only sixty-one. What's four years more or less from her point of view? That's why I tell you, it's like death, my youth is dead! Do you know something else? I miss the sex with her. Now I do think about it when I'm in bed with Elaine.

I faced the fact that I had become an old man without the assistance of a Katerina, said Schmidt. I found out about it from the mirror, and from the way I feel about myself and other people. It's not pleasant.

They sat in silence, Schmidt wondering how much time he had before Gil made his next move. The time to tell him was right now. Anyway, he wanted to. Without mentioning Bryan or the man. What difference did that make?

Well, well, how very nice. She's got real looks. I don't know that she could model. I wouldn't mind, though, setting up a screen test for her—since she wants to act.

Thank you. You will keep this just between us? She asked me to be careful.

Who would I tell?

For instance, Elaine. If you can help it, don't.

Do you know how you are going to play this out?

I have no idea. Perhaps I won't have any plan at all. I've already done an awful lot of planning in my life. Most of it hasn't turned out very well. The only advantage of my present situation is that I don't need to have plans.

And how about Charlotte? Are you going to let her find out about Carrie?

Ah, the question of Charlotte. Perhaps that's also a question that can be deferred. Have you time to hear about Charlotte and her new family? They were on my mind when I called you.

You bet I have time. Don't forget the mummy I have at home. She teaches you to count in units of eternity.

After Schmidt had finished, he asked Gil: Do you think I have gone off my rocker, or are they all insane, the shrink included?

No, I don't think you're nuts. I think you have been abused and all things considered have behaved very well. I would make a couple of observations though. How old is Charlotte? Twenty-six? Twenty-seven? She is a young adult, and you should hold her responsible as an adult for what she does. That's different from the way one sometimes tries to hold children to account. The other is that you shouldn't underestimate how strongly Jews feel about anti-Semitism—even when it's innocuous, one might almost say irrelevant, like yours. Take me as an example. I have heard myself say lots of times, I may have even said it to you, that I don't care whether people are anti-Semitic so long as they don't interfere with my work, or where I can live, and, above all, don't try to put me in an oven. That's only half true. Maybe only one-fourth. In reality, it hurts a lot to be disliked or denied some part of the respect you think you should get, without your having done anything to provoke it. It's like being treated as though you're ugly, when in fact you are not. You know that Louis Armstrong song—"All my sin is in my skin." One never forgets those hurts.

I am sorry, said Schmidt. Have I hurt you that way?

Long ago. But at the time practically everybody was like you or much, much worse. You stood out less. Anyway, now that I am who I am, and everybody is busy licking my backside, I really couldn't care less.

The kids want to do it their own way, a wedding in the city, he told Carrie late that night. At first it sort of stopped me dead in my tracks. Then I thought, Let them. So long as it's what they want. And they don't want to live here. They like some place upstate better; it will be near Jon's parents'. I think I will buy Charlotte's part of this house. Afterward I will probably be too poor to keep this house, so I will sell it and move into a much smaller place, but there is no hurry.

That's cool. You know, Bryan does construction too. If you want to look at some houses he's worked on he'll show them to you.

That gave Schmidt something to which he could look forward. One thought led to another. He wondered aloud how the man was doing.

Mr. Wilson? Why do you keep calling him the man? It kind of got heavy for him trying to hang out. I don't know. Probably he's in New York. What a mess!

I have a feeling he knows about you and me.

Yeah, he's smart! She giggled.

But how? Did you tell him?

He would've killed me. He figured it out when I walked you to that parking lot. He was somewhere around.

But there was nothing then!

I told you: he's smart. He could tell I liked you. He sure was pissed.

And Bryan? You told him about Bryan?

That's different. He doesn't give a shit about Bryan. Let's sleep, OK?

The next morning, after Carrie had left for work, he called Dr. Renata. She was with a patient. He asked to leave a message on her answering machine.

Renata, this is Schmidtie. About the house. Will you please tell Charlotte and Jon that I am ready to buy Charlotte out? They should talk to Dick Murphy at W & K. He's my lawyer.

XIII

On the following Wednesday, Carrie's day off—she had mumbled, No, no, no, and burrowed deeper under the covers when, after nine o'clock, he kissed her ear, asking in a whisper whether she wanted breakfast—Schmidt went to the post office as usual, at nine-thirty sharp, to pick up his mail. The daily expedition was a ritual; since he expected only junk and bills, he might just as well have gone only once a week, perhaps on Monday. It wouldn't have made any difference. He certainly didn't pay bills every day. This time, however, the assiduity was rewarded: waiting for him was a letter from Charlotte. He didn't think he wanted to read it while Carrie looked on, and she might be awake or walk into the kitchen before he had finished. Also, he might need a moment to collect himself. He decided he would open the letter at the candy store and read it over a cup of coffee.

Did the turtle doves have a laser printer at home? Had she written the letter at the office? He hadn't a doubt that, in either case, Jon would have reviewed it. That made it like a legal communication—you never know whether Mr. White or Mr. Brown who signed is the real author.

Here is what the letter said:

Hi Dad,

It isn't easy to speak to you on the telephone and it sure isn't easy to write this letter. I guess the letter is easier. So I'm writing. Jon and Renata thought I should to say "thank you" and "sorry." I'm saying both.

Jon and I are grateful to you for agreeing to buy my remainder interest. Jon has talked to Mr. Murphy who has told him there is no problem. I hope you are not inconvenienced. Bridgehampton has changed since I was a child, and I don't like the way that area has been developed. Ulster County, where Renata and Myron are going, is still rural. We will be near them, and near several couples from W & K and my office who have houses there or are actively looking. We don't have friends in the Hamptons and we don't know how we would meet couples like us. I don't believe we would meet them through your and Mom's friends.

Do you think I could have some furniture from the house? I am making up a list of the better pieces that belonged to Aunt Martha. I believe that Mom intended me to have them. I will send the list soon. When we buy a house, please send the furniture. Jon asked me to tell you that he thinks we should pay for the move. And could we please have the silver?

I guess you are glad in the end not to have the bother of the wedding, especially as almost all the guests will be people you don't know. Except the people from the firm. It would have been a lot of work for you, and now you can relax and carry on with your routine. It must be nice to be retired!

We have checked out several restaurants in Soho and

Tribeca. The one we like best is Nostradamus, at the corner of Broadway and Spring Street. I don't think that's an area you know. The restaurant has been there for just about two years. A man in my office is married to the chef. She does light Cajun cuisine. They can seat 250, and still have room for dancing. We don't need a band. We will use a DJ. The price they quoted is $200 per guest, everything included. They are reserved solid every evening, so they need a deposit of 20%, by the end of next week. You can make the check out to me. I'll pay them with my own check.

The wedding will be on June 20. We will be married at City Hall in the morning, and then the party will start at seven. Renata and Myron will be back from a Psychoanalytic Congress in Toronto early that week, and Jon has checked the date with the key partners. I guess you don't have too many scheduling problems!

So we hope you will come and see what a different lifestyle wedding is like.

You got up a head of steam about my becoming converted to Judaism. It won't happen right away, because I have to do a lot of studying even though I am choosing Reformed Judaism, but I am heading down that road. The Jewish religion is very beautiful and I never got that much out of being an Episcopalian. If we have children it will be less confusing for them. We will be able to give them a spiritual background. That does matter to some people.

I guess this has gotten to be a long letter so I'll say goodbye now.

Charlotte

Schmidt was one of those people who answer every business letter the day it is received and try to answer personal letters not more than one day later. Therefore, very little suspense, if any, will be sacrificed if the text of his reply is set out now, even as he ponders what he should say to his daughter.

Thursday

Dear Charlotte,

I haven't found much by way of gratitude or apology in your letter, but I won't quarrel with you about it. Not while I am writing in part about your wedding.

My check to cover the deposit at Nostradamus is enclosed. Are you familiar with the celebrated book of predictions by the XVIth century philosopher for whom that restaurant must be named? It might amuse you to consult it. Maybe prudent, too. I cannot do it conveniently on your behalf, because the Bridgehampton library doesn't have it. Incidentally, I assume that Jon has gone over a detailed listing of what is included in the all-inclusive price.

You were right; my calendar is clear of conflicting engagements. I intend to be there on June 20th.

Since I am not dead yet I don't think you will get Mom's and my silver just now. I will send candelabra, trays, and such like that belonged to Aunt Martha. You may not recall it, but your mother gave Martha's table silver to one of her assistants as a wedding present. That would have been about five years ago. For the same reason—my being alive—I will have to go over the list of furniture you want and decide what I can send to you without changing the look of the rooms here. I hope Murphy has told Jon that in the purchase of your remainder I am buying the contents of the house as well, I mean your rights to them after my death because all the furniture belongs to me for life anyway. They are included in the price. I also hope he has told Jon that the money is ready. We can close the deal anytime you wish.

I do not recall what you have told me over the telephone about your and Jon's plans in the weeks to come. Should you wish to come here of a weekend, you are most welcome, but I would like a few days' advance notice. Perhaps in the future I will have commitments.

Your

Father

Shouldn't I send a copy of Charlotte's letter to Renata? Schmidt asked himself. She has the tape. If she gets the letter, she'll be starting a real collection. In the end, he didn't do it: he felt too ashamed.

XIV

ONCE AGAIN, it's Carrie's Wednesday off: two
days short of the beginning of spring. Huge clumps of for-
sythia are in bloom across the lawn from Schmidt's back
porch. They seem to be a stronger color with each passing
year. The crocuses and narcissi are out too. Geese honk on the
pond beyond Foster's field. Every half hour or so, the great
wings begin to clap, and a helter-skelter squadron takes flight
toward the ocean, on the way sorting itself into an inverted
V. It's only an oafish joke, like the fat girls with chilblains
who marched in the St. Patrick's Day parade yesterday. These
birds aren't about to migrate anywhere. They'll wheel in the
sky and return to the pond, where they were born and will
die. Drunks on their way home after the last pub has closed,
lurching up Third Avenue toward the 86th Street subway entrance, pissing on grilles of closed storefronts.

It's so pleasant on the porch. Only one day in the week
when she can close her eyes like this and let her face absorb
the weak sun. Schmidt asks himself whether she must really
work so hard; suppose he offered to supplement her income.
Would that upset the balance, should he risk any change? She

is in the chaise longue. By now, she must have tried on all his clothes. The heavy white cardigan is very becoming. It makes her look even more exotic than usual. Is she dozing? They made love hard when they woke this morning; she drove him to his limit. The night before it was too late and she was too tired. She had to swing by Sag Harbor to drop off some package for Bryan. When Schmidt came down to the kitchen this morning, to make his and Carrie's breakfast, the fellow was already sitting there. He could have picked up the package himself and not have made her drive back and forth in the middle of the night. Unless. If Schmidt asks Carrie, she will tell him—more than he wants to know. Bryan and Carrie performing those gestures that are as monotonous as the antics of the geese. I belong to you, Schmidtie, like that, take me like that, she had whispered into the crook of his elbow just two hours ago. What more can he need?

It's just as well Carrie didn't come into the kitchen together with Schmidt, teasing him, her hands under his bathrobe, inside his pajamas. The official line is that Bryan doesn't know. Schmidt needed someone with more brains and less velocity than the Poles, not to replace them but to make sure the shopping gets done, the plants are watered, and so forth, and offered in return a private room and bath and a little money for extra work. She would say to Bryan, This old guy eats at O'Henry's. It's a good deal. His house is real near the restaurant. In the summer he'll let me use the pool when he's not swimming. Nobody wants Bryan to go crazy. In order to ease into the situation and, Schmidt is quite sure, to provide Bryan with a place to screw her that isn't under Schmidt's roof, or in the back of Bryan's half truck or his buddy's house in Springs, where she just won't go, she doesn't want to be gang-raped, Carrie is also holding on to the apartment in Sag Harbor for now. She wants to see how things will work out. And maybe that's the truth.

The advantage of this handyman-artist is that most of the time, unless something sets him off, he doesn't talk, and doesn't seem to mind if Schmidt is silent as well. When a question is put to him, he answers politely in a soft voice, his words gentle around the edges, like a little boy's. Before she left for Florida, his mother must have taught him not to use bad words and to speak carefully. You'd think he was sixteen, and yet he must be close to thirty! There is nothing childlike about his body: it is short but powerful. One can imagine him on the chin-up bar, putting in his five minutes every morning. The impression comes rather from the perfect oval face and cheeks that blush so easily under blond fuzz. There is another aspect, a little out of place: the tiny earring, the long, thin blond hair gathered in a ponytail, the fake elephant-hair bracelet, the fingers with nails that have been chewed raw, and something disagreeable about the eyes. At first the eyes seem "who? me?" Li'l Abner candid, but a careful observer cannot fail to notice that the whites are in fact yellow, and that Bryan doesn't look you in the eyes. He looks away, furtively. Is it better when he has on his aviator glasses? Hard to tell. It turns out that Bryan considers carpentry as only a means to get enough bread. In reality, he is an artist. He has brought over his paintings for Schmidt to look at. They provoke a similar unease in spite of their banality: huge canvases covered by tantric patterns. The boy has a weakness for poison green, magenta, purple, and pink. What of it? You wouldn't expect Carrie to have a beau from Skull and Bones!

Perhaps it's time for conversation? Schmidt asks him: Is this your day off, Bryan, or is business slow? The slump must hurt even on the South Fork.

It really does, Albert. Something awful.

Another redeeming grace. Although nine times out of ten, Bryan's kind of person proceeds immediately to a first-name basis, for instance on the telephone, calling you from the garage to say he's finished the lube job on your car, Bryan did not. It was Mr. Schmidt this and Mr. Schmidt that, although Schmidtie, seeking to ingratiate himself, told him early on to skip the Mr. and use the cozy, softened version of his name. Bryan replied with a pretty lisp: Gee, I just can't, it sounds so disrespectful! Would you mind if I call you Albert instead?

My buddy who lives in Springs is real worried. He's making payments on his truck. I'm lucky. I've got these other jobs.

Oh yes? Things you can do when the carpentry is slow?

That's right. I watch houses, like if you go on vacation to Florida or Europe, and for people who only come out on weekends. And I'm beginning to detail cars.

What's that?

You know, if you want your car to be superclean, cleaner than new! I get all the dirt and grease off, right down to the original surface, and then vacuum and wax. In this one garage where I work, there are customers that get brand-new cars detailed before they will drive them. I'm getting pretty good at it—it's artistic work.

He snickers, rolls a joint, and licks it until the paper is soaked through. Yes sir, a detail man! A particularly heavy fragrance spreads with the smoke.

You want to try it, Albert? Just once? It's the good stuff. Not the usual small-time goods.

No thanks. I'm about to light a cigar.

Hey, pass it to me, says Carrie.

Her eyes are open. Puff puff, lick lick. Back to Bryan. For Christ's sake, Schmidtie, will you relax! This is nothing: they regularly exchange body fluids.

Shit! You weren't kidding.

You know, Albert, if any of your friends would like some, I could get it for them. Other kinds of stuff too. Out here, rich people sometimes don't know the ropes. They want to make a purchase, and they want the best quality, but they don't know who to ask. I only go for the quality stuff.

Fuck off! You leave Schmidtie alone. He isn't interested.

Carrie's growl—it is the first time Schmidt hears it. A tigress! She would fight to defend him. Still, the tension is unpleasant.

It's a nonissue. I don't have many rich friends. Besides, I hardly ever see anybody.

But you know them, Albert, that's what counts. If any of them are interested, all I need is an introduction.

Will you fuck off, you shithead? I gave you your package last night. What're you doing here anyway?

Hey, Carrie, remember? You and I are going to show Albert that house that's come on the market. Don't hassle me. It was your idea.

I'm going to fix some lunch. Soup OK with you, Schmidtie? Of course.

Now he remembers. Carrie has told him Bryan and his partner work for a builder whose client didn't have enough money to close on a house. He said he would look at it.

Nice girl, that Carrie, and crazy over you, Albert. She'
never felt that way about me.

I'm just an old guy. I guess she enjoys having someone t
look after.

Sure, like last night. I'm with her, and, right away, th
party's over. She has to go to see if you're all right. How d
you think that makes me feel?

Schmidt shrugs his shoulders. I thought I just heard he
say she gave you a package last night.

Bryan rolls another joint and pats down the pouch.

She delivered it all right, he says. This stuff. That's wher
it came from. One hundred percent pure Moroccan hashish
Nothing but the best! You don't want to fool with that
Carrie's OK. She knows when I need her. But with you it'
something else.

Schmidtie, I want to drive. Can you get the top down?

She really can't keep her hands off the Saab. They cross th
highway and head for the stretch of scrub oak beyond th
railroad track. Scruffy, badly marked road: the center line i
hardly visible, the edges of the asphalt have been chippe
away by frost, winter after winter. The borders along it ar
half sand and half weeds. They are littered with debri
tossed from trucks like Bryan's and the cars of slobs who ow
or rent in this part of the world: paper plates, beer cans
Kleenexes smeared with lipstick, broken glass, cigarett
packs, and take-out cartons from Burger King. Here and
there, a busted white plastic bag surrounded by its load o
rotten vegetables, empty Evian bottles, and chicken bones
It's one way to avoid that trip to the town dump, and wh
wants to cart garbage to New York in the back of the statio
wagon and hand it to the doorman? They pass a grim old fel

low walking toward them on the other side of the road. He carries one of those white garbage bags and is actually picking up the stuff! A bum scavenging for food? No, he wears clean garden gloves, therefore, a deranged householder. Carrie toots the horn at him, but he doesn't look up.

What a yoyo, she cries out.

Hey, slow down, it's here on the right.

Bryan is in the backseat, behind Carrie. His hands reach over the driver's seat to her shoulders. Then one of them moves farther down, finds her breast, and squeezes.

Cut it out, will you? You want me to go off the road?

Schmidt negligently throws out his cigar. It's just tobacco, but immediately he regrets the gesture. Bryan will think he's OK, behaving just like Mr. Schmidt, when he next heaves a broken muffler pipe over to the side of the road.

They turn into a driveway, really a curving swath cut by a bulldozer. At its end the site, also raw—the contractor hasn't returned to haul away his litter, never mind finish the grading—an odd-looking one-story house, shaped like the letter **X**. The dumpster placed near what should be the front door overflows with sheetboard, scraps of timber, and corrugated wrapping.

Shangri-la, says Schmidt.

Bryan whines: Don't look at the plot, Albert. It can be landscaped any way you want.

Of course.

I swear to you. McManus didn't clean up the land because the guy broke the contract. I have the key. You want to go in?

One entire segment of the **X** is a long room with two fireplaces and a kitchen that's all counters and no walls placed toward the farther end, the other two half segments that cut across it are like separate wings and contain sequences of bedrooms and bathrooms. Oak floors with a chic finish and white walls. Even though the sky has clouded over, the house is very light.

Schmidt has never been the first occupant of a house or an apartment. It must be a strange experience. Every nick in the paint, every scuff mark on the woodwork, would be one's own. He walks around, opens closet doors, looks at the plumbing and kitchen fixtures as though he knows what he is doing, asks about the cellar.

It's great, Albert. Come on, take a look.

In fact, it is a nice, clean cellar, with two crawl spaces. *Basta*. In another minute Bryan will whip out the contract for him to sign. He must be working on a commission.

Thanks, Bryan. Nice house. Shall we go now?

Carrie has been doing some looking of her own.

You could put me in this room, she announces, and leads Schmidt to the bedroom at the end of one of the wings. It has a door that opens on what will be the garden.

That's a deal.

If Albert buys the house you can look after him without sleeping here. It's real close to Sag Harbor. Right?

Bryan puts his arm around her waist.

At the Sag Harbor hotel, Carrie has a rum and Coke, Bryan has two beers, and Schmidt a brandy. During the short ride over, Bryan has smoked another reefer, sharing it with Carrie. Schmidt feels dreadfully put-upon. He asks for the check, pays with cash because it's quicker, and gets up, saying, See you soon, Bryan. I'll think about the house.

It doesn't work. Bryan has left his truck sitting in

Schmidt's driveway. Carrie races along the turnpike. If the police stop her, they will find Schmidt in a car blue with hashish smoke, driven by a local waitress, with a pusher in the back. That's front-page news for the local press. But they make it back safely.

Bryan doesn't roar away in his truck. He follows them into the house. Carrie has gone upstairs without a word, perhaps meaning to shake him off. What is Schmidt to do? He fusses with his mail while Bryan sits in the corner of the library, working on his nails. Some time passes before Schmidt finds the solution. He walks over to Bryan, holds out his hand, and says, I had better take a nap now. We'll see each other soon.

Bryan rises to shake his hand and sits down again.

I'm waiting for Carrie, he informs Schmidt.

In Schmidt's room, the bed is turned down. Carrie holds out her arms to him. What took you so long?

Bryan. How to make him leave. In the end, I told him I needed a nap. But he's still here. He said he is waiting for you.

Yeah. He wants me to go back to Sag with him.

Do you have to?

He gets crazy when he's like this. Come on, Schmidtie.

She is already naked. Squatting on the bed, she unbuckles his belt, opens his trousers.

Later she renews her question: You still love me?

More and more.

And Bryan. You're not mad at me?

I wish he'd drop dead.

I belong to you, Schmidtie. Please love me. I'll be early. You'll wait for me?

The truck is pulling out, going too fast on the gravel. He

had been so deep inside her, and now she is going to get under this guy and open her legs, her buttocks. Whatever time she returns, she'll nuzzle his neck and whisper, Let's go to sleep, darling. Fatigue? Satiety? Perhaps it's also a sort of modesty: wanting to be fresher when he takes her.

The photographs of Mary and Charlotte, alone and with him, that cluttered up the top of the double chest of drawers to the left of the bed are gone. They are on a shelf in the closet, easy to reach when he wants to look at them. That's his form of modesty. The pain Mary suffered in this bed during the last weeks: Was it a form of retribution? Schmidt can't think what grave sins she had committed to deserve it. The past is both distant and recent, and yet they all seem venial: small lies, short-lived fits of anger, perhaps pride. But it was a Miss Porter's and Smith College alumna kind of pride, a quality girls used to be praised for. They were to have self-respect and remember who they were and how much they had to be grateful for. Mary certainly did. As for his own case, the scourge of Charlotte's unnatural dislike, icy loneliness, the trap of Bryan and of the man, which condemns him to live in desire and without hope? If it is retribution meted out ahead of time, it must be for Corinne, confirming that there is symmetry in the Almighty's arrangements. Of course, it was unthinkable that someone was actually bothering to balance separately billions of individual accounts. The job had become too big for the just gods who "of our pleasant vices / Make instruments to plague us." The final solution was global: endless torment, distributed randomly, but with no one left out. It was enough to remember that all lives end badly.

One simplifies these things, especially for children. He remembers how, when Charlotte was eight, Mary and he played their LPs of *Don Giovanni* for her over and over and explained the plot before taking her to see it performed at the Metropolitan Opera. When they got home from the matinee, he asked her what she had liked the best. It's when the statue comes to dinner and walks like this: ta ta ta ta, she told him, and kept on repeating, ta ta ta ta. He was delighted with her answer, and told her she had gotten it exactly right. First, Don Giovanni kills the Commendatore. Then he taunts the dead man by inviting his marble statue to dinner. Then, on top of it, he has the bad manners to forget the invitation he has issued, sits down to dinner, without waiting for his guest, and starts gorging himself. Here Schmidt gave his off-key rendition of *Ah*, *che piatto saporito* and *Ah*, *che barbaro appetito!* No wonder the man of stone walks into the banquet room angry ta ta ta ta and pulls the Seducer down into hell!

When retribution is so neatly personalized, Schmidt thinks he can understand it, perhaps even, *à la rigueur*, for a moment believe in the system. According to the librettist, and Tirso de Molina before him, Don Giovanni could have escaped. If he had not mocked Elvira, if he had obeyed the ghost of the Commendatore, if only he had repented! How is he, Schmidt, going to be saved? By letting go of Carrie? *Sei pazzo!* Not for all the tea in China! It should be possible, for a sum of money that he could afford, to buy off Bryan. And if the man reappears, he can have him arrested and put away for a good long time in a booby hatch, enough time so that, if he is let out again, it won't matter. For instance, in Wingdale, if that place is still in business: he would call his old friend, the governor's secretary, and ask him to speak to the right people. That fellow is obviously a dangerous public nuisance. But Bryan might not stay "bought." He might pocket the money and laugh at him. When in the past he counseled clients against paying bribes and thought that arguments derived from moral principles or the likelihood of getting caught weren't working, he usually concentrated on the ghastly inefficiency of such methods. You couldn't be sure whether it was necessary to pay—the government official might do what the client wanted anyway, without the money—and if he took the money and did nothing, you had no recourse. He might now for once listen to the voice of his own wisdom. On the other hand, Wingdale has a chance of working.

But then he realizes that, even if effective, neither solution is acceptable. Carrie might find out what he has done: he can't take that risk. It is better not to have a plan.

When he woke up—in the end he did take a nap—it was dark. He dressed rapidly, feeling the need to get away from the house to a place where there were other people. Inside his house, wherever he turned, he felt mocked: Charlotte's presence and Charlotte's absence, like twin masks of Comedy and Tragedy in some allegory he was unable to decipher. On any other night, he would have driven straight to O'Henry's. That was out of the question.

Right after law school, before he had met Mary, he went out with a receptionist at W & K who was a cousin of the debutante from Boston brought so vividly before his eyes through the magic of involuntary memory as soon as he heard Gil Blackman's fickle assistant on the telephone. The receptionist was nice to him, but not so nice as he had wished. He suspected that a senior associate, whom, as it turned out, she eventually married, was allowed to take certain liberties. During a short but shameful period, on evenings when he was working late, or she had refused to see him, he would telephone her. If she didn't pick up, Schmidt would immediately conclude that she was with his rival, and gave his imagination free rein. The thought that she might have activities outside of work that weren't connected with dating, for instance going to a concert or the movies with another woman, never crossed his mind. The age of the answering machine had not yet arrived: he could not keep calling just to savor one more time the sound of the promise that she would call back. If she did answer, he would cover the receiver with a guilty hand, listen, and hang up after a minute or two. But to hear Charlotte! It occurred to him that unless Riker was already back from the office he would be certain to hear her voice—at least a recording of it. He dialed the number and let it ring until the answering machine took over.

Eight-thirty. There had to be a nine o'clock show in Southampton, in one of the odd shoe-box rooms into which the old movie theater that smelled of mold had been divided. Any film would do.

He parked his car around the corner. Fifteen minutes to show time. There was no line. He bought a ticket and went to look at the vans and convertibles through the window of the General Motors showroom next door. What should he do with Mary's car? Give it to Carrie. It was absurd to let her drive an old jalopy while the Toyota was just sitting in the garage. Or he could trade the Toyota in for another car and give Carrie that one. He would lose money, and it was foolish to get rid of a car that had maybe twenty thousand miles on it, but that would be the more elegant thing to do. There was also Charlotte's car, which she had left on her last visit. She hadn't mentioned it in her letter. Perhaps now that she was being advised by both attorney Riker and Dr. Renata she had come to think that the car, registered in Schmidt's name, wasn't really hers. They must have counseled in their tactical discussions: Don't ask for the VW at the same time you make a grab for your old man's silver! He'll flip out!

He looked at his watch. There was time for a quick drink across the street. He started in that direction. But in the entrance to the alley next to the bar, as if carved in stone, staring at Schmidt and registering no surprise, stood the man. He held a brown paper bag at chest level. In anticipation of the season, he wore a beige duster. On his head perched a stained gray fedora.

Get over here, you bastard, you old goat, he cried to Schmidt. I've been waiting for you. You and I have business to settle!

Schmidt turned tail. Once inside the movie theater, he found a seat toward the front, in the middle of the row, with people on both sides. He felt calmer when the movie ended. The man's unspeakable filth and stench—it was that, not his physical strength, that terrified him. Like fear of rats feeding on garbage. He would overcome it.

Mary took long baths. Carrie prefers showers. There is a white wicker armchair in the bathroom. Schmidt sits in it, watching Carrie take a shower. She has returned from Sag Harbor—not long after his return from the movies. Seeing her like this is overpoweringly exciting: her body is so young, so free of imperfections. The contrast between the heft of her breasts and the elongated body that seems always at the edge of fatigue is not a defect; Schmidt finds in it an ineffable charm. It reminds him of the sadness of certain Degas dancers—that girl, for instance, with a questioning upturned face, one foot on a chair, tying her slippers. When Carrie makes love she grows so serious that in the beginning Schmidt wondered whether he was hurting her, whether she needed to be consoled. But it's never that: she is serious because the gift she makes of herself is total, and the force of the climax overwhelms her. He has come to think that her violent, prolonged orgasms are a reward for her seriousness and generosity.

She has been washing with extreme care. Schmidt laughs at the attention she has given to her belly button. She has told him, pointing to a tiny pinprick, That's where I wore a ring. It was crazy! Schmidt would like to know which one of her boyfriends had this wish to mark her. He hasn't asked; he is afraid it was Mr. Wilson, although that seems so preposterous. When she finishes, Schmidt stands up and holds a towel for her, wraps her in it, and pats her down until she is dry. She has already brushed her teeth. He takes her in his arms and, turning out the lights on his way, carries her to bed. Too bad for the little guy, she whispers this in his ear, and, a moment later, I love you, darling, I can't tonight. He dicked me for an hour. It was brutal. That asshole was so freaked out he couldn't come. Her fingers continue. Do you still love me? You like it like this, Schmidtie?

Later, when her head is already in its nest on his chest, Schmidt tells her that he has seen the man and asks whether she knows that he has come back. She does; he has waited at the restaurant.

Carrie, does the man dick you?

You sound funny! Can't you say Mr. Wilson? That's his name.

Does he?

When he first came here, he tried. He got cleaned up at my place and tried and tried. No way! He couldn't. He got so pissed he hit me. No, it wasn't bad, just knocked me around.

What will you do if he tries it again?

He won't. He just won't. Not while I'm with you.

Why? How do you know?

He told me. Like you've got the things he used to have. He doesn't want me to compare.

Then he will want to kill me.

XV

QUOGUE HAD FOUGHT VALIANTLY and with considerable success to stop Jews from invading the bay properties that made it such a desirable beach community in the eyes of many of Schmidt's partners and clients. Nevertheless, Schmidt had a deep-seated, generalized prejudice against Quogue and its entire population—locals and summer and weekend residents.

To start with, Schmidt's canon held that all townies living in the western part of Long Island's Suffolk County were avid, mercenary riffraff: the more enterprising among them built on speculation the houses that were defacing Schmidt's landscape, while the rest busied themselves selling cars and insurance. So far as he was concerned, regardless of geographical considerations, Quogue belonged in that part of the county. The East End locals were more likely to be found cutting lawns, servicing septic tanks, and growing vegetables (activities of which Schmidt approved and that, in his opinion, lifted them to a higher sphere of existence), unless they were fishermen, an ornery but noble and endangered order. But Schmidt's loathing for Bryan was not at all related to

Quogue's being his birthplace. He detested Bryan for being devious and exacting access to Carrie's body. Whether and to what degree these demands were unwelcome, Schmidt had not yet chosen to investigate.

And Schmidt's view of Quogue was not enhanced by the presence of those very partners and clients who had houses there. They were the sort of people whose links with Schmidt Jon Riker had used to illustrate for Charlotte her father's anti-Semitism, but Schmidt did not feel at ease with them. As a species, they were too genial and too gregarious for his taste, given to planning jolly activities at which they were sure they would have great fun together, and to relating later, in detail that suggested the gift of total recall, how swell everything had in fact turned out to be, even though Jimbo had broken his kneecap falling down the Spanish Steps and Mary Jane's doctors were unable to cure the dysentery she caught in Cancún. It will be plain by now that bonhomie was not one of Schmidt's characteristics. Besides, the men had used to irritate Mary by not understanding what she did, while their wives, with existences defined by raising children and good works, had bored her, made her impatient.

His first inclination, therefore, when he opened the Walkers' lengthy, many-times-folded-over invitation to their thirtieth wedding anniversary celebration to be held at their house in Quogue on the second Saturday in May, was to decline. The invitation had been addressed to his office; he didn't recall receiving a letter of condolence from them; the past was the past; they weren't intimate anymore. There would be other people at the party in the same embarrassing category of former friends: couples who made up Schmidt's circle when he was at law school or with whom he and Mary had dined regularly in the years that followed, and the flotsam and jetsam of divorces. As for the latter category, it was hard to predict whether the wife or the husband was more likely to have been salvaged. Looks and charm were often dispositive, the more attractive partner sailing on to other waters.

These were friendships that had bloomed long ago, when most of them lived on the Upper West Side or between Washington Square and Gramercy Park. At that time the grand firms for which the men worked paid young lawyers pitifully low salaries but the old partners fully expected the associates and their wives to dress up like Mommy and Daddy and live like miniatures of Mommy and Daddy, on the assumption that everyone had a small trust fund that made that sort of thing possible. Therefore, they coped; knowing how to cope was a tribal skill, like knowing how to rig a sailboat. Sometimes two couples—inseparable, good looking, and exuberant, with their perfect, picture-pretty, towheaded, and exuberant children—would jointly rent a large house near the beach in Amagansett or on the north side of the highway in Water Mill. The husbands had all been law school classmates, give or take a year. They would ask strays like Schmidt to come out on the train with them for a weekend of corn on the cob, gin, and watching the children play at the edge of the surf. It was during such a weekend at the Walkers', to which Ted Walker had invited him, that Schmidt was able to dazzle Mimi, Walker's willowy Philadelphian wife, by poaching for her a whole salmon, and then decorating it with rich-looking, yellow mayonnaise he had made from scratch in a bowl, just stirring peanut oil into egg yolks with a little whisk. Anyone other than Schmidtie would have simply reached for a jar of Hellmann's, became the universal many-times-repeated comment.

Still, why should he go to that party? Did he any longer care about them or they about him? One couldn't begin to explain over a drink or a plate of cold roast veal the games life had played with the Walkers or with him since they had drifted apart, soon after his marriage to Mary. And the rest of that group! He expected it would be a challenge even to recognize half of them, requiring instant restoration of hair color, if not of hair itself, airbrushing potholes left in the skin by removal of little cancers, whittling down bellies and rear ends. Nevertheless, after breakfast, as he read the text of the invitation—it was really an illustrated family history, punctuated at every turn by exclamation points, with pictures of the Walkers and their children at various ages—he was overcome by curiosity. Ted and Mimi's story seemed so happy and their lives so wonderfully simple. What was that like? How did they manage it? He should find out: it would be a sociological expedition of a sort he would not be easily able to undertake if Carrie should accept his various imprudent suggestions that they live together and she quit her job. It was a buffet dinner: he could leave when he wanted. No one would miss him.

Once he had driven the thirty miles from Bridgehampton and found himself in Ted and Mimi's house, he remembered his tergiversations and curiosity, and might have burst out laughing, because it was all so simple, if it had not been for the envy that stabbed him. The house was much like his, a brown clapboard affair with screened porches and sky-blue window shutters, surrounded by old trees. On the neat lawn in the back a band was playing New Orleans jazz. Pleasant-looking locals were handing drinks and canapés and other finger food to older types, many of whom he could identify without captions, and to young people cut from the same selection of cloths as the more presentable latter-day associates at W & K, and just as wholesome. Those would be the friends of the Walkers' lawyer and banker kids. There was no tent; he supposed the house was big enough to feed this crowd, and anyway the night air would be too cold for a tent unless it was heated. For Charlotte's wedding, he had planned to have a big tent close to the back porch, so that people could drift in and out. That was one difference. The other was his rotten luck; it was nothing but that: first Mary and then the dreadful business with Charlotte. Without that unseemly row, he could have managed. Ted didn't have any more money than he. He could have given a great party—Mary and he could have done it with both hands tied behind their backs. All he needed was something to celebrate. But hold it: Why not throw a bash to introduce Carrie to society? With Bryan parking cars and the man in blackface behind the bar—if he could be found and cleaned up! Decidedly, there was no riddle to be answered here. This was just another catered party, given by a nice couple whose lives had not yet been broken. Their time would come.

Despite his own indifference to the fortunes of the Walkers and his other former friends scattered among the guests, Schmidt took it hard that people he had once known well, and had not seen for an age, should not feel curious about him. For instance Ted: he had been perfectly polite and cordial, but then ditched Schmidt with the "Stay right here, I'll be right back" of a busy host, not bothering to make sure he had someone to talk to. Abandoned, Schmidt crisscrossed the lawn, drifting in and out of groups, putting forward views and asking questions he knew were of no interest to himself or whomever he had happened to buttonhole. Resenting the intrusions of others into conversations he had begun only to feel excluded from them, drinking more and faster than usual in the hope that the repeated trips to the bar made his meanderings less conspicuous. A voice he knew well hailed him. It belonged to his former partner, Lew Brenner. What a surprise: Had the walls of Jericho fallen down?

He said, Nice to see you, Lew. What are you doing at the Walkers'?

I guess the same as you. Having a great time! Isn't this a grand occasion?

I mean I hadn't realized you knew them.

We've been friends for years. In fact, Tina and I play doubles with them once a week in the city, unless one of us is on the road. You know how that is!

Behind Schmidt's back! This too was hard.

That's nice, Lew. How are things at the firm?

Not bad, we're pulling out of the slough. Earnings for '92 should be flat. That's not great, but it's better than '91! Partners were going around saying they'd kill for a deal. Of course I couldn't complain then and can't complain now, because foreign work never dropped off, and that Jon Riker of yours and the rest of the bankruptcy gang are doing great things!

Good for you, Lew. Good for Jon. You know, I never hear much about W & K anymore.

That's your fault! You should drop in, come to firm lunch. People miss you.

I can't believe that! Lew, tell me, are you having a good time here, do you have a good time at this sort of party?

What do you mean? Sure, I'm having a fine time this evening.

I can see that. What I really meant is how do you do it, how do you get to enjoy this?

Tonight is special, because we like Ted and Mimi and the children so much. But generally? I don't know. Parties are just for having a drink or two, talking to a couple of people, and soliciting clients! Right? I don't take them seriously.

I suppose you're right, Lew. But these things always leave me discombobulated.

You want to come and say hello to Tina?

In a moment, I should say hello to Mimi first. You're a good man, Lew. I wish we had been closer during all those years.

It's never too late!

Although it was past eleven, he was among the first to leave. The band had moved indoors and was working its way through "St. Louis Woman." Through the frame of the tall windows, he could see the older set dancing 1950s style, women clinging to the men. No problem: he would be home before Carrie.

By the time he reached the end of the divided highway, the fog had thickened. That didn't faze Schmidt. A man's Saab is his castle. He turned on the fog lights, fixed his eyes on the freshly painted center line, and stepped on the gas. On the radio, a panel was discussing racial rage and violence: LA cops beating Rodney King and LA blacks beating Reginald Denny.

Schmidt had seen both on television. No one was asking the crucial question: How does a man not get sick when he hears his stick go thwack on the head, the shoulders, the back of another man? Why doesn't he feel the blows on his own squirming body and stop? Is it the adrenaline rush of rage? It was clear to him that he suffered from an adrenaline deficiency. Why else hadn't he by now turned Sergeant Smith loose on the man without worrying about the old thwack? That's because he wasn't Sergeant Schmidt. Very funny! Meanwhile, the man was closing in. Cuckoo here and cuckoo there. One would think he was shacked up in the pool house! Perhaps he was: fed on the sly by Carrie.

He turned off Route 27 at the first opportunity, and before he had gone a half mile realized he had made a mistake. This was no fog; it was like driving through a cloud. What to do? To turn back to the highway wasn't that simple, and in the end he would have to head toward the beach anyway. To hell with it! He knew every turn of these roads by heart. There weren't any other cars to worry about. The panel of experts on human nature was getting under his skin. He fiddled with the radio knob looking for jazz. There wasn't any; just talk or country music. To hell with that too. He would sing to himself. Full steam ahead to the tune of *L'amour est enfant de Bohème*. No humming: words please. *Toreador, toreador, l'amour, l'amour t'attend*. How apt! No, he wasn't in a cloud; he was in a black Saab convertible inside an immense, unending bottle of milk. Schmidt's excitement mounted. Was he a horse smelling the stable, or could it be, at last, an adrenaline rush? This was almost the end of the first straight segment of Mecox, he felt in his bones the turn was coming up, then another straight stretch, and then Ocean Avenue. A piece of cake. If he could only see, his own driveway would be in sight. Schmidt's operatic repertoire was limited. He launched into *Vivan le femine! Viva il buon vino! Sostegno e gloria d'umanità!* The Walkers' wine was not bad, and as for Carrie—brava! He could sing that aria all the way home. But then a thud like the whole percussion section gone mad fills the car, its force throws Schmidt forward until the belt across his shoulder bites, and Schmidt squints, trying to make out the intentions of the great white fish swimming gracefully in the milk over the hood of the Saab, the face coming to meet his face across the windshield. Of course, the man! Although Schmidt has stopped singing, the music continues. Two terrifyingly slow measures, a pause that's even more frightening, then the strings play in unison for all they're worth, and the brass supports them. It's the "Theme of the Steps"!

The window shades in his bedroom were all up, letting in the early afternoon sun, and the air smelled of lilacs. They were there, white and night blue, in vases of all sizes, on the double chest of drawers once cluttered with photographs of Mary and Charlotte, on the long Chippendale table centered between the windows, on the tip table in the far corner of the room. He had told Bryan to keep cutting them. Since he wouldn't be able to walk about in the garden before it was past its glory, he might as well have them in the room to look at and smell. Bryan had brought his lunch and later taken away the tray, leaving only the bottle of Gewürztraminer Schmidt hadn't finished with his meal and a glass. Schmidt took little sips of the wine. It turned his head very pleasantly. His convalescence was as good an excuse as any for drinking at lunch. As Bryan had put it, he wasn't going anywhere so he might as well enjoy himself.

Would you like to watch a film, Albert? asked Bryan just at that moment. I've got what you wanted. *The Lady Vanishes* and *How to Marry a Millionaire.*

Schmidt didn't want to. And he didn't want to read or to be read to. He wanted to think his thoughts, drink his wine, and then drift off into a catnap until Carrie got back from the restaurant, took her shower singing and leaving the door open for him to hear, and then came to his bed all cool, slightly wet, like an African Venus risen from the sea foam. His broken ribs and broken left shoulder did not interfere with all forms of pleasure. In the meantime, while he was waiting for her, the painkiller the surgeon had prescribed—he had to keep a hawk's eye on Bryan to make sure the stuff wasn't looted—procured for him exquisite dreams. He was sure he would make a fortune if only he could charge admission to them.

Bryan brought him the pipelike contraption with little blue balls enclosed in a plastic globe at its end. He was to breathe into it regularly and hard, and thus keep the balls dancing, for five minutes twice every hour. This country fair activity was supposed to prevent his left lung from collapsing again. It had collapsed twice already, once in the Southampton hospital and once when he was already at home, in Bryan's care, which was galling to Bryan. It was extraordinary how seriously that boy took everything. Schmidt thought he had never been as clean as he was since Bryan began washing him. Those awful fingers could be very tender.

Could it be that he had come to think of Schmidt as a broken piece of furniture? For instance, a Victorian rocking chair that one of the ladies whose houses he watched had bought at a yard sale and asked him to restore? Or was he "detailing" him? It had occurred to Schmidt that he could be underestimating Bryan when he suspected he might filch the Percodan. In normal times, yes, but so long as his patient needed it? That was a different story. When Carrie suggested to him in the hospital that Bryan would be better and more useful than a practical nurse when he came home, Schmidt's reaction had been to think that he had helped her develop a nice gift for black humor. Bryan? he had replied. Why not the man himself? For you, he will rise from the grave! That crack made her cry, and he took her hand and agreed very quickly to hire Bryan. But Carrie was entirely right. Bryan had a real future in geriatric total care—according to *The New York Times,* a business with unlimited growth potential. He came to discuss the terms of his employment during Carrie's working hours. Schmidt was alone.

Albert, he told him, I appreciate this. I know I'm not your favorite person. I promise I'll do a good job. You'll see.

Of course.

I think I can learn a lot from you, Albert. It's like I went back to school!

Heavens!

I'm not kidding. If you let me stay on in your house after you get well, I'll take care of the house just for the room. I'll fix anything that needs fixing and take care of anything you want done in the garden that Jim Bogard doesn't do. If you want, I could go on living in the room off the kitchen.

Aha! Schmidt hadn't realized he was engaging a live-in keeper. A rather odd successor to Corinne in that room! On the other hand, what Bryan might get into his head to do with Carrie, he could do as well in the day as in the night, probably more easily during the day, because at night Carrie would be in bed with Schmidt, one would hope otherwise engaged.

The room off the kitchen is all right while you're nursing me to health. If I ever get well! Afterward, we'll talk. I can't think that far into the future.

He was beginning to feel tired, and wondered whether he should discreetly ring for the floor nurse.

Albert, you know it's over between Carrie and me. You've won.

Schmidt smiled wanly. Was this a trap?

You know I figured it out right away, even before she moved into your house. It's OK. We were just into some sex. It isn't like she cared. Man, she really likes you!

Perhaps that's how it really was and how it was to remain. One would see. We'll talk about it when Carrie's here, he told Bryan.

The previous day, before his lung collapsed, which happened in the afternoon and caused the nice intern to panic because, it being Sunday, he couldn't get hold of the surgeon, Charlotte and Jon came to see him. When he asked whether they had just driven in, they said no, they had spent the night at the house. Counting the silver, thought Schmidt. He had spoken to them, Charlotte and then Jon, on the telephone, as soon as he got out of emergency care. Jon showed right away how having been trained at a first-class New York law firm makes a man useful, in all circumstances.

You know, the bum you ran into was dead when the police

and the ambulance got there. Fortunately, the autopsy showed he was really tanked up. Besides, according to the skid marks, you were in your lane, going at a normal speed. I talked to Vince—that was the senior litigating partner, a former prosecutor—he doesn't think they'll charge you. To be on the safe side, we've hired that Shaugnessy fellow in Riverhead. He knows his way around the courthouse.

I wonder what was in my blood, thought Schmidt. Could it be that they didn't test it?

Renata called the surgeon. He says you'll be just fine. There's no concussion. We'll come out to see you on Sunday.

So there they were, right on time. No flowers, Schmidt observed, or anything else that might spoil him. Perhaps within the family one skipped these sentimental gestures. He noted with satisfaction that Charlotte's skin sparkled. What a beautiful girl she was! He told her so, and added that she looked more and more like Martha, the Anglo-Irish beauty. Did Anglo-Irish with its High Church connotations (if she knew about them!) strike the wrong note? She got right down to business.

Dad, the Saab was totaled. If they don't take away your license, I guess you can drive Mom's car. What about the VW? Is it still mine? If it is, we'll drop off the Avis car here and drive the VW to New York.

I gave it to you. The only reason it's in my name is insurance. You know that.

All right, so that is settled. Dad, what is that Hispanic girl doing in the house, and what is she doing in your and Mom's bedroom?

Holy cow! He had forgotten. It was bound to come up, sooner or later.

You mean Carrie? She sleeps there.

With you!

When I'm there. Yes.

Dad, how long has that been going on? That girl must be younger than me.

She is. What's the expression for it? Winter-spring romance. Or do you say spring-winter?

We don't think it's funny. She looks like someone out of a movie about gangs.

Possibly. I think they look for the prettiest girls for those parts.

It was time for the lawyer son-in-law to intervene.

She'll rob you blind, Schmidtie. You've got every right to do what you want and live your life, but you should be protected. I'll speak to Dick Murphy. He'll set up something to stop her from getting hold of your money.

I think I can talk to Dick myself if that becomes necessary. By the way, Carrie works hard as a waitress and saves her money. She doesn't show any interest in mine.

Someone will tell her to get interested. Just wait! That was Charlotte's contribution. Anyway, I don't want her at our wedding. I hope you weren't planning to bring her.

Lord Harry, Charlotte! You really are old-fashioned. So you are planning a semirestricted event: People of the Hebrew faith are welcome, people of color need not apply! Very nice! Have you checked that against the firm's equal opportunity policy, Jon?

You are off the reservation! Stop talking like that!

Don't raise your voice, Jon. I told you when you were still a young associate that's always bad form, a sign of insecurity.

They left shortly afterward, and he began to feel he couldn't breathe right.

Don't make plans. That was a deep insight, although, as Schmidt would be the first to admit, not one that applied to every situation. Before the problem with the man was solved, Schmidt had intended to call his former partner Murphy—in his thoughts always that clown Murphy—to ask if he could get away with not paying a gift tax if he paid Carrie's tuition at Southampton College and any other costs directly, instead of giving her the cash. Why should he give the government more money than he absolutely must to waste on the space program and making Afghanistan safe for Western values? And he had planned to ask Murphy, as an aside, about the law that had come out of palimony suits and the like. But after that clown Riker—another one!—had opened his mouth he felt he was goddamned if he was going to stoop so low. The circumstances had changed.

He tried to reach for the mail on the night table. The pain stopped him.

Albert, is there anything you want? You shouldn't be moving around in the bed.

Yes, thanks, that thick certified mail and my glasses.

He read the papers for the third time. The lawyers for his stepmother, Bonnie, were notifying him that she had died suddenly, in her sleep, probably from a heart attack, and bequeathed to Schmidt her entire estate, including what was in the trust her first husband had set up for her with the assistance of Schmidt's father. The will was enclosed, as clear as possible. Also a letter from Bonnie. Dear Schmidtie, she wrote, in the laborious handwriting that had always amused him,

I felt bad when your Dad left everything to me, because poor Sozon had already left me more than enough. I told your Dad that was what I thought but he wanted to do it. He said I was good to him—goodness knows, I tried and he was such a sweet man, so gentle! He told me if you behaved well and I kept feeling that way I could leave you what was left over in my will. You were sweet to me during that difficult time, and you never let on that you were disappointed! So I'm doing the right thing now. I am also leaving to you everything in Sozon's trust. Your Dad worked it out so I could give it to anybody I like, he said that was good for taxes. Sozon's sons have too much already and they weren't ever nice to me.

Probably, I'll live another fifty years, at the rate I'm going, but if I die you have fun, and get some more suits at your poor Dad's tailor. You liked them so much! Those nice people in Boston your Dad got to look after the money have done a real good job. Believe me!

The letter was dated Christmas Day, 1990. He had sent her a card with his wishes just before that Christmas and, as usual, she had replied. Apparently she didn't hold it against Schmidt that he had skipped the following Christmas. He had written to her about Mary; she knew that things were not as they should be.

Bryan, he said to his keeper, I have a feeling that when I get better I'm going to need someone to look after a large house in Florida. In West Palm Beach. It's a big job. Practically everything will need fixing or replacing. It will take a lot of work and a very long time. Do you think you could manage that?

A NOTE ABOUT THE AUTHOR

Louis Begley lives in New York City. His earlier novels are *Wartime Lies*, *The Man Who Was Late*, and *As Max Saw It*.

A NOTE ON THE TYPE

The text of this book was set in Van Dijck, a modern revival of a typeface attributed to the Dutch master punchcutter Christoffel van Dyck, c. 1606–69.

Composed by NK Graphics,
Keene, New Hampshire
Printed and bound by Quebecor Printing,
Martinsburg, West Virginia
Designed by Peter A. Andersen